OF DOPPELGÄNGERS, DUPPIES, AND DEADS . . .

"Tan-Tan and Dry Bone": *"Duppy Dead Town is where people go when life boof them, when hope left them and happiness cut she eye 'pon them and strut away . . ."*

"Slow Cold Chick": A strange horror hatches out of an empty fridge—and a strange wonder hatches out of an empty life . . .

"A Habit of Waste": *"I was nodding off on the streetcar home from work when I saw the woman—wearing the body I used to have . . ."*

"Ganger: Ball Lightning": Their passion was all that kept them together—until the day that passion wanted a life of its own . . .

"Greedy Choke Puppy": *"Inside my skin I was just one big ball of fire, and Lord, the night air feel nice and cool on the flame! When your youth start to leave you, you have to steal more from somebody who still have plenty . . ."*

UNIVERSAL ACCLAIM FOR NALO HOPKINSON

MIDNIGHT ROBBER

"A unique voice . . . refreshingly original."
—*Denver Post*

"Fusing Afro-Caribbean soul and speech in an intriguing landscape of spirits . . . a terrifying battle between good and evil."
—*Black Issues Book Review*

more . . .

BROWN GIRL IN THE RING

"Hopkinson lives up to her advance billing."
—*New York Times Book Review*

"An impressive debut precisely because of Hopkinson's fresh viewpoint."
—*Washington Post Book World*

"A parable of black feminist self-reliance, couched in poetic language and the structural conventions of classic SF."
—*Village Voice*

"Excellent . . . a bright, original mix of future urban decay and West Indian magic . . . strongly rooted in character and place."
—*Sunday Denver Post*

"A wonderful sense of narrative and a finely tuned ear for dialogue . . . balances a well-crafted and imaginative story with incisive social critique and a vivid sense of place."
—*Emerge*

"A book to remember."
—*Cleveland Plain Dealer*

"Active, eventful . . . a success."
—*Philadelphia Inquirer*

Also by Nalo Hopkinson

Brown Girl in the Ring
Midnight Robber

NALO HOPKINSON

SKIN FOLK

ASPECT®

WARNER BOOKS

An AOL Time Warner Company

"Riding the Red" © 1997. First appeared in *Black Swan, White Raven*, edited by Ellen Datlow and Terri Windling. AvoNova, USA, 1997.

"Money Tree" © 1997. First appeared in *Tesseracts 6: the Annual Anthology of Canadian Speculative Fiction*, edited by Robert J. Sawyer and Carolyn Clink. Tesseract Books, Canada, 1997.

Copyright information continued on page 259.

Aspect® name and logo are registered trademarks of Warner Books, Inc.

Warner Books, Inc., 1271 Avenue of the Americas, New York, NY 10020

Visit our Web site at www.twbookmark.com.

For information on Time Warner Trade Publishing's online publishing program, visit www.ipublish.com.

 An AOL Time Warner Company

Printed in the United States of America

First Printing: December 2001

10 9 8 7 6 5 4 3 2 1

Library of Congress Cataloging-in-Publication Data

Hopkinson, Nalo.
    Skin folk / Nalo Hopkinson.
      p. cm.
    ISBN 0-446-67803-1
     1. Science fiction, Canadian. 2. Life on other planets—Fiction. 3. West Indies—Emigration and immigration—Fiction. I. Title.

PR9199.3.H5927 S58 2001
813'.54—dc21

2001026416

Book design and text composition by L&G McRee
Cover design by Don Puckey
Cover illustration by Mark Harrison

Acknowledgments

Heartfelt thanks to any long-suffering soul who ever workshopped one of these stories with me. You are Legion, and you know who you are. And blessings and grace, too, to Betsy Mitchell and Jaime Levine of Warner Aspect, and to my agent, Don Maass. As ever, love and appreciation to my mother, Freda Hopkinson, my brother, Keita Hopkinson, and my partner, David Findlay. Thank you to the Ontario Arts Council and the Toronto Arts Council for the grants that helped to support me while I completed this manuscript.

Contents

SKIN FOLK

Throughout the Caribbean, under different names, you'll find stories about people who aren't what they seem. Skin gives these skin folk their human shape. When the skin comes off, their true selves emerge. They may be owls. They may be vampiric balls of fire. And always, whatever the burden their skins bear, once they remove them—once they get under their own skins—they can fly. It seemed an apt metaphor to use for these stories collectively.

RIDING THE RED

She never listens to me anymore. I've told her and I've told her: daughter, you have to teach that child the facts of life before it's too late, but no, I'm an old woman, and she'll raise her daughter as she sees fit, Ma, thank you very much.

So I tried to tell her little girl myself: Listen, dearie, listen to Grandma. You're growing up, hmm; getting dreamy? Pretty soon now, you're going to be riding the red, and if you don't look smart, next stop is wolfie's house, and wolfie, doesn't he just love the smell of that blood, oh yes.

Little girl was beginning to pay attention, too, but of course, her saintly mother bustled in right then, sent her off to do her embroidery, and lit into me for filling the child's head with ghastly old wives' tales. Told me girlie's too young yet, there's plenty of time.

Daughter's forgotten how it was, she has. All growed up and responsible now, but there's more things to remember than when to do the milking, and did you sweep the dust from the corners.

Just as well they went home early that time, her and the little one. Leave me be, here alone with my cottage in the forest and my memories. That's as it should be.

But it's the old wives who best tell those tales, oh yes. It's the old wives who remember. We've been there, and we lived to tell them. And don't I remember being young once, and toothsome, and drunk on the smell of my own young blood flowing through my veins? And didn't it make me feel all shivery and nice to see wolfie's nostrils flare as he scented it? I could make wolfie slaver, I could, and beg to come close, just to feel the heat from me. And oh, the game I made of it, the dance I led him!

He caught me, of course; some say he even tricked me into it, and it may be they're right, but that's not the way this old wife remembers it. Wolfie must have his turn, after all. That's only fair. My turn was the dance, the approach and retreat, the graceful sway of my body past his nostrils, scented with my flesh. The red hood was mine, to catch his eye, and my task it was to pluck all those flowers, to gather fragrant bouquets with a delicate hand, an agile turn of a slim wrist, the blood beating at its joint like the heart of a frail bird. There is much plucking to be done in the dance of riding the red.

But wolfie has his own measure to tread too, he

does. First slip past the old mother, so slick, and then, oh then, isn't wolfie a joy to see! His dance is all hot breath and leaping flank, piercing eyes to see with and strong hands to hold. And the teeth, ah yes. The biting and the tearing and the slipping down into the hot and wet. That measure we dance together, wolfie and I.

And yes, I cried then, down in the dark with my grandma, till the woodman came to save us, but it came all right again, didn't it? That's what my granddaughter has to know: It comes all right again. I grew up, met a nice man, reminded me a bit of that woodman, he did, and so we were married. And wasn't I the model goodwife then, just like my daughter is now? And didn't I bustle about and make everything just so, what with the cooking and the cleaning and the milking and the planting and the birthing, and I don't know what all?

And in the few quiet times, the nights before the fire burned down too low to see, I would mend and mend. No time for all that fancy embroidery that my mama taught me.

I forgot wolfie. I forgot that riding the red was more than a thing of soiled rags and squalling newborns and what little comfort you and your man can give each other, nights when sleep doesn't spirit you away soon as you reach your bed.

I meant to tell my little girl, the only one of all those babes who lived, and dearer to me than diamonds, but I taught her embroidery instead, not dancing, and then it was too late. I tried to tell her quick, before she set off on her own, so pretty with her little basket, but the young, they never listen, no. They're deaf from the sound of their own new blood rushing in their ears.

But it came all right; we got her back safe. We always do, and that's the mercy.

It was the fright killed my dear mam a few days later, that's what they say, she being so old and all, but mayhap it was just her time. Perhaps her work was done.

But now it's me that's done with all that, I am. My goodman's long gone, his back broke by toil, and I have time to just sit by the fire, and see it all as one thing, and know that it's right, that it must be so.

Ah, but wouldn't it be sweet to ride the red, just once more before I'm gone, just one time when I can look wolfie in the eye, and match him grin for grin, and show him that I know what he's good for?

For my mama was right about this at least: the trick is, you must always have a needle by you, and a bit of thread. Those damned embroidery lessons come in handy, they do. What's torn can be sewn up again, it can, and then we're off on the dance once more! They say it's the woodman saves us, me and my daughter's little girl, but it's wolfie gives us birth, oh yes.

And I haven't been feeling my best nowadays, haven't been too spry, so I'm sure it's time now. My daughter's a hard one, she is. Never quite forgot how it was, stuck in that hot wet dark, not knowing rescue was coming; but she's a thoughtful one too. The little one's probably on her way right now with that pretty basket, Don't stop to dawdle, dear, don't leave the path, but they never hear, and the flowers are so pretty, just begging to be plucked.

Well, it's time for one last measure; yes, one last, sweet dance.

Listen: is that a knock at the door?

MONEY TREE

Silky was having dreams of deluges. They'd started soon after she got the news about her brother, Morgan. The dreams frightened her: mile-high tidal waves that swallowed cities; vast masses of water shifting restlessly over drowned skyscrapers.

In one nightmare, she was living in a cottage on a mountaintop. She was cooking a meal for Morgan, barbecuing fat pink prawns on an outdoor grill while she and her brother laughed and talked. Far away on the horizon was the outline of another mountain range, a wide plateau. She heard water running. It irritated her that Morgan had left a tap on—what a way the boy was lazy!

She turned to tell him to go and turn it off, and saw the plateau in the distance. Water was spilling over the top of it, billions of gallons rushing over that mountain range miles away. That's what she'd been hearing.

Morgan shouted, "The water table! It's rising!" Before Silky could stop him, he ran down the hill, yelling that he had to go and get his wallet. She knew that the flood would drown the city below, then rise to engulf her, and there was nothing she could do about it.

Morgan would have called the dreams apocalyptic. He would have hauled some tatty paperback about "mysticism and the psychic power of dreams" off the bookshelf and launched into a speech about how she was tapping into her archetypal consciousness, or something.

In her mind's eye, Silky could just see his earnest expression as he tried to convince her, the eagerness that could usually make her smile, ever since they were children.

She made herself a cup of tea and took it to the kitchen table. She shoveled a tablespoonful of sugar from the sugar bowl into her mug. Demerara brown sugar, damp with molasses and moist as mud. The glimmering crystals swirled like chips of gold, then sank slowly to the bottom of the cup. She loved the rich taste, hoarded the Demerara sugar for herself; guests could have the white. In Jamaica it was the other way around; the costly refined sugar was for guests, and the everyday brown sugar was cheap. Mummy would have been horrified at how expensive Demerara sugar was in Toronto.

Silky was aware that her mind was wandering, skittering over mundane things to avoid thinking about Morgan. The Jamaican police hadn't found him. It was horrible not knowing whether she should be grieving or not. She stood up and walked over to the kitchen window, leaned out to look at the pear tree just outside.

The moist heat of the summer past had been good for

the tree. In the crisp fall air, its branches drooped with heavy fruit. The pears looked like the bodies of plump, freckled green women. Through the leaves of the tree, the sun cast pale disks of gold onto the pears. The autumn light was muted, as though everything were underwater. If she stretched a little, Silky could touch one or two of the pears, stroke their smooth skin. Many of them were about to ripen. Soon she'd be able to pluck sustenance from the watery air. The pear tree was the main reason that Silky had persuaded Morgan that they should buy this little old house with the silverfish living in the cracks. Besides, it was what they could afford, what with Morgan only doing casual work at the car parts plant. He was angling for full time, but until then her job as research assistant for the Ministry of State just barely brought in enough to keep them both going.

Morgan had been fed up of never having enough money, and he thought he'd found a quick way to make his fortune back home. He wouldn't tell her about it, had wanted to surprise her. He'd flown to Jamaica, where Silky had had one phone call from him. His plans were going well, it looked like his hunch was going to pan out. Then he disappeared.

The cold air through the kitchen window was making her eyes water.

When they were children, Silky and Morgan used to fly with their parents to Gaspar Grande island off the coast of Trinidad to spend the summer holidays there. That was before it became a fancy resort. At the time, there were only a few rambling cottages and the small house where the caretaker lived with his old dog. Silky and her brother would dig sea cockroach barnacles out of the rocks for bait, then fish all morning for little yellow grunts, mimicking the fishes' croaking sounds as they pulled them up out of the water. They would take their catch for their mother to gut. The rest of the day, the island was theirs to roam. They would climb sweetsop trees for the green-skinned, bumpy fruit, sucking out the sweet, milky pulp and spitting the black seeds at each other. During those holidays, Silky felt that she could want no other food, need no other air to breathe.

She remembered her mother diving from the jetty into the dark water, circling down past the parrot fish and the long-snouted garfish, until Silky could barely make her out, her plump body shimmering greenish in the deep water. She seemed to stay under forever, and it scared Silky and Morgan, but Daddy would simply smile.

"Is by the riverside I first met your mother. She was in the water swimming, like some kind of manatee. Mamadjo woman, mermaid woman. Happy in the sea, happy in the river!" He laughed. "What a man your daddy must be, eh, to make a fair maid from the river consent to come and live on dry land with him?"

The children wouldn't be reassured, though, until she burst to the surface again, not even winded.

Their mother had tried to teach them both to swim, but the sight of her sinking into the black water appalled them. Morgan refused to be coaxed in any deeper than the shallows. Silky remembered him shaking his head no, how the sunlight would make diamonds of the water flying from his tight peppercorn curls. For herself, she had loved the feeling of body surfing, but wouldn't put her whole head under the water. She'd stick her face in just far enough to be able to see the grunts flit by. She never learned to dive beneath the surface the way her mother did. "Just try to go deeper, nuh, sweetheart?" Mummy would say, undulating her arms to show her how to stroke through the water. "You and Morgan can both do it; you're my children. I'm right here. I won't let anything happen to you."

But Silky hadn't wanted to be swallowed up by that dark wetness.

She had another dream that night. In it, she had survived the flood from the previous nightmare. She was swimming on the surface, above the drowned lands. Bloated corpses bumped her from time to time. The horror made her skin prickle. She put her face into the water to inspect the damage below her. She could see submerged roads, tiny fish nibbling at dissolving lumps of flesh, a sea anemone already blossoming on a disintegrated carcass that had sunk to the sea bed.

The sea gave a greenish cast to the rotting flesh of the drowned people. In the rigor of death, a man clutched at a slab of coral the size of a dinner table. The coral glowed reddish gold in the flickering water. The man's face was turned up towards her. His dying gasps for air had contorted it into a ghastly scream. Watery light glistened off his teeth, turning them to gleaming coins. Silky was terrified. Just then, a freak wave rose and slammed her down into the depths, tossing her against the drowned man. The current rearranged his features. It was Morgan. His eyes opened and he reached a beseeching hand out to his sister. She couldn't stop herself; she screamed. She expected the brine to flood her lungs, burning them, filling them like sponges, but it entered her body slowly; sweet and sustaining, like a breath of air. In disbelief, she heaved, trying to expel the liquid from her stomach.

She woke in terror, blowing hard. She was lying in bed, a few strands of her hair crushed between her face and the pillow. Some of it had worked its way into her mouth. The hair tasted brackish as the sea, as though she'd been crying in her sleep.

Silky lay shivering under the icy sheets, trying to get rid of the image of herself drowned, swollen full of salty water. She was afraid that if she hadn't woken up, the sea would have changed her, rotting the flesh of her dream hands and feet into corrupt parodies of flukes, while eels snapped at her melting flesh. Her mamadjo mother could live in the sea like a mermaid, but she could not.

The pears were ripe. Silky climbed the tree with a basket hooked over one shoulder, a long scarf inside it. She wedged the basket into a crook of the tree so that she would have her hands free to pick. Shards of golden sunlight struck her eyes. She looked down. A light breeze was rippling the grass in waves. She was sailing on a green sea.

When they were children, she and Morgan would climb the julie mango tree in the back of the house and pretend that they were old-time pirates, scaling the mast to spy out ships to plunder. Other little boys in Mona Heights had had cap guns. Morgan had a plastic sword. He used to jab Silky with it, until that time when she punched him and broke his nose. Grandpy had been so mad at her!

As she reminisced, Silky picked a fat, golden pear, but with a liquid sound it collapsed in her hand, rotted from within. "Ugh! Nasty!" She flicked the soggy mush off her fingers and wiped her hand on her jeans.

After Mummy and Daddy died, the children's grandfather came from Spanish Town to take care of them. He was the one who had told them the story about Jackson, a man who had lived just outside Spanish Town in the 1600s. People hadn't known it at the time, but Jackson had been a carpenter turned pirate. He was a greedy man. He had drugged the crew with doped rum and scuttled their ship at sea while they were still in it. He had drowned his mates so that he could retire rich with their booty.

"Guilt drove Jackson crazy," Grandpy told them. "The ghosts of the drowned pirates called from their grave in the sea and asked the river spirit for her help. They said she could have their gold if she gave them revenge.

"River Mumma loves shiny things. She agreed. She would come to Jackson at night. As he tossed and turned in his bed, he could hear the river whispering in his ear that he was a murderer and a thief. River Mumma told him she would have revenge, and she would have his gold. Jackson was afraid, but he was more greedy than scared. He wasn't going to let her have the doubloons. He used his carpenter's skills to make a huge table of heavy Jamaican mahogany, then he nailed every last gold coin onto it. Hid it in his cellar. He stopped bathing, stopped talking to his neighbours, stayed in his house all the time."

"Then what happened?" Silky had whispered, holding tight to Morgan's sleeve for reassurance. He looked just as scared as she.

"Jackson didn't even notice the heavy rains that year. It rained so hard that the Rio Cobre river that ran beside his property swelled up big. He was in his cellar admiring his gold when the Rio Cobre broke its banks and gouged a new course for itself, right through his home. The house was demolished.

"River Mumma sent the water for him," Grandpy said. "The last thing the neighbours saw was a big golden table rising to the surface of the rushing water. It floated for twelve seconds with Jackson clinging to it. Then it sank. If he had let go, they might have been able to save him, but he refused to leave his treasure."

"What happened to the table?" Morgan had asked. He was eleven and already he had a taste for money. Grandpy was looking after his two orphans as best as he could, but things were tight.

"No one ever fetched the golden table out of the Rio Cobre. They say that at the stroke of noon every day, it rises to the top of the water, and it floats for exactly twelve seconds, then sinks again, dragging anything else in the water down with it."

Silky's basket was full. She tied the scarf around the handle and lowered it to the ground, climbing down after it. She lugged it inside the house. Morgan loved pears. She would make preserves from them, stew them in her precious Demerara sugar to keep them until he returned.

The Jamaican police had sent her Morgan's effects. Some clothes, a letter he hadn't mailed. She had put the letter with the month's stack of bills on the bookshelf. At least the insurance was covering Morgan's half of the mortgage payments.

Morgan used to say to her, "Back home, they tell you that when you come up to Canada, it's going to be easy, not like in Jamaica; that you'll be able to reach out your hand and pull money from the trees. Money will just fall into your lap like fruit. I wonder where my money tree is," he said.

He had explained his plan to her in his unmailed letter: he had gone back to Jamaica to look for the Golden Table. *I think I can really find it, Silky! The Rio Cobre has altered its course twice since the pirate Jackson built his home beside it: once when he drowned with his treasure, and once more when they built the Irrigation Works in the 1800s. The works have drained off so much water onto the plain that you can actually walk on parts of the river bed in the dry season. That's when I'm going to go looking for the Golden Table. I can dig late at night when nobody will see me. I even know the spot where the old people say it is—it's a deep sinkhole that doesn't dry up until the height of the dry season.*

No one looks for the Table, you know. They're afraid. People out here still tell stories about a plantation owner way, way back who tried to have his slaves pull the Table out of the water when it rose at noon. Six men drowned that day, and twelve yokes of oxen, dragged under when the Table sank to the bottom again.

Suppose it's really there! All that gold! It's almost dry season now. Just a few more weeks, and maybe I'll be coming home rich. I'll see you soon.

If Silky had known what Morgan had been up to, she would have talked him out of it. When they were children, her mother had made it clear that she was to look out for her younger brother.

"You're the eldest one, Silky, and a girl to boot, so you have to have more sense. That boy's so full of mischief, always getting himself in deep water. You have to be ready to pull him out. Your daddy and I won't always be around, you know."

Silky had resented the burden placed on her. She loved Morgan, but at the time, she'd been a child too, just like him. Why did she have to take care of him? Isn't that what her parents were for?

After their parents were killed in the car crash, Silky sometimes wondered if her mother had known that they wouldn't be around to see their children into adulthood. Like Silky, Mummy used to dream things. And if Mummy had known that, had she also known how to save Morgan? Did she die before she could tell her daughter what to do?

Silky had another dream. *Morgan was standing beside her on the bank of the Rio Cobre. He put an arm around her shoulders to draw her close, and pointed into the murky water.*

It's time, he said. Look into the water, Silky. No, bend your head like so. Quickly! Twelve seconds and it gone. See it? Rising towards us through the river water? That big round of pure gold, that tabletop, shimmering like the promise of heaven. Getting bigger, coming closer . . . four, three, two . . . gone again. Sunk back into the depths of the river. You can't take it out, you know? The spirits drag you down. If I jump in, Silky, you will pull me out? I can't swim.

She didn't answer him, just stared down into the roiling water that would melt her flesh and change her if she went into it.

Morgan had been staying with a cousin in Spanish Town; Leonie and her husband, Brian. In a phone call, Leonie told Silky that Morgan had started going out late at night, returning while it was still dark. Leonie had surprised him coming in at four o'clock one morning. He was laughing softly to himself, and she could smell stale sweat on him, like he'd been doing hard labour. When he saw her, he hid a pouch of some kind behind his back, scowled at her, and went to his room. She had heard the key turn in the lock.

After that he kept to himself. He took a knapsack with him when he left the house in the evenings. Sometimes they saw him when he brought the knapsack back late at night, bulging with whatever was inside it. He cradled it to his body like a lover. He stayed in his room during the days, but they knew when he was in the house by the reek of sweat that followed him. Morgan had stopped using the shower, muttered that he didn't want the water to wash him away, then had tried to pass it off as a joke. They had been afraid he was going mad.

A few days later, a tropical storm hit Jamaica hard. The Rio Cobre swelled its banks again, and by morning, Leonie's house was flooded knee-deep in water. She and Brian knew they had to leave the house until the storm was over. They had called for Morgan through the bedroom door, but there was no answer. Finally, Brian broke the door down. The room was empty. All they found were his clothes and his knapsack with a few water-logged splinters of wood inside it. The police told Leonie that Morgan had probably used it to carry marijuana. They assumed it was a dope deal gone bad, and they expected to find his body at any time, shot and dumped somewhere.

In Toronto, fall went by and winter settled in, gelid and sullen. Silky stuffed towels into the house's old cracks to keep the wind out. She moped, barely able to drag herself through work every day. Her colleagues tiptoed around her, speaking quietly. She overheard her boss whispering to another manager over the coffee machine: "brother," and "drugs." She didn't care. All she could think about was Morgan. Her body felt heavy, earthbound.

She started taking long, hot baths in the evenings, soaking in the deep old claw-footed tub in the darkened bathroom. The water and the dark soothed her, sank into her bones. It felt as though she could float away on the water like an otter, buoyed up from the sorrow that was weighing her down.

One evening, face bathed in tears, Silky decided to give her body to the water. She let herself sink completely under the surface of the bath. She held her breath for a long time, feeling at peace, listening to the whispering of the water. Then she inhaled. It burned into her lungs, but she fought her body's thrashing and stayed under. Strangely, the pain in her chest soon stopped. It seemed like she stayed submerged for a long time, waiting for death, but nothing happened. She sat up in the bathtub, and warm water drained harmlessly from her mouth and nose. She felt a curious contentment. She got out of the bath and went to bed. For the first time since Morgan's disappearance, sleep felt like a benediction.

Silky didn't really notice spring come and go. She had no more dreams of Morgan. She started smiling at work again, even went out for drinks one evening with a couple of the women from the office. She drank only water all night, though, glass after glass, until her friends teased her that she would burst. But she was feeling so dry! It had been hours since her last soak in the tub. She dipped a napkin in her glass and dabbed it on her chest and arms. The first thing she did when she got home was to have a long bath, reveling in the feel of water on her skin.

She was amazed when she looked out the kitchen window one Sunday afternoon and saw that the pear tree was in full leaf; tender, bright green leaves dancing like tiny fish in the balmy air currents.

It was late May, nine months since Morgan had disappeared. In that time, Silky had birthed herself again. After her failed attempt at suicide, the odd sense of peace had stayed with her. She still grieved for her brother, but no longer felt as though she would die from the pain. In fact, she felt almost invulnerable, as though she could swim through air, or breathe in water.

Silky looked at herself in her bedroom mirror that Sunday afternoon, wondering if the change in her was apparent on her face. Over the winter, she'd become as portly as her mother had been. She actually found the plump curves of her new full pear shape pleasing, but she was feeling the effects of nine months of inactivity.

"It's spring, Morgan," Silky said to the air. "Time to get into shape."

No time like the present; she grabbed workout gear and a bathing suit and walked over to the YMCA. She tried the weight room, but after a few painful contortions on the Nautilus machines she decided to go to the pool instead. It had been years, but she was sure that she'd remember her mother's lessons. It was five minutes to midday. The noon public swim was just about to start.

Silky wrinkled her nose at the smell of chlorine. The

space rang with the laughter of children, sleek and plump as seals as they splashed in the water or raced around the pool deck. She went to the three lanes roped off for doing laps. An old woman moved with slow grace through the water, blowing like a walrus when she came to the turns. Feeling a little nervous, Silky eased herself in.

She did the breaststroke so that she could keep her head out of the water. After a few laps, she settled into the rhythm of lane swimming. She no longer heard the noise of the children playing. She kept swimming, always a few feet behind the old woman, who seemed tireless. As usual, her thoughts turned to her lost brother.

Silky believed that Morgan had found the Golden Table. She believed that by night, he pried the doubloons out of the rotten wood, and brought them back bit by bit to Leonie's house. But the money was not his to take. River Mumma had claimed it. Grandpy used to say, "Want all, lose all." Silky believed that because Morgan stole that treasure, River Mumma had stolen away his wits, made him afraid of the water, and when he still wouldn't return the gold, she came to get it herself, and took him into the water as punishment, the way she had done with the pirate Jackson before him.

The summer sun shot rays of light through the windows to the pool deck. The light refracted in the blue water, flickering so that Silky couldn't see below the surface of the pool. With one hand she shaded her eyes from the glare. It was noon. The time the Golden Table rises up from the bed of the Rio Cobre.

Ahead of Silky, the old woman stopped, treading water until Silky drew level with her. The woman's skin was brown, and her eyes were like those of Silky's mother. The old woman smiled at her. "He always getting into deep water," she said. "Stubborn, greedy boy. But he's my son from your mamadjo mother, so I'll let you pull him out. You have to dive, though. You're changed enough to do it now. But hurry, daughter's daughter! Only six seconds left!"

The glare brightened until Silky could no longer see River Mumma. The light seemed to be coming from beneath her now. She felt her heart slamming in her chest, beating the seconds away. The water was rushing and swirling around her. The river had found her. Looking down into it, Silky saw a great golden disk, glowing as it rose to the surface. She was dimly aware of squeals of alarm all around her, people clambering out of the pool, the lifeguard shouting, "Get out! Everybody out of the water!"

She could see Morgan clinging stubbornly to the Golden Table, refusing to relinquish all that gold.

If she gave herself to the water, would she become a mamadjo like her mother?

No time for doubt. Silky dove, inhaling as she went. The Rio Cobre waters bubbled cool and sweet as air into her lungs. She was truly her mother's daughter.

Morgan was closer now. She could see his upturned face, but couldn't read his expression. Would she be able to pluck Morgan from the Table, like fruit from a tree? Or would his need suck them both down to drown and rot in the green, greedy depths?

Breathing in the strength of the river, she swam down with strong strokes to get her brother.

The title of this story comes from a response a student once wrote on a test, if one can believe any of the endless e-mail spam one gets. I wish I knew who that student was so that I could thank the person. It really is one of the most inspired definitions I've ever read. (The student's complete response is up on the Web at http://www.thefreedmans.net/jokes/bloopers.htm.)

SOMETHING TO HITCH MEAT TO

Artho picked up a bone lying in the street. No reason, just one of those irrational things you do when your brain is busy with something else, like whether you remembered to buy avocados or not. The alligator-tail chain of a day care snaked past him, each toddler hanging on dutifully to one of the knots in the rope by which they were being led. One of the young, gum-popping nannies said:

"So then little Zukie draws herself up real tall, and she says, 'No, silly. The purpose of the skeleton is something to hitch meat to.' Really! I swear, I nearly died laughing, she sounded so serious."

The woman eyed him as she walked past, smiled a little, glanced down. She played with her long hair and stage-whispered to her co-worker, "God, Latino men are just so hot, don't you think?" They giggled and moved on, trailing children.

The gears of Artho's brain kicked back into realtime. He was standing at the southwest corner of King and Bay, holding a chicken thighbone. Fleshless and parched, it felt dusty between his fingers. He dropped it and wiped his hand off on his jeans. Latino? What the hell?

Streetcar coming. Artho got on, elbowing himself some rush hour standing room between an old man with a bound live chicken that lay gasping in his market basket and three loud, hormonal young women, all politics and piercings. Artho reached for a steady strap. Traffic was gridlocked. He stared blankly out the window as the streetcar inched its way past a woman struggling with two huge dogs on leashes. Bergers des Pyrenées, they were; giant, woolly animals bred for rescuing skiers trapped under alpine avalanches. They were so furry that Artho could barely make out their legs. They lumbered along in a smooth, four-on-the-floor gait. The dogs' handler tugged futiley at their leashes, barely able to keep up. The beasts could probably cover miles in effortless minutes, snowshoeing on their woolly feet. Artho fancied that they would move even faster, smoother, if you changed them to have six legs, or eight. They would glide along like enormous tarantulas. Artho looked at their handler's legs and had the oddest feeling, like when an old film skips a frame, and for an instant, you can see the hole-punched edges of the film strip, black and chitinous on the screen, and then it jerks back into place, but now you're looking at a different scene than you were before. It was like that, Artho looking at this woman walking on ordinary woman legs, then reality skipped frames, and he was seeing instead a being whose natural four-legged stance had been twisted and warped so that all it could manage was this ungainly two-legged jerking from foot to foot. Made into something it wasn't.

Alarmed, Artho blinked. He made himself relax. Tired. Too many hours at work in front of a computer screen, staring at all that skin. He leaned his head against the streetcar window and dozed, thinking hungrily of the stewed chicken and rice he would have for dinner, with avocado—his dad always called them alligator pears—on the side. He could see the fleshy avocado in his mind's eye: slit free of its bumpy rind; pegged and sitting on a plate; beads of salt melting on the sweating, creamy skin. He imagined biting into a slice, his teeth meeting in its spineless centre. His mouth watered.

It wasn't until he reached his stop that he realized he really had forgotten to buy the damned avocados. He found some tired, wrinkly ones in the corner store near his apartment. The man behind the counter, who served Artho at least twice a week when he came in for cigarettes or munchies, grumbled at the fifty dollar bill that Artho gave him, and made a big show over holding it up to the light to see if it was counterfeit. Artho had seen the same man cheerfully make change from bills that large for old women or guys in suits. He handed Artho a couple of twenties and some coins, scowling. Artho held each twenty up to the light before putting it into his pocket. "Thank you," he said sweetly to the guy, who glared. Artho took his avocados and went home. When he sliced into them, one of them was hard and black inside. He threw it out.

"So," Artho's brother said, "I'm out with the guys the other night, and . . ."

"Huh? What'd you say?" Artho asked. Something was obscuring Aziman's voice in the phone, making rubbing and clicking sounds over and around his speech. "What's that noise?" Artho asked the receiver. "Like dice rolling together or something."

"One dice, two die. Or is it the other way around? Anyway, so I'm . . . "

"What're you eating? I can't make out what you're saying."

"Hold on." Silence. Then Aziman came on again. "This any better?"

"Yeah. What was that?"

"This hard candy the kids brought home. Got me hooked on it. These little round white thingies, y'know? I had a mouthful of them."

"Did you spit them out?"

"Well, not round exactly. Kinda egg-shaped, but squarer than that. Is 'squarer' a word?"

"Did you spit them out?" Artho was just being pissy, and he knew it. He could tell that Aziman had gotten rid of the candies somehow. His voice was coming through clearly now.

"Yeah, Artho. Can I tell my story now?"

"Where'd you spit them?"

"What's up with you today? Down the kitchen sink."

And Aziman started in with his story again, but Artho was distracted, thinking on the tiny white candies disappearing into the drain, perhaps washed down with water.

" . . . so this man walks up to us, a kid really, y'know? Smart-ass yuppie cornfed kid with naturally blond hair and a polo shirt on. Probably an MBA. And he says to me, ''s up, man?' only he says it 'mon.' I mean, I guess he's decided I'm from Jamaica or something, you know?"

"Yeah," said Artho. "I know."

"He gives me this weird handshake; grabs my thumb and then makes a fist and I'm supposed to touch my fist to his, I think, I dunno if I did it right. But he says, ''s up' again, and I realize I didn't answer him, so I just say, 'Uh, nothing much,' which I guess isn't the lingo, right? But I dunno what I'm supposed to say; I mean, you and me, we're freaking north Toronto niggers, right? And this white guy's got Toronto suburbs written all over him, too. Probably never been any farther than Buffalo. So what's he trying to pull with that fake ghetto street shit anyway, you know? And he leans in close, kinda chummy like, and whispers, 'Think you could sell me some shit, man?' And I'm thinking, *Like the kind you're trying to sell me on right now?* I mean, he's asking me for dope, or something."

Artho laughed. "Yeah, happens to me, too. It's always the same lame-ass question, never changes. I just point out the meanest-looking, blackest motherfucker in the joint and say, 'Not me, man, but I bet that guy'll be able to help you out.'"

"Shit. I'll try that next time."

"Though I guess it isn't fair, you know, my doing that. It's like I'm picking on guys just 'cause they're blacker than me."

"Heh. I guess, if you want to look at things that way. You going to Mom's for Easter?"

"Is Aunt Dee going to be there?"

But Aziman's only reply was a rustling, shucking type of noise. Then, "Shit!"

"What?"

"I stuck my hand into the bag for more candy, y'know? Just figured out what these things are."

"What?"

"Skulls. Little sugar skulls, f'chrissake."

Dead people bits. That's what the candy was. It was all in the way you looked at it.

"No," said Artho. "It'll be just like last year. I'm not going to Mom's for Easter."

A few days later it happened again, a weird unfamiliarity when Artho looked at human bodies. He was in the mall food court on his lunch hour. When he went back to work, it would be to spend the rest of the day updating the Tit for Twat site: *Horny Vixens in Heat! No Holes Barred!*

The food court was crowded. People in business suits wolfed down Jolly Meals, barked on cell phones. The buzz of conversation was a formless noise, almost soothing.

Not many empty spaces. Artho had to share a table for two with a thirtyish man in fine beige wool, engrossed in the financial pages of the *Globe & Mail* newspaper. The man had shaved his head completely. Artho liked it. There was something sensuous about the baldness, like the domed heads of penises. Cute. Artho was thinking of something to say to him, some kind of opener, when the man's ears caught his gaze. They jutted out from the side of his head like knurls of deformed cartilage. There really was nothing odd about the guy's ears—that's just how ears were—but they still gave Artho a queasy feeling. With one hand, he worried at his own ear. He looked around at other people in the food court. All their ears seemed like twisted carbuncles of flesh sprouting from the sides of their heads, odd excrescenses. Nausea and doubt squirmed like larvae in

Artho's chest. His fingers twitched, the ones that he would use a few minutes from now to point, click, and drag his mouse as he smoothed out the cellulite and firmed up the pecs of the perfect naked models on the screen, making them even more perfect. He closed his eyes to block out the sight of all those ugly ears.

Someone was singing. A child's voice, tuneless and repetitive, threaded its whiny way through the rumble of lunchtime chatter:

> "Tain't no sin,
> Take off your skin,
> And dance around in your bones.
> Tain't no sin . . . "

Artho opened his eyes. Wriggly as only seven-year-olds can be, a little girl slouched beside her father at a table for four, sitting on her spine so she could kick at the centre pole supporting the table welded to its four seats. Her wiry black hair was braided into thousands of dark medusa strands. The brown bumps of her knees were ashy with dry skin. The lumpy edge of a brightly coloured Spider Man knapsack jutted out from behind her back.

"Tain't no sin . . . " She kicked and kicked at the pole. An old man who'd been forced to share the table with them looked up from his chow mein and gave her a strained nice-little-girl smile.

"Quit it, Nancy." Not even glancing at his daughter—was she his daughter?—her father reached out with one hand and stilled the thin, kicking legs. With his other hand he hurriedly stuffed a burger into his mouth. Green relish oozed between his fingers.

The little girl stopped kicking, but all that energy

had to have some outlet. She immediately started swaying her upper body from side to side, jerking her knapsack about so that something thumped around inside it. She bobbed her head in time to her little song. Her braids flowed like cilia. She looked around her. Her gaze connected with Artho's. "Daddy," she said loudly to the man beside her, "can you see me?" She wore glasses with jam-jar-thick lenses, which refracted and multiplied her eyes. She didn't look up at her father.

And he didn't look down at her, just kept gnawing on his burger. "Can't see you at all, little girl," he mumbled. "I only think I can. You're nowhere to be seen."

She smiled at that. "I'm everywhere, though, Daddy."

Must be some kind of weird game they had between the two of them. Then she started singing again. Artho found himself swaying slightly from side to side in time with her song. He looked away. He'd always hated Spider Man. As a kid, the comic book character had frightened him. His costume made him look like a skeleton, a clattery skin-and-bone man that someone had painted red as blood.

" . . . dance around in your bones!" the little girl shouted, glaring at him from the depths of her specs.

Artho leapt to his feet and dumped the remainder of his lunch in the garbage, fled the girl's irritating ditty. His table partner still had his nose buried in his paper.

As Artho walked the last few feet to the elevator of his office building, he suddenly became aware of the movement of his legs: push off with left leg, bending toes for leverage; contract right knee to extend right leg, heel first; shift weight; step onto right foot; bend right knee; repeat on the other side. For a ludicrous moment, he nearly tripped over his own feet. It was like some kind of weird jig. He stumbled into the elevator, smiled I'm-fine-really at a plump young woman in a business suit who was gazing at him curiously. She looked away. Then he did. They stared politely at the opaque white numbers, knobbled as vertebrae, that indicated each floor. The numbers clicked over, lighting up one at a time: 10 . . . 11 . . . 12 . . . *Roll the bones*, thought Artho.

"Um . . . do you know what time it is?" the woman asked him.

He checked his watch, smiled at her. "Almost ten to one." The deep rust of the suit made her flawless cinnamon skin glow, hinted at the buxom swell of breast, belly, hip, and thigh. Yum. Artho's mouse fingers stopped twitching.

She smiled back nervously. The smile quirked friendly lines at the corners of her mouth. "Thanks. Guess I'm on time after all, then."

"Job interview?"

"Uh-huh. Marketing. Up at Joint Productions."

"The design place? Cool. They've done some great stuff."

She looked even more interested, leaned forward a little. "Oh, you work there?"

Shit. "Uh, no."

"In the building, then?"

"Yeah. Web design. For, um, Tri-Ex Media."

She frowned a little, took a bit of a step back. "Another design place?"

"Yeah, sort of. We . . . "

The elevator stopped and the door slid noiselessly open.

"Oh, my stop," she said. "Nice talking to you."

"Yeah. Bye." If she got the job, that'd be the last civil

conversation he had with her. The people at Joint acted like Tri-Ex Media was the very source and centre of evil in the universe. She'd probably get bitten by the same bug. Artho got out at 17.

Cold air prickled his forearms into goose bumps when he opened the door to Tri-Ex Media. The office was air-conditioned year-round to protect the expensive computer equipment. The not-so-pricey staff just wore sweaters. "Close the fucking door!" growled Charlie, his boss. Artho uncurled his spine to stand tall. He stitched a smile across his face and stepped inside, gently pulling the door shut behind him. "Miss me?" he cooed at Charlie.

People just look really weird, Artho thought. He contemplated the image up on his screen: a buff, tattooed man in a shoulder stand who'd curled himself tight as a fiddlehead fern so as to suck his own cock. Well, actually, he hadn't quite been able to reach it. His searching tongue was just a few inches away. Probably would have helped if he'd been interested enough in the procedure to have a hard-on. That was where Artho came in. He giggled, began the process of stiffening and elongating the man's dick. "Virtual fluffer, that's me," he said, aiming the comment at the general air.

Only Glenn looked up, scowling over the top of his terminal and flicking a lank lick of Popsicle pink hair out of his eyes. "Yeah? Just keep it in your pants, Mouse Boy." He grinned a little to take the sting of the comment out.

That uncomfortable little grin. Taboo subject at work, sex. Staring all day at pictures of spread, penetrated flesh—flesh more shapely than any of them in the office had: plump, perky breasts, impossibly slim waists; muscled thighs and ever-ready cocks—but *talk* about any of it?

"Hey, Artho?" Tamara called quietly from across the room.

"Yeah?" Today her thick wool sweater had a picture on it of that guy from the Fabulous Four comics, the one who turned into fire? *Flame on.* Johnny, his name was? Where in hell did Tamara find the stuff she wore?

Tamara pulled the sleeves of her sweater down over her hands, trapped them against her palm with three fingers on each hand, kept typing with the free forefingers and thumbs. "You doing anything for Easter?"

Easter again. Long-distance phone call from Vancouver Island from his father. "I long to see you and your brother," he'd say. But it never happened. And if Artho visited his mother with her stiff, dead, pressed hair and the pale pink lipstick blanching her full brown lips, she'd ask if he was still working at *that place* and whisper prayers under her breath when he said yes. Aunt Dee would be there too, with her look of fearful hunger and her Doberman's knack of going for the soft underbelly of all their relatives: *Uncle James starting to lose his hair; Cousin Melba have neither chick nor child to look after; and eh-eh, look at old Uncle Cecil, taking up with a twenty-year-old chick in his dotage.* Aziman would be sitting in the basement with the basketball game turned up loud. Holidays always made him morose about his own divorce. He'd get steadily drunker on Wincarnis Tonic Wine (sugar code 17) while his boy and girl screamed and romped and fought around him. "No," Artho told Tamara. "Gonna stay home, where it's quiet."

There. The autofellatio man looked like he was sucking his own dick now. It was moderately convincing. It'd do.

Easter meant that Aziman, after fueling himself with enough of the sugary wine, would flare, shouting insults at the players on the TV, yelling at his kids to quiet down, brown face flushing burgundy with the barely contained heat. Their mother would make him and the children spend the night at her place. "You can drive tomorrow, when you cool down," she'd say. Artho hoped that one day the fire inside Aziman would come busting out, fry away the polite surface he always presented.

How did that Johnny guy's flame really work? Artho wondered. Was he always flame on the inside?

On his screen, Artho checked out the autofellatio man's skin and hair; this one was going on the "Banjee Boys" page, whatever a banjee was, and Charlie thought a light brown black man just didn't fit the image. Good thing the position the man was in now obscured that aquiline nose, those thin lips. Smiling to himself, Artho painted another tattoo on the man's beefy shoulder; "nkyin kyin," the West African Adinkra symbol for "always changing oneself." He bet Charlie'd never recognise it in a million years.

Charlie came huffing by, glanced at the screen. "Artho, you still working on that fucking thing? Time is money here, y'know. I want Tit for Twat uploaded before you leave tonight. And no whining at me about overtime, either."

Artho sighed. "It'll be done before five." As if. But so long as it was up and running when Charlie came in on Monday, he'd never notice.

"Better be. And make that guy blacker. Looks like a

dago." Charlie turned away. Stopped. Turned back and peered at the screen. Guffawed, "Jesus, Arth! He's darker than you! Well, whaddya know 'bout that? Betcha his dick's no match for yours, though. Eh? Eh?" Charlie cackled and elbowed Artho in the ribs, then shaking his head and chuckling at his own wit, stumped his way out of the office. He slammed the door behind him. Everyone jumped at the thump. People avoided Artho's eyes.

Artho sighed and got to work again with his mouse, sticking cocoa-coloured pigment to the man like tar on the Tar Baby. He ignored the feeling of his ears burning. It went away eventually.

He finished blackening the man up, then opened up the working files Tit for Twat. He imported the new images, new inane text (*"When Daddy's not home, see these blond sisters work each other up!"*) The "blond" was bleach, the "sisters" Tania and Raven no relation at all, and they were doing their best straight guy's lesbian fantasy. As soon as they got out of the studio, they shucked the whole act like corn trash from corn and hugged each other good-bye before going their separate ways. Raven was a CGA student, blissfully married to a quiet, balding guy with a paunch, wore hightop sneakers everywhere, showed around pictures of her kids every chance she got. And Tania, as she walked out the door, would be peeling off her false two-inch nails, muttering that her girlfriends would never let her near them with knives on the tips of her fingers.

" . . . good weekend, Artho."

"Huh? Oh, yeah. Bye, Glenn," he said as Glenn let himself out.

Artho looked around for the first time in hours. It was well past five. He straightened up, groaning; he could feel each of his vertebrae popping as he uncurled from the computer screen. And he was freezing. Charlie was long gone. He and Tamara were the only ones left.

"Lost in the land of skin?" she chuckled at him.

"Yeah. Be done soon now, though." He set the files to render, moved to the next computer over—Rahim worked at that one, but he was gone too—and called up Tomb Raider. Artho'd gotten pretty good at the game. Masquerading as the impossibly firm-breasted Lara Croft, he hunted in a nightmare landscape of demons. He was just killing a ghoul in a spray of blood and bone when the door to the office whispered open. A tiny face poked round it.

"Hey, Artho?" Tamara said, waving sweater-covered fingers at him. "Relative of yours? This isn't exactly the place for a kid, you know."

It was the little girl, the one from the food court.

"What're you doing here?" Artho blurted out. "Where's your dad?"

"Daddy's always busy making stuff," came the scratchy response from the tiny face hanging in the doorway. "We do his work for him instead."

"Huh?" was all that Artho managed in response.

"Yeah. Each one of us has different jobs. Mine is that I get to go wherever I want, keep an eye on stuff." The little girl stalked on spindly legs into the room. Her knees were still ashy, the lenses of her specs still woozily thick. The wormy mass of her long, messy braids seemed to be wriggling out from their ribbons as Artho watched.

"That's ridiculous! It's"—Artho glanced at the clock on his screen—"almost seven-thirty in the evening! You can't be more than seven years old! Who're your parents? Why are you alone?"

"So you don't know her, then?" asked Tamara. She got up, went and knelt by the child. "What's your name, little girl?" she asked sweetly.

"Didn't come for you. Came for him." And the child stomped right past an astonished Tamara. "Whatcha doin?" On the screen, Lara Croft waited to be activated by a mouse click. "Oh," said the little girl. "Do you like that?"

Artho shrugged. "It's something to do."

She turned to the other screen with its bodies frozen in mid-writhe.

"Don't look at those!" Artho said.

"Just skins sewed together," she replied, grinning. "Do you like those, then?"

"Artho, do you know this kid or not?"

Artho found himself answering the child instead of Tamara: "No, I don't like them so much. I like people to look more real."

"Well, why do you make them look not real, then?"

From the mouths of babes and sucklings. "That's why they pay me the big bucks," he said ruefully, thinking of how far his paycheque wouldn't stretch this month.

"Do you like people making *you* be not real?"

Artho thought how he'd been late for work that morning because six taxis in a row had refused to stop for him. Thought of the guy in the corner store inspecting his money. Of Charlie elbowing him in the ribs a few hours ago. He felt a burn of rage beginning. "No, dammit!"

The ugly child just stood and stared at him from the depths of her ugly glasses.

"But it's not like I can do anything about it!" Artho said.

"Do you wanna?" She was shrugging out of her Spider Man knapsack.

He turned so he could scowl at her face straight on. "Shit, girl, what d'you think? Yes!"

Tamara giggled. Fuck, why was he talking to a kid this way? He started slamming pens and pencils around on the desk.

"Well, change things, then!" the child squealed. She lunged at Artho and swung her Spider Man knapsack right at his forehead.

It was like slo-mo; Artho could see the oddly muscular bulge of her lats powering the swing, almost had time to wonder how a seven-year-old could be that built, then he had barely focused on the red and black image of Spidey coming for him, reaching for him, when *bang*, the knapsack connected and something exploded inside Artho's skull.

Tamara yelled. Artho shouted, tried to reach for the kid through the stars flaring behind his eyes. Jesus, felt like a bag of bones the damned child had in there. "Shit, shit, shit," Artho moaned, holding his aching head. He dimly saw the child slither out of Tamara's grasp and run, no, glide out of the room on those skin-and-boneless legs. She had a big butt, too, that child; as she ran, it worked under her little plaid skirt like that of someone three times her size.

"Artho, you okay? I'm calling security."

He paid Tamara no mind. He was dizzy. He put his head down between his knees. It was wet, his forehead was *wet* where he was holding it. He was bleeding! Damned girl. He took his hand away, raised his head enough to inspect it.

"Yeah, Muhammed? Can you come up to Tri-Ex Media on 17? We got a little girl loose on this floor. No, don't know where she came from. Look, she just *hit* Artho, okay? I think he's hurt. Yes, a kid did it, she's little, maybe six, seven. Little black girl, school uniform, thick glasses. Says her parents aren't with her. Okay. Okay." She hung up. "He's coming."

There was no blood. At least, the stuff leaking out of him didn't look like blood. The liquid on his hand seemed to glow one minute and go milky the next, like a smear of syrup. "What is this shit?"

"Here, let me see." Tamara crouched down by him like she had by the little girl. Nancy. That's what her dad had called her. What kind of dad let his young kid roam around loose like that?

Tamara frowned. "Yeah, you're cut, but there's this weird . . . stuff coming out. Oh. Never mind, it's stopped now. How d'you feel, Artho?"

"What the hell was in that knapsack? Where'd she go?"

"I'll go see." Tamara jumped up, left the office.

Artho's head was clearing. It didn't hurt so much now. He touched where the cut was, couldn't feel one. The goop was still on his fingers, though. He rubbed the fingers together to smear the stuff away. His fingers kind of tingled.

But really, he felt a lot better now. He chuckled a little, thinking of the comic books he'd read as a kid. He'd been bitten by an overactive spider.

His computer pinged to tell him that it was done rendering. Shit. Had to get that stuff done tonight, or Charlie'd have his head. He moved back to his terminal to upload Tit for Twat. He reached for the mouse. He clicked on it, and the click felt like it traveled all the way through his arm. No, like it had come *from* his arm, down through his hand, to the mouse. Weird.

Tamara came back. "Found a little girl with her dad in the elevator. Could have been her. Looked a little bit like her, I guess. I mean, I can't tell, you know, they all look . . . I mean . . ." She stopped, blushing.

They all look alike. The superintendent of Artho's apartment building always mixed him up with Patrice who lived on the 27th floor, never mind that Patrice was dark café cru to Artho's caramel, was balding, had arms like thighs, and spoke with a strong French accent. Tamara had always been nice to Artho, though. And she knew what a bonehead she'd just been, he could tell. Right? Right. He swallowed, didn't say anything. Let Tamara believe he hadn't guessed what she'd almost said.

"Anyway," Tamara continued, "she's gone now. Muhammed's gone back to his desk. You feeling any better?"

"Yeah, thanks."

"Well." She stood there, still looking sheepish and uncomfortable. "Um, I'm going home now."

"See ya." He watched her put on her coat. He waved good-bye to her. Then he uploaded the site, ignoring the odd clicking feeling in his mouse arm. God, it made him feel clumsy. He'd have to get that checked out. Probably some kind of overuse thing. He clicked the file closed. Behind it was the autofellatio man. Hadn't he uploaded that one too? He went to do it, but the hand with the mouse slipped, and he ended up instead selecting the "changing oneself always" symbol he'd put on the man's arm as a joke. Yeah, better take that off. Just in case Charlie did figure out he'd done it. Didn't want to get his ass in trouble. He dragged the nkyin kyin symbol off the guy's arm, and what the fuck, it came all the way *off* the screen, skidded right across the keyboard, and came to rest on his thigh. Alarmed, he released the mouse. The symbol melted through the cloth into the meat of his leg. "Shit!" It tingled for a second, then faded.

Ah, fuck. Bloody weird day. He reached for the mouse again. When he clicked on it this time, something subtle changed about the autofellatio man. Artho stared hard at the image on the screen to try to see what was different. Yes, the nkyin kyin was back on the man's shoulder. And he was a little pudgier. And were those crow's-feet around his eyes? A hint of a smile around his wide-stretched mouth?

Whatever. Artho shrugged and uploaded the damned thing, ignoring the weird feeling in his arm every time he clicked the mouse.

Enough. Time to go home. Artho grabbed his coat, locked up, and left.

By the time the elevator had made it to the first floor, Artho was feeling really odd. Not sick, really, just faintly unreal, like when he smoked a joint too fast, or took sinus meds. He sighed, hoping he wasn't going to spend the weekend with the flu. At least it'd give him an excuse to skip going to his mum's. He put his hand on the door of the building to let himself out. *Click.* When he took the hand away, the nkyin kyin symbol was on it. He peered at the handle. Had it always been ornate worked brass? In the form of some kind of bug? No, now it looked like . . . a skeleton? Artho touched the handle again, double-clicked. And the handle was a plain aluminum strip once more.

Artho's skin began to prickle. Not with fear, not with fever. With hope. He rushed outside the building, put his palm against its dull brick exterior. Clicked. The walls flushed red, then purple. Fluted columns started to sprout beside the doors, which were quickly changing from sliding glass and steel to intricately joined oak. With big knockers. Artho giggled. Pretty damned tarty. He wondered if that had been the builder's original dream for the building. He double-clicked. The building reverted to its usual form.

"You're getting it."

When he turned towards the voice, Artho wasn't at all surprised to see the little girl. She was crouched down beside the steps, jam-jar glasses winking at him. Her hair knotted and unknotted itself.

"Can I change everything?" Artho asked.

"Course not, silly! Changing things isn't *your* job. You're not changing things; that'll happen anyway. You're just helping them peel off the fake skins."

"How's that work?"

"You'll just have to try it and see." She stuck her tongue out at him too. It was too pointy, and more lavender than pink. She leapt, stuck to the side of the building, started climbing smoothly up it, with two legs, with four. No wonder her behind had looked so, well, well-endowed. Must have had the other pair of legs hitched up under her skirt. The little girl was far above Artho now. He could just make out white panties with her legs sticking out of four leg holes. She climbed with two arms, with four. Ah. That well-muscled back. Artho smiled. He watched her until she disappeared into the darkness. He'd figured out who, what she was. Appeared as a skeleton sometimes, in a top hat. Watcher at the boundaries, at the crossroads. Sometimes man, sometimes woman. Always trickster. He couldn't really tell in the dark, but she seemed furrier now, or more bristly, or something. Sometimes spider? He wondered if this was the kind of thing her dad had really meant her to do.

Ah, well; she was notoriously capricious. She might decide to take her gift away again, so he'd better use it while he could. He set off for the streetcar stop, almost bouncing, dancing along in his excitement, thinking where he'd like to implant the Adinkra symbol next. On Charlie? Maybe Charlie really was the way he appeared to be. Oog. His Aunt Dee? What would Dee be like if she could peel away all that unhappiness?

How about on Aziman? All these choices. "Good evening," Artho said to the tired people waiting at the stop. One white woman clutched her purse tighter when she saw him. Hmm. Maybe he should work that nkyin kyin thing on himself; it was in him, after all. He wondered what she would see then.

"Tain't No Sin (To Dance Around in Your Bones)," words by Edgar Leslie, music by Walter Donaldson, 1929.

In 1995, I was accepted into the Clarion Science Fiction and Fantasy Writers' Workshop at Michigan State University. Going to Clarion had been a dream since I was a teenager. I begged and borrowed enough money to attend. I had no idea how I was going to repay it. I went to Clarion with no story ideas, no confidence that I had the talent to be a writer. For the first long, expensive week, I wasn't able to write at all, and I was terrified that the whole six weeks would be like that. Writer-in-residence Joe Haldeman warned that perhaps the worst way to try to break writer's block was with alcohol. Well, nothing else had worked, so on the Friday evening, desperate, I went on what for me is a mini-bender—probably three beers. Then I slept for a few hours, woke up in the late evening, and wrote the first draft of a story that I imbued with a terror that was alarming even as I was writing it.

SNAKE

He never wore any bright colours, nothing remarkable. Wouldn't want anyone to remember that he'd been hanging around. Faded jeans, scuffed running shoes. He bought cheap white T-shirts three to a pack from the nearby K-Mart. He always paid cash. He had a battered old van, but he walked to work, rarely drove. He saved that for special occasions.

He'd been drawn to this city by its peacefulness. Lots of open, green space, almost no crime, a good place to raise children. The city's main source of pride was that it was a bird sanctuary. Anyone who so much as flipped a rock at a pigeon had to pay heavy fines. The sign at the entrance to the city even boasted: "Where the Birds Come Home to Roost."

The sounds of the school playground tugged at him

every morning: the bright, happy laughter of the children; even their squabbles and scuffles. He enjoyed the small, twittering voices chanting jump rope games, the giddy shrieking as little bodies hurtled down the slide, one last game before the school bell rang and the children took flight like spooked birds. It made him sad to watch the schoolyard quickly empty when they ran inside.

If he woke early, he could spend a few minutes sitting in the large public park beside the school. He would buy a small cup of coffee, heavily sweetened, and a jelly doughnut (never from the same coffee shop twice in a row). He'd take his breakfast to one of the park benches—always a different one—and sit there, watching the children play. Starlings and sparrows would gather at his feet, cocking their heads at him, hoping for crumbs, but he ate too tidily for that.

The morning ritual soothed him: the milky smell of the coffee; the jammy, sticky doughnut. Two sips of warm, syrupy coffee to every bite of doughnut. He ate meticulously, being sure never to let the jelly touch his fingers. He'd been taught the virtues of cleanliness, and he practised them scrupulously. He would take small bites of his doughnut, then, with a little gulp, swallow each morsel whole, so that he wouldn't have to endure the sodden mass of chewed food in his mouth. When he was finished, he would carefully fold the brown paper bag in half, then again, and once more, firmly creasing each fold between the fingernails of his thumb and forefinger. He always made sure to deposit the wad of paper and the empty coffee cup in the garbage cans with the heavy swinging lids: litter disgusted him. The sight of gulls rooting in open bins for stale french fries sickened him. He hated the quarrelsome, messy birds.

In his mind, he had names for some of the school-children, the ones who caught his eye. The small but boisterous little girl who loved to climb to the very top of the jungle gym, she looked like a Jenny, his jenny-wren. Some might call her plain, but he noticed the way her pigtails bounced saucily on either side of her head as she played. She often beat the boys at marbles, crowing triumphantly as she claimed all the best taws and aggies. He could watch her for hours. She must have bruised her knee last week; a fall, perhaps. All week, she'd worn a Band-Aid on the knee. It mesmerised him, the contrast between her strong, muscular brown legs and the pale pink of the Band-Aid. She was left-handed, and had a loud, joyful laugh.

Then there was the thoughtful one. He'd christened her Samantha. She played happily enough with the others, but she liked to be alone, too. He could understand that. Samantha often sat nestled in the tire swing, one leg tucked up beneath her, the other trailing in the dust as she rocked gently back and forth, reading a book. She loved to read. He would squint at the covers from his park bench, but it was hard to make out the titles of the books. Samantha had straight, chin-length blond hair. As she read, she would trail some of her hair into her mouth. He often thought of her lips, sucking like that on her hair. There were other girls; Laura, Michelle, and Deb, or so he imagined their names to be. He never thought of names for the boys.

He would watch the children romp and argue, play and fight and scream and laugh. They were lively, messy little things. It fascinated him that no one punished them for spitting, for farting, for letting their hair come undone. He would study them until the bell rang, then go to his job in the mail room of the local public library.

It was routine, solitary work. It suited him well, he felt, the orderly routine of sorting the mail into its tidy cubbyholes.

There was a spry old couple who usually took an early-morning walk in the park, a brisk stride along the paths that wound through the trees. They brought stale cake in greasy brown paper bags from a pastry shop, and scattered crumbs for the birds as they walked. Sometimes they sat on a bench near to his, enticing the birds to peck from their open hands. "Look, Thomas," he heard the old woman say once, "that pigeon there; that's old Helga, I'm sure, the one whose broken wing you set? She's come along well, hasn't she?"

He took care never to make eye contact with the couple.

City Central Library was a huge, squat structure, nine floors high. Two stone creatures guarded the steps to the entrance, a griffin and a sphinx, weathered wings outstretched in what had once been majesty. Now, their stern faces were obscured by the bird fæces that had been drizzled down their heads by the gulls that roosted there. He didn't understand why the city went to such great lengths to protect the filthy creatures.

The mail room of the library was a musty, sprawling storage room in the basement. The heavy white enamelling of the stucco walls gathered dust; he spent a lot of time scrubbing at the years of dirt that had gone unnoticed by previous employees. Delivery trucks offloaded directly from the back door, large boxes of books, new library materials, magazine subscriptions. When he was done sorting the mail he would load it onto wheeled book trucks for each department. He would deliver them upstairs twice a day to the supervisor of each department: Media/Technology at 9:30 A.M. and 2:30 P.M.; Arts/Humanities at 9:45 and 2:45; Languages at 10:00 and 3:00; Children's at 10:15 and 3:15. He was never late. The supervisors were friendly, in an offhand way: "Hi, Stryker. Keeping well?"

"Yes, Miz Grady."

"That's good. Just put the box over here."

Mostly they didn't much notice him. People didn't. Except sometimes. Mrs. Herbert in Children's had let him have a poster to tape above his desk, a glossy picture of a little freckled girl flying against a backdrop of stars that formed words. He liked her mischievous grin and the knowing look in her eyes. "Books let your imagination soar," read the poster.

Some mornings he reached the park very early, before any of the parents had brought their children to school. It was quiet then, except for the birds. The park was always full of them, even in winter. Raucous starlings disputed the best spots on the power lines. Tiny house sparrows squabbled in the branches. There was even the occasional lurking crow.

In the mornings, as the wind whispered in the leaves of the old oaks, maples, and weather-twisted crabapple trees, people would walk their dogs in the park, picking up their pets' steaming excrement in plastic grocery bags. He approved of the cleanliness bylaw, but didn't see how the dog owners could bring themselves to touch the steaming, foul waste, even through a layer of protective plastic.

The park was a favourite spot for people practising Ta'i Chi, retirees trying to keep their joints limber. He'd become accustomed to the slow, crane-like gestures that they performed in unison, arms sketching strange patterns in the air while they bent their legs in a series of odd, consecutive movements. He was sure it didn't do them any good. The movements were too slow for any real exertion, and most of the exercisers were so old that they seemed near death anyway. But there they were, every morning, a gaggle of undignified eccentrics wearing old cardigans, loose pants, and soft slippers.

Some of them were loners, he'd noticed. One man always stayed off to one side of the main group, flapping his outstretched arms through a mysterious warmup. A bowed old Asian lady with one blind eye went through the movements with a plastic sword in one hand, a ridiculous instrument with a feathery yellow tassel hanging from its pommel. If that wasn't peculiar enough, she brought her pet with her, some kind of hunting bird with a wicked beak. It clutched her right shoulder as she swung about, bating its wings for balance. The bird *stared* all the time, as though if it looked at everything hard enough, it could make up for her unseeing right eye.

This afternoon, Stryker left work promptly at 3:45. He wormed his way through the rows of book trucks in the mail room, packed high with books to be returned to other branches, and slid out through the basement door. He'd been feeling restless and irritable all day— for weeks, in fact, but today was particularly bad. People had been bumping into him all day, as though they didn't see him. Even Mrs. Herbert in Children's hadn't greeted him as she normally would. It always happened. Sooner or later, everybody would walk all over him, like soil on the ground. Dirty. The tension was building up in him, it was starting to seep from his skin like ichor, thick and green, a sullen poison that would need to be leached soon.

Today, he took the quickest route home. Needed to be home. His apartment building was an old, low-rise brownstone, four floors of small, stuffy one-bedroom apartments with sealed windows and no balconies. He climbed the stairs to his fourth-floor unit. It was the easiest way to avoid striking up conversations in the elevator. He locked and barred his door behind him, removed his shoes in the entranceway, carried them immediately to the bathroom sink, where he washed them, inside and out, with soap. He dried them and applied a new coat of polish to the leather. Then he placed them just inside the front door, ready to wear the next day. He washed his hands three times, fronts and backs, and cleaned under his fingernails, too. There. That was a little better.

By now, the restless, irritable feeling had built to an almost delicious tension. He was leaking it.

Now. He took a plastic grocery bag from a drawer in the kitchen. Went into the small, orderly bedroom. Neatly made bed. Tiny dresser in the corner, no mirrors, no decorations. Reaching under the bed, he pulled out the shoebox. Now. Cross-legged on the bed, he opened the box. Took out the photographs. Fanned them out on the bed in front of him. His little pretties, his little birds. Plump Angelica, eight and a half, Toronto, September 1990; flighty Pauline, ten years old, Edmonton, December 1992; pouty Barb, nine years old, Vancouver,

July 1994. Now. The images flashed in his mind; smooth, hairless chests, soft as down. The sweet bite of rope into flesh. The soft cries. Now. Now. Yes. He unzipped the fly of the cheap jeans. Reached in. Freed the Snake. He wrapped the grocery bag around his stiff penis, took it in both hands. Closed his eyes and let the pictures in his mind flow as he drained the sticky poison. Now. Now. Yes.

He was going to have to move on soon, as soon as he'd made a new addition to his collection. He always moved immediately after doing that. He hated the inconvenience of it, but he was on edge all the time now. He had to do something about it, as he always did. After that, find another town, another cheap apartment, live on his savings for a few months until he'd found a job. By now, he had the sequence down pat. Two months' notice to the building superintendent. One month and a week after that, give two weeks' notice at the library. Be gone a week before the superintendent expects him to. Soon. As soon as he found a way to get what he needed. In the meantime, he rented a van under the name of Charles Coral, presenting Coral's driver's license and smiling pleasantly for the clerk around the cotton wadding in his cheeks. The fake moustache tickled his lip. He'd get rid of the false I.D. along with the van, afterwards.

But it was long weeks before the opportunity came. He had just made his last delivery to the Children's department one afternoon and was pushing his truck back towards the elevator when he heard a girl's excited voice. She was talking to a librarian at the information desk.

" . . . you mean, Gabrielle Singer is actually going to be here? At the library?"

"Yes," replied the librarian.

"No way! She's my favourite writer of all time!"

"It's a March Break program. She's going to be reading from her last book, you know the one?"

"*Madeleine Feldman, Girl Astronaut*? Oh, that's the best story! Especially the part where the girl, you know, Madeleine? The part where she saves the moon colony from blowing up? Gabrielle Singer is going to read from that?"

"Next Wednesday, seven o'clock, in the auditorium. It's free."

"Oh, I have to be there!"

Stryker casually stopped the truck behind one of the shelves of books, picked something at random off the shelves. *The Tale of Henny Penny.* He opened it, pretended to be reading it. Then he turned his head to look towards the information desk through the open rows of books.

It was his Samantha, his little chicken. His hands started to shake. He flicked his tongue out over and over to lick his dry lips. *Stay calm.* He replaced the book and kept on about his rounds, but his mind was working hard, planning the details. This was perfect. He'd have to cut his notice short at the library, but that was easy. He'd make up some excuse like a sick mother he had to nurse. Same excuse for his building superintendent, maybe even get his deposit back if she took pity on him.

Next Wednesday he'd finally be able to talk to Samantha, stand close to her, have her to himself for a little while. It couldn't have been better. He imagined that she had come here today especially for him. Sweet, flirtatious dove. A week to wait. The time would just crawl by.

At first he thought he would miss his chance. He'd come back to the library at 8:30, when the reading was supposed to be over. He waited behind the stone griffin, where none of the library employees would see him. The summer sun was just beginning to set. His heart fluttered when he saw Samantha skipping out the door, but she was laughing and chatting with two other girls. He couldn't speak to her with them watching. Mad with frustration, he had already turned away when he heard Samantha say, "Look, it's Old Helga! Mr. Peck fixed your wing up real good, didn't he, girl? I still have a cookie left from the reading; would you like some?"

He turned back to see his girl crouched on the library steps, hand held out to a pigeon in front of her.

"Come on!" urged Samantha's friends. "We can still catch the ice cream shop before we have to go home."

The bird cocked an interested eye at her and waddled closer. She took a cookie from her pocket and began crumbling one edge of it to feed the bird. "You go on ahead," she told the other girls. "I'll be right there."

"You and your old birds," one of them said. "Well, we're going." Arms held out like planes, the two girls swooped down the library steps, startling a flock of house finches in front of them.

"They can be such poopy-heads," Samantha whispered to the pigeon. "Laura always does what Katy says. Come on, Helga." She let the crumbs fall to the ground. The bird came closer, started pecking them up with one wary eye on her.

Stryker looked around. No one was watching. He walked up to the girl, touched her bare shoulder. "Samantha?"

She frowned up at him. "Huh? My name is Patty."

Mistake. Make something up. "I'm sorry. They told me inside . . . well, don't you want to get Gabrielle Singer's autograph?"

Patty shot to her feet, making the pigeon step back with a surprised burble. "No kidding? She's giving autographs?"

"Yes. It's a . . . special signing. Downstairs. I'll show you where."

"That's so cool. Those guys will be so jealous!" The girl brushed the rest of the cookie crumbs off her hands, waved at the ruffled old bird. "Bye, Helga. See you again soon." She followed Stryker around the back of the library, chattering happily about how good the reading had been. He opened the basement door with his key, escorted her inside. The lock clicked behind them. She turned to him with bright eyes. "Where's the signing going to be?"

He pointed behind her. "There." Now! She turned, he muffled her mouth with one hand, wrapped his other arm around her torso. The skin of her arm was velvety as down. He picked her up, but she struggled, kicked, nipped viciously at his hand. It hurt. He hissed, pulled the hand away.

"Hel—!" Patty shouted. He quickly clapped his hand to her mouth again.

"Sshh, little one, little bird. Stop fussing now. I'm not going to hurt you, I just want to spend some time with you."

She fought, kicked some more, tried to scream

against his palm. He held her firmly, loving her squirming warmth against him.

"They won't hear you down here anyway. The walls are too thick. Don't make me mad now. You wouldn't like me mad."

Her eyes went wide.

"Will you be good?" he asked her.

She nodded. Slowly, he let her go, but she bolted for the locked door, screaming. Bad, bad girl. It was easy to knock her to the floor, secure her hands behind her with the duct tape in his pocket. He took his time with the gag. He'd told the truth about the walls being soundproof. He'd experimented himself, turning up his radio to full volume as he worked. No one had ever complained. No one to hear her, no one to see him drag her into the van, waiting at the loading dock.

He wished that she could sit beside him as he drove. It would be nice to go for a drive with his girl, but he couldn't chance a passerby seeing the gag. He apologized for putting her in the back of the van, but he'd made it nice and comfortable, lined it with blankets, a soft nest. He took a minute to look at her before he closed the door. So sweet she looked. He told her that she wouldn't be in there for long.

He could hardly wait. His whole body was humming with triumph. He felt drunk on power, on anticipation, barely able to focus on the road ahead of him. He'd made her notice him. These were the moments he lived for. He took the road that would lead to the outskirts of the town, was zipping along, happy as a lark, when he saw the turnoff for the park with the adjacent school playground. He went warm with nostalgia for the hours he'd spent in that park. And it extended for acres, was practically a woods as you went farther out. The park would be the perfect place, their secret bower. He drove into the park, the empty, quiet, dark park. Once there, he doused the headlights. The van coasted almost silently; the clerk at the rental place had boasted that it would. He drove until the road became crunching gravel, then a narrow, hard-packed dirt path; kept going as the path gave way to scrub and shrubs that whipped the underside of the van as it clambered over them. It was getting more difficult to manœuvre the van now. Small birds, spooked, flew up out of the underbrush as he passed. He imagined those that hadn't gotten out of the way in time; their small bodies would be popping like grapes under his wheels.

There. Over there. The van would just fit inside that stand of trees. He drove it in amongst them, parked. Shut the engine off. He could almost hear his heart drumming. Soon. He sat for a bit, breathed slowly, felt his body go calm, cool.

He took the camera out of the glove compartment, slid out of the van, opened the back doors. She was so pretty, lying there with tears streaming down her soft cheeks, her bosom heaving, tiny cheeping noises escaping from the duct tape gag. Her nose was running too. How disgusting. But this had happened before, with other darlings of his. He used some tissue from the box he'd stored in the back of the van just for mishaps like this one. He wadded it thick so none of her snot would touch him, and lovingly cleaned her up, though she tried to yank her head out of his hands.

What was that clicking sound? A soft *tap-tap-tap*, like birds pecking at crumbs. He put the tissue down and peered through the stand of trees, looking back the way he'd come. In the dark he could just make out two people coming down the path, arm in arm, walking carefully, as the elderly do. It was the old couple that walked the park in the mornings. They moved purposefully, scrawny limbs pumping in jerky, almost avian motions as they made their way closer. Shit! What were they doing out in the woods this late at night? Bloody busybodies probably spent their time beating other lovers out of the bushes who just wanted some peace and quiet. Stryker went utterly still, trusting in the dark camouflage colours of his clothing and the van. Aging eyes wouldn't make him out, aging ears wouldn't hear Samantha's soft noises.

But they kept coming. He had to distract them. He quietly shut the doors on Samantha. She would stay put, she had no choice. He unzipped his fly, turned, and made his way to the dirt path. He stepped onto the path ahead of the couple, zipping himself up as nonchalantly as possible, just a guy out for a walk who'd stepped into the bushes to take a piss. He feigned startlement, embarrassment when he saw them, nodded in their direction.

The old man glared beadily at him. Stryker attempted a smile, a nod, just a neighbourly greeting. He felt his lips pull back into something more like a snarl. "Evening." He'd never been good at the niceties. They nodded back, silently. "Nice night for a stroll," he ventured. "Peaceful."

"Yes," they said, in unison.

Damn, they just stood there! He hoped they wouldn't spot the tire tracks. He couldn't do anything that would draw their attention over to where the van was. He moistened his lips with his tongue tip. "I'll just be on my way back, then." He tried to say the words cheerfully.

"Yes, we must too," they chorused.

Stryker brushed past the two. He swore he could feel the warmth of their bodies. He strolled back down the path, back the way he had driven a few minutes earlier. Were they turning to follow? Yes! Oh, soon, little chick, I'll be back for you soon!

The park was restless tonight. A capricious breeze made the branches of the trees flap fitfully, as though they would take flight. Stryker kept walking, forcing his feet into a slow, aimless glide. It seemed as though he'd been walking, carefully calm, for hours, but he was still only a few hundred yards from where he'd nested his van. Suddenly, a shadow swooped across the path, stopped directly in his way. He squinted into the dark, trying to see what it was. He didn't believe his eyes: the old, half-blind bag with the fake sword! She was holding it en garde, motioning with the other hand for him to stop. She must have weighed all of ninety pounds. He hissed his amusement at her, made to slide past her—and cried out as the blade struck with a horrible thud, biting deeply into the warding arm he was holding up. Pain burst like lightning through his body. Tonight, the sword was real. And she handled it with a master's ease. Incredulous, he clutched at the gash with his uninjured hand, curled the damaged arm against his body. It was already erupting blood in dizzying amounts. He couldn't move his fingers. He was in agony, he felt sick. He started backing away from the woman. She cocked her head at him, focused with her one good eye, and prepared to swing the sword again. Swallowing bile, he turned to run, and stumbled straight into the arms of the couple.

"You!" The old woman clawed at the front of his shirt, poking sharp fingers at his chest with each word. "What have you done with our Pat? Helga told us she was shouting for help!"

The pigeon told them? Stryker didn't answer. Blood slithered wetly from the gash in his arm. He tried to hold the slippery edges of the cut together. He felt his own blood; hot, sticky. Dirty. It was all over his hands. Dirty. He felt weak.

"Where is she?" screeched the old biddie's husband, thrusting a beaked nose inches from Stryker's eyes. Panicked, he wriggled out of their grasp, went running down the path. He'd get ahead of them, pop back into the woods when he was around a bend in the path, out of sight. He could lose them that way. But as he ran, he could see other figures converging on him. He recognized some of the morning exercisers. They waddled and hopped as fast as their aging legs would carry them. It would have been ludicrous if he hadn't been so dizzy from shock and blood loss. He *hurt!* He stepped off the path, staggering. He made as quickly as he could for some sheltering trees. He could move very quietly, hide in the tiniest spaces. As he approached the copse, a cloud of birds swooped down on him from their branches, all types of birds. They dug their tiny claws into his already bruised body and pecked at any exposed flesh, twittering, cawing, screeching their rage. He smelt his own coppery blood in the night air. He struck the birds off, crushed and stamped on the tiny bodies like fleas, but more replaced them. As many as he pulped underfoot, there were more. The air boiled with them. The heavy smell of blood and feathers made his head reel. He stung all over from the bite of claws and beaks.

And the old people were on him now, drawn by the sound. They poked him with their canes, jabbed at him with umbrellas. "Yes! Keep at it, Robin; don't let the slimy bastard get away!"

Huge claws tangled in his hair. A massive pair of wings beat about his head, blinding him. The cry was the challenge of a hunting bird. He stumbled, fell, writhed quickly onto his back so he could see his attacker. Screeching, the old woman's pet landed on his chest, stabbed at his eyes. He tried to bat the great hooked beak away, but the bird struck at his hand. He felt two fingers snap in its talons. He put his hands up to protect his eyes. The bird set its beak in his throat and tore it out. Spreading its wings, it hopped up to its mistress's shoulder, where it swallowed the gristly lump of flesh.

Air rattled in Stryker's ragged throat, whistled out from his neck. He could feel his body arching, his heels drumming on the earth. The old guardians just watched, alert.

It took a little time for asphyxiation to kill him; long enough for his darkening eyes to see his Samantha, his darling pigeon, being escorted from the van by a clutch of old women, a brood of old hens, straightening her clothing and clucking soothing words at her.

Boston subway stops have the oddest names: Braintree. And Alewife (which, Bostonians will explain helpfully, is a fish). One day, traveling on the Toronto subway system, I could have sworn that the driver announced Saint Mare Wash as the next stop. The mundane Saint Clair West paled in comparison. In parts of Toronto, they wrap the trees with burlap in winter to protect them. And then, I've always liked Hans Christian Andersen's fiction . . .

UNDER GLASS

Lying on the chilly bank of the splinterswirling river, Sheeny shook the obsidian rectangle of the playscreen in her hands, then swiped her palm over its blankened surface. In response, its opalescent screen swarmed with vague, sluggish forms: something large and blocky, a building, maybe; smaller somethings moving around it; motes fluttering. Did that tiny shape in the foreground look like Kay? No, no; stop it. Create instead a new story in the masses on the screen. Cobble a fake story out of tales that Jeff used to tell, of worlds that used to might could be, places that she'd never seen, could only imagine.

The shapes were curdling into solid images. A tiny old woman stood inside the picture blossoming on the playscreen:

The cold morning light was the soft grey of a dove's breast feathers. Old Delpha, old lady, stood on the wintry street corner, looking at the construction site that had been sprouting there for the past few months like a stop-motion film; of ice crystals, maybe, growing branch by angular branch upon each other like frozen towers.

Kneeling on the second-floor girders of the skeleton building, a welder flipped her mask down and put her lit torch to a joist. A hissing tongue of blue flame jutted. To the burring sound of the torch scouring the metal—a tongue-lashing, Delpha giggled to herself—a myriad motes of orange light sprang from the join, fountaining red-gold to the ground. A flock of fat pigeons descended eagerly on the sparks, wings pumping the birds whup-whup-whup down. They quarreled and jostled for space, pecked up the glowing embers as fast as they could. Smart pigeons. They knew how to keep their insides warm, anyway. Wouldn't be them turning to cold glaze when the glass wind hit. They'd be warm, from the inside out.

The welder didn't pay any attention to them, nor to the first icy fingers of wind flicking at the collar of her orange flameproof. Delpha wouldn't bother to warn her, either. Silly woman.

"There's a glass wind coming," Old Delpha muttered to the girl who was watching her from the other place. Interfering little chit. Little voyeur. Delpha felt a teeny twitch of uncertainty from the girl who was sensing a thought she hadn't birthed; Delpha's thought. Serve her right.

Glass wind. Winter flinter. Delpha could feel it in her achy bones. Fracture-streamy glass wind blowing up screeling across the river from the mountains into the city. Screaming like the angry dead through the valley; glass grinding the city's more glass windows into shivershatter-splinters. A breaking wind. It would be here soon, stinging *singing cold, rattling the leafless branches of the wind-scoured trees, whipping icy slivers into hair and eyes. The Whetherman had said so this morning on the radio. Indications were, he'd said. But opposing opinions, he'd said. Never know whether. Idiot. Delpha hummed the jingle that was perfect for the Whetherman: "Whether the weather is cold, or whether the weather is hot, we'll weather the weather, whatever the weather, whether we like it or not." It'd be cold and hot and cold again. And no, they wouldn't like it.*

It was all that stupid girl's fault, playing with her toy.

Tinkling, twinkling, the river ground coldly by. A swirl of breeze abraded Sheeny's cheek. Kay's lips, his cold-chapped lips had brushed across her cheek so. Absently she wiped her hand over the irritated spot on her face, and brought it away blood-streaked. "Shit!" Alarmed, she yanked her concentration from the playscreen. Untended, the picture froze.

Sheeny looked up the valley. Damn. There *was* a glass wind coming, like she'd thought her head had said: blowing down the valley out of the deadlands, making the splinter-scoured trees rattle their deceasing branches. She got to her feet, no longer interested in the spring tumble of water chuckling between the river's banks, roiling with masses of ground glass too fine to see, too deadly to drink unless it'd been sifted and filtered and filtered again. She looked up the valley; across parched, bare, red earth for miles, nothing to relieve the eye but a few almost-expired trees like clutching hands, towards the two mountain shoulders with the deadlands sitting between their collarbones.

No head, only that deep, parched, hollowed-out valley. She could just make out the dark haze of the glass wind swirling down. She could hear it now too; a pleasant tinkling sound at this distance, like ornaments on the Christmas trees, Before. So Mumsie said they'd sounded.

She shouldn't have been by the riverbank, daydreaming of Kay. But it was the only place to go to avoid the eyes of her neighbours, gone cold with blame at the sight of her. And Mumsie's accusing eyes. How could Sheeny have known what would happen? She tugged at the filter hanging from weathered elastic at her neck, pulled it up over her nose and mouth. Fat lot of good that would do if she got caught out in the wind. She hugged the playscreen to her chest and started running for home.

The rhythmic pounding of her feet covered a little the sound of the wind whistling down. She sent her mind wandering, to keep it calm . . .

She'd read about Christmas trees, seen pictures in Kay's old picture book, the one possession he'd brought with him when her family took him in. Christmas trees used to have this green . . . fuzz on them, not just bare, sandpapered branches that only stayed up one day and were used for fuel the next. Christmas trees didn't have glass ornaments anymore. Mumsie said the soft clinking sound would drive people crazy with fear, thinking they were hearing the glass wind, the crazed, screeching, splinter-whipping gale that would flense flesh from bone in seconds. Sheeny ran faster, ignoring the way her boots pinched where she had outgrown them.

Never mind the Whetherman. Old Delpha knew what the weather would be: Glass. Winter's cold first, then a great big bang boom, then glass. Molten hot, running like rivers and beautifully red. Cold again, descending with the dark ash cloud. A keening, cold iridescence that could freeze your eyes solid as marbles. Then all you saw, peering through ashy light, was the last thing before the freezing. If a glass wind got into your eyes, you had only one point of view forever after. If it slid into your heart, then you were really in trouble. There you'd be, your heart hardened to a lump of frigid, frozen meat, just offal from the butcher's. Shake the picture up all you want, this one won't change. Unless the girl made it home safely, re-drew her playscreen. Could happen. The picture wasn't solid yet. Weird, how it had made a world where the girl could hear her, only her. "Run," Delpha whispered into the otherworld, the one behind the glass.

Mumsie had a cow's glass-scoured thigh bone. Thick, like a young tree trunk, and half Sheeny's height. Mumsie kept it on top of the bookshelf, to remind herself and to scare Sheeny.

"Was Dodder, that," she would tell Sheeny, jerking her sharp chin in the direction of the bone. "An old cow of ours, born Before. Me and Jeff, we'd taken the cattle out to the water troughs and she wandered off. Didn't have the sense to get in when she heard the glass wind coming. We shoved in the house with the cows and all, but Dodder, she was way out, heading for where she remembered the pasture to be, never mind it's just dirt and rock there now. No time to roust her back. Wind singing through the valley, blowing down fast.

Me and you—you were just two, you wouldn't even remember—and Jeff, we all clambered with the cattle down the basement, hunkered down there in the mouldy hay. The cow farts smelt like fermented grass."

Mumsie didn't tell the story much anymore, because she'd have to say Jeff's name when she did. Sheeny'd been with her stepdad Jeff when he'd coughed his last. Mumsie'd come home with her buckets of splintery water to find Sheeny cradling his head, weeping. Sheeny'd looked up to see sorrow and blame burning deep behind Mumsie's eyes. Sheeny never knew whether Mumsie blamed herself for not having been there in Jeff's last moments, or whether she blamed Sheeny because Sheeny had.

Sheeny ran, the howler at her back.

"Just keep going, girl!" Delpha hissed. The child obliged, pounding her bounding way to home and safety. And when she got there, she'd make a new picture with her toy. She didn't know that the thing altered worlds. No one knew, yet.

Delpha had to admire the little chit's strong lungs, not even thinking of tiring yet. She was so young, hadn't breathed in much glass. Yes, Run. Like that. Be a gingerbread girl, not yet baked solid. Run. Save us all. Run.

Slamming across bare earth, Sheeny trod on a stone in her too-small boots. It shifted under her foot; she stumbled, crying out as she felt her ankle twist. The playscreen went tumbling. Something cracked inside it. No time to mind that. Sheeny straightened, gritted her teeth against the crunch of pain, and ran on, leaving the playscreen making unhappy grinding noises on the ground. Behind her, the wind sound was louder now, a buzzing like the sky was full of angry bees.

She shouldn't have been by the river. It was too far away from home, from safe windowless cement enclosures and steel doors abraded to a smooth shine by the wind. But the river, it called her. Mumsie knew that's where Sheeny was nowadays, if she couldn't be found. Mumsie scolded her for it, beat her sometimes, but she couldn't stay away. She needed to spend time just crouched by the river, away from Mumsie's silent accusations, staring at the only thing that lived free beneath the sky, never needing shelter. Kay had jumped into that river when he couldn't face living under glass any longer.

"That wind hit dead soon," Mumsie had told her. The Dodder story. "Scraping, scraping against the house, and screaming 'cause it couldn't get at us. I dunno if Dodder screamed too, when it caught her. Couldn't hear nothing but that scraping, screeching wind. Could feel you though, sobbing in my arms, clutching at my bodice, and me sobbing right back, but soft, so you wouldn't feel it. So you'd learn how to be strong.

"Jeff, he went up the basement steps, checked to make sure the hatch was bolted. Good, thick steel, that door. He'd checked it twice already, and anyway, no wind would have made it all the way through the tunnel upstairs, but that was Jeff. If he could do something, he felt better."

Sheeny's ankle stabbed with each step; sickly jolts of pain that made metallic-tasting saliva squirt in her mouth. She glanced over her shoulder. In the distance, an army of black cones twirled, screeling. The wide, flat land made it hard to tell how close; too close. The sound they made was a granular scraping, like sandpaper grinding away. She sobbed, stumbled on.

"When it was over," Mumsie had said, "we went out. Up to the upper level, out through the tunnel. We had to unhook the carpets from the wall. Laid them down, crawled through the tunnel on them. Glass all the way inside the first two doors. The outside one was blasted open. Mound of glass sand as high as my knee in front of it. Left Jeff sweeping up, you trying to help. I went to find Dodder. Was still a bit of breeze. The glass had gone on in front though, so it was safe enough by then.

"All left of Dodder was great ropes of flesh that the breeze was stirring about on the ground. They glittered with grindglass, so pretty . . . And the ground soaked in blood, and bones scattered everywhere, scoured smooth and white like they'd been bleaching in the sun for years. And her skull. I remember. Gaping up blind at me from the ground. After that, we slaughtered all the cows, gave the meat out to the whole town. We couldn't look out for them all the time anymore. Besides, the mouldy hay was making 'em sick, and we couldn't grow no more."

Something had gone crack in the world when the playscreen broke. Something big and silent. Only Delpha knew it had happened. The world picture had slipped sideways, was grinding distressfully on the ground. It was the

damned girl had gone and done it, blowing her troubles back in all their faces. This is how it started. Delpha whimpered. Time and history would all be crazed now, like broken windows.

The welder turned her torch off. Their meal gone, the birds flew away.

Old Delpha could hear how the wind would come, screaming. The centre one of the giant triple mountains had bulged, puffed its cheek out, ready to blow. Delpha wished her eyes were strong enough to see the scientists clambering about it, taking measurements. Any day now, they said. Whether or not. Some of them would get off the mountain in time, get into planes and fly away to safety, if this new cracked-crazed world held any such. She'd get on a plane too, if she could afford a ticket. If she could stop mumbling and shuffling and could remember to keep her hair combed for long enough to pretend normal so that they'd let her on.

Striped yellow and black and bumbled as bees, a school bus pulled up to the corner. Little children tumbled out, all squeals and shrieks and gambols and galumphs and Gumbie sneakers and Maximal Morphin' Mounties lunch boxes going creak-creak as the kids swung them by their handles. The children were so sweet, it hurt Delpha to watch them.

On the grass verge (brown grass now it was winter, going to become even Fimbul-er, but nothing to be done about that), three trees that had been wrapped in burlap against the cold shuffled creakily out of the children's way. Crazed-crazy time. They moved like old ladies in shapeless coats, shuffling with swollen ankles. The sight made Delpha chuckle a little. The old lady trees huddled at the side of the road, their spiny green-tongued needles chatterly gossipping to each other from under their dumpy burlap coats while the soon to be groundglass wind sang around them, dumping shivery ice splinters into their burlap folds, making them twinkle in the sun like movie stars in the camera's glare, like ropes of twirled raw gut. Could no one else hear the grinding?

"Next stop, Saint Mare Wash, Fishwife, and Brainstem," yelled the driver. "Hurry home, kids. Your parents are packing." The little bus waddled off, lumpy with its weight of rambunctious children. Poor children.

Delpha had never heard of those schools before. Saint Mare Wash she understood. She guessed somebody had to learn how to keep the old Night Mare clean. Yeah, she was a goddess, but she probably got dirty, galloping through people's dreams all night, making them gasp with terror. Old workhorse. She probably got all lathered. So Saint Mare Wash made sense. But Fishwife? Brainstem? Delpha started walking, trying to figure it out. Was there a way out? Out from under? She thought about fishwives and tongue-lashings and scolds and shrews and tried to keep it all straight in her mind, how she might get out, but it made no sense. It made her brainstem hurt. A school for fishwives? Cold as a fish, people said. "Shut up!" she screeched at the burlap tree women.

"Scold; cold scold," one of them taunted her. They were shuffling along the grass, keeping up with her as she walked. "Where's your warm one now?"

Seemed to Delpha she'd had one who kept her warm. But gone now. Left her when Delpha's brain broke—that's the story the world was telling now—broke, and they tried to glue it back together with pills. "Old broads," she muttered at the tree hags. "Old broad beams. High blow shatter you."

They gasped, offended, then froze where they were, pretending to be trees again. But she could hear them still windily whispering to each other about her. Their needle tongues rustled. Doc in this new story would say there were *no talking trees, just her meds, new stuff they had tried on her that had broken her brain apart. But it was everything that was broken, not just her. Shattered everything seven ways from Sunday, they had. With those damned toys, those screen things that trapped stories under glass. Pieces all the way into the future, the past, the never. And when the blasted things broke, they were all stuck with that story. Delpha glared at the tree ladies, kept walking. They wouldn't last the heat of the glass wind out, nor the cold neither.*

The breath was burning, burning past Sheeny's throat. Felt like she'd swallowed glass. Maybe she had. Glass wind roaring down to strip flesh from her bones, it had probably blown dust ahead of it before she'd put her filter on. Glass to catch in her throat and scrape it raw, fill her lungs with glistening sand, harden her heart to stone. Always silicone sand in the air, glistening on the ground, even without the glass wind. Old people died from it, coughed to death, spitting gleaming red sand. Stained glass. So lovely.

Sheeny had been nine when her family took Kay in. His dad was his last people, the rest blown sky high when the mountain went. Pneumonia took Kay's father, and so he'd come to them. Eleven years old. And pretty. Skin just beginning to pimple; swollen, perfect lips; and that delightful, husky, breaking voice. Was about three years before Sheeny really took all that in though— how much she enjoyed the sight of Kay, the smell of him when he'd been working all day, helping Jeff build another shelter over someone's basement. Concrete igloos with long, curved tunnels for entranceways. You had to stoop to get inside, then crawl through five doors for keeping glass out. She took to helping Kay make those tunnels, so she could watch his heart-shaped backside proceeding ahead of her as he smoothed walls with his trowel.

And soon he'd noticed her noticing. Was in one of those tunnels that she and Kay had first kissed. The touch of his lips and tongue against hers had lodged a sliver of something in her heart. His hand had grazed over her canvas jumpsuit, thick weave to keep glass out. His hand brushed over where her breast hid, under layers, and her nipple jumped to attention. Her heart pounded and pounded, but couldn't dislodge the sliver. She'd pulled back to look at Kay. Glass in her eye? He looked different, he glowed. She leaned in again, laid the warm flat of her tongue against the hollow of his neck. He groaned. She sighed.

Sheeny hadn't meant for Kay to go away and never come back, didn't Mumsie understand? Sheeny'd wanted a boy who would divine her true nature, and love her passionately forever for it. She'd wanted love to blow her world apart, to fall on her like houses. That's what she'd thought. But when it had finally happened, everyone, everyone could see. In the hitch of her breath when Kay walked into a room; in the way her eyes filled up with him, her fingers moved by themselves to clutch his. They could all see! And they'd looked at her and Kay differently. Some wanting what they had, hating them for having it. Some hoping that something so fragile could survive weeks huddled in concrete huts, hours sifting water glass through gauze and filters for its moisture, days watching the spidery crops in the watery light and hauling the troughs in at the first sign of a breeze. She had hated being so transparent, hated that everyone could see. Love had snuck into her heart and lightened it, made it clear, easy to see through. Kay wanted to love her warm. She couldn't stand it, couldn't let herself melt into another's contours. She made herself cold to him again to keep separate, to keep eyes off her. She'd learned to look at Kay again with obsidian eyes, like everyone else.

First love feels like everything. It was too much; Sheeny couldn't stand to let it overtake her. And Kay couldn't stand losing it, not when he'd already once lost all he'd loved. It was her gaze gone cold that had put him under glass, sent him stumbling to the river. Jeff gone, then Kay. Mumsie's blaming eyes found Sheeny's more nowadays. Now Mumsie never filtered the water one last time for Sheeny anymore before she poured her a drink. Never shook the sandy glass out of Sheeny's gloves anymore when she left them in the tunnel.

The pain in her foot made Sheeny retch. Nearly home. The low cement domes were only about a minute away, steel doors battened against the wind. No one out looking for her. No time, when the wind came down. Time to get inside then. Had Mumsie locked the doors already? Sheeny's right thigh knotted, brought her crashing to one knee. She didn't feel the splinters slipping into her skin like bamboo slivers under fingernails. She heaved back up to her feet, ran on, her legs wobbling.

A sovereign for a sovereign remedy . . . Fuck, it was cold. Fuckcold. Cuckold. No, she'd be faithful. Had no choice, no plane fare, no way to unbreak the glass. But she had enough for two bottles of bitters from the corner store.

The guy behind the counter gave her an extra one, then hurried her out. "Gotta close up, lady. Getting my ass outta here. Radio says. You should leave too."

The story was hardening to bone, stone, silicone. Delpha clutched her three bottles. They made hard little squeaks as they rubbed against each other. Forty percent cold ethyl times three, and then Delpha wouldn't care what came. 'Cause it was coming. The nighttime air was crackling with it. Stupid, stupid girl, with her games and her hard gaze.

Delpha stepped outside the store, squinted at the mountain. Her eyes too glassy to see if the peak's cheek was bulging bigger. Look, I'm a zit. Pop.

She fumbled one of her bottles open, tasted the dark, astringent potion inside. Nice. Bent her head back, swallowed. More. All gone. Her belly warming, molten. All around her, loaded cars full of goods and their people, faces stiff with panic. Everyone leaving, end to end, not going fast enough. "Hey!" she yelled into the window of a deep green family van, "I don't wanna be under glass either! Take me with you!" The woman at the wheel put her head down, gunned the engine. It took them all of six feet before they had to stop behind the ass of the fat rich Cadillac in front of them. Two kids in the van twisted their heads round to look at her. The older boy was holding a playscreen, shak-shak-shaking it to make a new image. Imagine unblown, Delpha thought at him. Imagine unglass. But that screen led to another world, not this one. In this one, the groove of all their tracks was set, was lying on a desert floor, grinding down. She spat at the van, watched the spittle hit pavement, freeze into a lump of pearlized glue chip. She waved the van away, shuffled into the road. Horns blew. "Take me!" she yelled. Horns blatted. She made it to the other curb.

Delpha swigged back another bottle of bitterness. Her feet were a little shaky now. Cold, so cold. Shivershatterday *cold. Tomorrow would be Noneday, ever after. All the girlie's fault.*

Not so much noise in the streets now. Plenty of folks gone.

Cold. The doorway to the crazy people place yawned at her, belching warmth. She swayed towards it, but its avid lips snapped together while she was still out of reach. She swung her fist in triumph at the building. "Missed me!" She could see the flagstone fangs sticking out. She flung her nearly empty bottle to shards against the building's face. Shatter, splatter. The façade snarled at her, but couldn't reach. With a crackly cackling, she opened the last bottle of warmth in glass, toasted the squatting concrete structure. The building hissed, spat. She drank, kept moving.

"Jeff, where'd it come from, the glass?" Those days, Jeff had still been around, lungs intact, to answer Sheeny's questions. They were sitting on little stools just outside the house, reading by the last few rays of daylight. Books on cement construction, on water filters. At her question, Jeff had looked over at her, squinting. He took his spectacles off, polished the lenses on the sleeve of his shirt, put them back on. Wouldn't help him see any clearer, though. He'd dropped the specs on the ground too many times. Glass dust had ground the lenses to a pearly finish. Eyes were pretty ground down too. Jeff went outside too much.

"Well, Sheeny-girl," Jeff had drawled at her. "Your Mumsie has a theory about that." He'd flicked a look at Mumsie, who just turned the ends of her mouth down and kept knitting by the fading daylight. "Yeah," he continued. "She says that when the mountain blew and took the city with it, all those skyscrapers with their millions and millions of windows, it must have blown shatterglass high into the air to be picked up by the winds. Yeah. She says that the glass house people have finally thrown the biggest stone they could, and broke the whole kit and kaboodle. Time to come, she says, the glass'll grind itself back down to sand, and then there'll be just one big desert."

Mumsie knitted faster, mouth pursed like a bumhole, cracking the needles together.

"Y'know that playscreen you and Kay are always staring in? Used to make them up on that mountain. Big factory. Gone too."

Wind keened. Sheeny ran, her ankle jabbing and stabbing.

As she shuffled and shivered on her way, near asleep, Delpha's fingers loosened. Crash woke her. Crunch of glass underfoot made her jump alert. She licked clear ice off broken lips, tasted salt slurry of blood starting up again. Her mouth stung. Her stomach and head were woozy with bitters. She looked up the valley. Dark, too dark to see the looming mountain.

There was a turgid slush and wash sound. The air smelled sodden, rotting. She was down near the docks, at the mouth of the river. How had she come so far?

The skirling of the dancing winds tore at Sheeny's back. The sound drove ice picks into her ears. She eyeballed the nearest shelter. Leon's. She pulled her coat off, tied it around her head. Hands in front of her, she ran for Leon's. Tripped on rocks, kept going. A sword was jabbing up into her ankle. She barely registered the thud of her hands hitting Leon's shelter. Whimpering, she fumbled round and round it until she felt the tunnel, patted frantically along it till she was kneeling at its entrance. She pulled on the door. Locked. She pounded on the tunnel walls, yelled. She couldn't hear herself above the grating howl.

No one opened. The glass wind hit with a ululating joy, tumbled her off her feet, shrapnelled the skin of her exposed hands into a bloody screaming mess. Somewhere back in the wasteland, the playscreen was scoured and pummelled into pieces. The fragments scattered into glittering dust.

The glass wind skirled.

The frigid sky was still cyan, staining fast to black. Glacial black all around her. Delpha staggered past blocky storage, feet tramping now over the thick wooden planks of the jetty. Hollowthump. Clump. Again. She could feel her toes only too well, throbbing and burning.

No ships more, all gone. The crushed ice water, half frozen, gleamed and washed, gleamed and washed. Delpha was shivering like a kite in the wind now, like a burlap lady in a storm. It was coming, the blow was coming, it would tear her apart. She was shaking with cold and with hatred for the careless child who'd brought them to this. She hoped that in other worlds they'd understood the danger of the playscreens.

Delpha slowly removed one ratty coat, fingers pushing numbly at the buttons to make them work. The air rushed in, came at her in stabbing shards. She unbuttoned the second coat, the one with the torn lining. She shucked both coats to the ground. She trembled belly-deep. She hoped she knew the way, hoped it wasn't just her speech that could cross worlds in this new physics the girl had made. "I'm going to get out from under." She pulled her clothing away until she was banana-peeled, standing juddering on the jetty, wearing only the crusted socks in their sole-thin boots with missing laces. Nothing of this place to weigh her down. Stiff-legged 'cause she could no longer feel how to bend at the knee, she lurched to the end of the jetty. Nutty banana, all she needed was creamy ice to make it complete. Dessert time. Time to lose it all. She tried to grin at the grinding water, her new love. Not a warm one. Her teeth chattered, made her smile a rictus. Muscles shuddershaking into cramps, she couldn't jump. She just leaned. Fell. The splash of landing in the unspeakable lump-ice water froze the scream in her chest. She sank briefly, then rose to the surface again, a bobbing Delpha-sicle finally come to the yearning, intimate cold.

With sullen, icy fingers the wind lovingly circled and circled and circled Delpha's tumid nipples, making them crinkle and jut painfully long and hard. She gasped and panted hot breath. The wind supped it from her mouth and blew it back changed, a cooling fog. Yes, take it all away. Frigid air slid over her breasts, pooled in her navel, lapped lazily at her cunt like winter lakes, making her flow. She was all goose bumps, laved in ice, shivershivering. The viscous wash of the water's tongue carried her on its slow tide, lick, lick, lick, and she was trembling uncontrollably, chilled through to her core. Her limbs were frost-coated. They would shatter with her shuddering. Come for me, I'll come for you. She managed to spread her legs, open the heat of her. The sea sucked at the hard knot of her clit with a tonguetip dipped in ice. Orgasm crackled her jangling into fragments. She was half *aware of the water surging the length of her body like ice floes to cover her. The last thing she saw was a steely wash of it that loomed above her, then crashed, entered eyes, mouth, all her holes. She screamed, impaled by cold glassy ice.*

In a concussion that could shatter eardrums, the mountain exploded. Molten flame poured out. Delpha never knew.

Mumsie's house was next. Wind stripping her, Sheeny ran. Stumbled. Ran. Carommed off the side of her house. Found the tight-locked tunnel door and banged and banged with bleeding hands. Would Mumsie forgive?

Huddling alone in her stone igloo, Sheeny's Mumsie Adelphine had dozed off. The hollow banging sound startled her awake. She opened her eyes, looked around. Delpha had made it to the other side, had always been there now. She remembered bearing Sheeny, remembered losing Dodder. And Jeff, and Kay. All the warm ones gone; only that hated bleeding girlchild with so much to learn, the one who had shaken the world and broken it. Adelphine sat up, her hands curling into the position where she'd held a tiny two-year-old head once between her breasts, protecting the child and stilling her sobbing. Teaching her to be strong, hard-hearted; ice to the heat of the hurtful world. Sheeny'd always been a quick girl.

There was a story once about mirrors and cold. Adelphine had read it, somewhere in another sometime. Glass splinters freeze your heart, but it's still in you. Still sitting there in your chest, sullen, solid. Letting nothing in or out. Not blood, not anything. You lose heat and colour from being so bloodless, and there you are, no feeling. Solid and pale, merciless as the glass wind itself. Under glass.

The hollow thumping demanding to be let in was still strong. Mumsie swung her unfamiliar feet to the floor and stood, considering.

In my anthology Whispers from the Cotton Tree Root: Caribbean Fabulist Fiction, *I introduced the following story with these words: "Eggs are seeds, perfectly white on the outside. Who knows what complexions their insides might reveal when they crack open to germinate and bear fruit?"*

THE GLASS BOTTLE TRICK

The air was full of storms, but they refused to break.

In the wicker rocking chair on the front verandah, Beatrice flexed her bare feet against the wooden slat floor, rocking slowly back and forth. Another sweltering rainy season afternoon. The arid heat felt as though all the oxygen had boiled out of the parched air to hang as looming rainclouds, waiting.

Oh, but she loved it like this. The hotter the day, the slower she would move, basking. She stretched her arms and legs out to better feel the luxuriant warmth, then guiltily sat up straight again. Samuel would scold if he ever saw her slouching like that. Stuffy Sammy. She smiled fondly, admiring the lacy patterns the sunlight threw on the floor as it filtered through the white gingerbread fretwork that trimmed the roof of their house.

"Anything more today, Mistress Powell? I finish doing the dishes." Gloria had come out of the house and was standing in front of her, wiping her chapped hands on her apron.

Beatrice felt the shyness come over her as it always did when she thought of giving the older woman orders. Gloria was older than Beatrice's mother. "Ah . . . no, I think that's everything, Gloria . . . "

Gloria quirked an eyebrow, crinkling her face like running a fork through molasses. "Then I go take the rest of the afternoon off. You and Mister Samuel should be alone tonight. Is time you tell him."

Beatrice gave an abortive, shamefaced "huh" of a laugh. Gloria had known from the start, she'd had so many babies of her own. She'd been mad to run to Samuel with the news from since. But yesterday, Beatrice had already decided to tell Samuel. Well, almost decided. She felt irritated, like a child whose tricks have been found out. She swallowed the feeling. "I think you right, Gloria," she said, fighting for some dignity before the older woman. "Maybe . . . maybe I cook him a special meal, feed him up nice, then tell him."

"Well, I say is time and past time you make him know. A pickney is a blessing to a family."

"For true," Beatrice agreed, making her voice sound as certain as she could.

"Later, then, Mistress Powell." Giving herself the afternoon off, not even a by-your-leave, Gloria headed off to the maid's room at the back of the house to change into her street clothes. A few minutes later, she let herself out the garden gate.

"That seems like a tough book for a young lady of such tender years."

"Excuse me?" Beatrice threw a defensive cutting glare at the older man. He'd caught her off guard, though she'd seen his eyes following her ever since she entered the bookstore.

"You have something to say to me?" She curled the Gray's Anatomy *possessively into the crook of her arm, price sticker hidden against her body. Two more months of saving before she could afford it.*

He looked shyly at her. "Sorry if I offended, Miss," he said. "My name is Samuel."

Would be handsome, if he'd chill out a bit. Beatrice's wariness thawed a little. Middle of the sun-hot day, and he wearing black wool jacket and pants. His crisp white cotton shirt was buttoned right up, held in place by a tasteful, unimaginative tie. So proper, Jesus. He wasn't that much older than she.

"Is just . . . you're so pretty, and it's the only thing I could think of to say to get you to speak to me."

Beatrice softened more at that, smiled for him and played with the collar of her blouse. He didn't seem too bad, if you could look beyond the stocious, starchy behaviour.

Beatrice doubtfully patted the slight swelling of her belly. Four months. She was shy to give Samuel her news, but she was starting to show. Silly to put it off, yes? Today she was going to make her husband very happy; break that thin shell of mourning that still insulated him from her. He never said so, but Beatrice knew that he still thought of the wife he'd lost, and tragically, the one before that. She wished she could make him warm up to life again.

Sunlight was flickering through the leaves of the guava tree in the front yard. Beatrice inhaled the sweet smell of the sun-warmed fruit. The tree's branches hung heavy with the pale yellow globes, smooth and round as eggs. The sun reflected off the two blue bottles suspended in the tree, sending cobalt light dancing through the leaves.

When Beatrice first came to Sammy's house, she'd been puzzled by the two bottles that were jammed onto branches of the guava tree.

"Is just my superstitiousness, darling," he'd told her. "You never heard the old people say that if someone dies, you must put a bottle in a tree to hold their spirit, otherwise it will come back as a duppy and haunt you? A blue bottle. To keep the duppy cool, so it won't come at you in hot anger for being dead."

Beatrice had heard something of the sort, but it was strange to think of her Sammy as a superstitious man. He was too controlled and logical for that. Well, grief makes somebody act in strange ways. Maybe the bottles gave him some comfort, made him feel that he'd kept some essence of his poor wives near him.

"That Samuel is nice. Respectable, hard-working. Not like all them other ragamuffins you always going out with." Mummy *picked up the butcher knife and began expertly slicing the goat meat into cubes for the curry.*

Beatrice watched the red lumps of flesh part under the knife. Crimson liquid leaked onto the cutting board. She sighed, "But, Mummy, Samuel so boring! Michael and Clifton know how to have fun. All Samuel want to do is go for country drives. Always taking me away from other people."

"You should be studying your books, not having fun," her mother replied crossly.

Beatrice pleaded, "You well know I could do both, Mummy." Her mother just grunted.

Is only truth Beatrice was talking. Plenty men were always courting her, they flocked to her like birds, eager to take her dancing or out for a drink. But somehow she kept her marks up, even though it often meant studying right through the night, her head pounding and belly queasy from hangover while some man snored in the bed beside her. Mummy would kill her if she didn't get straight A's for medical school. "You going have to look after yourself, Beatrice. Man not going do it for you. Them get their little piece of sweetness and then them bruk away."

"Two patty and a King Cola, please." The guy who'd given the order had a broad chest that tapered to a slim waist. Good face to look at, too. Beatrice smiled sweetly at him, made shift to gently brush his palm with her fingertips as she handed him the change.

A bird screeched from the guava tree, a tiny kiskedee, crying angrily, "Dit, dit, qu'est-ce qu'il dit!" A small snake was coiled around one of the upper branches, just withdrawing its head from the bird's nest. Its jaws were distended with the egg it had stolen. It swallowed the egg whole, throat bulging hugely with its meal. The bird hovered around the snake's head, giving its pitiful wail of, "Say, say, what's he saying!"

"Get away!" Beatrice shouted at the snake. It looked in the direction of the sound, but didn't back off. The gulping motion of its body as it forced the egg farther down its own throat made Beatrice shudder. Then, oblivious to the fluttering of the parent bird, it arched its head over the nest again. Beatrice pushed herself to her feet and ran into the yard. "Hsst! Shoo! Come away from there!" But the snake took a second egg.

Sammy kept a long pole with a hook at one end leaned against the guava tree for pulling down the fruit. Beatrice grabbed up the pole, started jooking it at the branches as close to the bird and nest as she dared. "Leave them, you brute! Leave!" The pole connected with some of the boughs. The two bottles in the tree fell to the ground and shattered with a crash. A hot breeze sprang up. The snake slithered away quickly, two eggs bulging in its throat. The bird flew off, sobbing to itself.

Nothing she could do now. When Samuel came home, he would hunt the nasty snake down for her and kill it. She leaned the pole back against the tree.

The light breeze should have brought some coolness, but really it only made the day warmer. Two little dust devils danced briefly around Beatrice. They swirled across the yard, swung up into the air, and dashed themselves to powder against the shuttered window of the third bedroom.

Beatrice got her sandals from the verandah. Sammy wouldn't like it if she stepped on broken glass. She picked up the broom that was leaned against the house and began to sweep up the shards of bottle. She hoped Samuel wouldn't be too angry with her. He wasn't a man to cross, could be as stern as a father if he had a mind to.

That was mostly what she remembered about Daddy, his temper—quick to show and just as quick to go. So was he; had left his family before Beatrice turned five. The one cherished memory she had of him was of being swung back and forth through the air, her two small hands clasped in one big hand of his, her feet held tight in another. Safe. And as he swung her through the air, her daddy had been chanting words from an old-time story:

Yung-Kyung-Pyung, what a pretty basket!
Margaret Powell Alone, what a pretty basket!
Eggie-law, what a pretty basket!

Then he had held her tight to his chest, forcing the air from her lungs in a breathless giggle. The dressing-down Mummy had given him for that game! "You want to drop the child and crack her head open on the hard ground? Ee? Why you can't be more responsible?"

"Responsible?" he'd snapped. "Is who working like dog sunup to sundown to put food in oonuh belly?" He'd set Beatrice down, her feet hitting the ground with a jar. She'd started to cry, but he'd just pushed her towards her mother and stormed out of the room. One more volley in the constant battle between them. After he'd left them Mummy had opened the little food shop in town to make ends meet. In the evenings, Beatrice would rub lotion into her mother's chapped, work-wrinkled hands. "See how that man make us come down in the world?" Mummy would grumble. "Look at what I come to."

Privately, Beatrice thought that maybe all Daddy had needed was a little patience. Mummy was too harsh, much as Beatrice loved her. To please her, Beatrice had studied hard all through high school: physics, chemistry, biology, describing the results of her lab experiments in her copy book in her cramped, resigned handwriting. Her mother greeted every A with a non-committal grunt and anything less with a lecture. Beatrice would smile airily, seal the hurt away, pretend the approval meant nothing to her. She still worked hard, but she kept some time for play of her own. Rounders, netball, and later, boys. All those boys, wanting a chance for a little sweetness with a light-skin browning like her. Beatrice had discovered her appeal quickly.

"Leggo beast . . . " Loose woman. The hissed words came from a knot of girls that slouched past Beatrice as she sat on the library steps, waiting for Clifton to come and pick her up. She willed her ears shut, smothered the sting of the words. But she knew some of those girls. Marguerita, Deborah. They used to be friends of hers. Though she sat up proudly, she found her fingers tugging self-consciously at the hem of her short white skirt. She put the big physics textbook in her lap, where it gave her thighs a little more coverage.

The farting vroom of Clifton's motorcycle interrupted her thoughts. Grinning, he slewed the bike to a dramatic halt in front of her. "Study time done now, darling. Time to play."

He looked good this evening, as he always did. Tight white shirt, jeans that showed off the bulges of his thighs. The crinkle of the thin gold chain at his neck set off his dark brown skin. Beatrice stood, tucked the physics text under her arm, smoothed the skirt over her hips. Clifton's eyes followed the movement of her hands. See, it didn't take much to make people treat you nice. She smiled at him.

Samuel would still show up hopefully every so often to ask her to accompany him on a drive through the country. He was so much older than all her other suitors. And dry? Country drives, Lord! She went out with him a few times; he was so persistent and she couldn't figure out how to tell him no. He didn't seem to get her hints that really she should be studying. Truth to tell, though, she started to find his quiet, undemanding presence soothing. His eggshell-white BMW took the graveled country roads so quietly that she could hear the kiskedee birds in the mango trees, chanting their query: "Dit, dit, qu'est-ce qu'il dit?"

One day, Samuel brought her a gift.

"These are for you and your family," he said shyly, handing her a wrinkled paper bag. "I know your mother likes them." Inside were three plump eggplants from his kitchen garden, raised by his own hands. Beatrice took the humble gift out of the bag. The skins of the eggplants had a taut, blue sheen to them. Later she would realise that that was when she'd begun to love Samuel. He was stable, solid, responsible. He would make Mummy and her happy.

Beatrice gave in more to Samuel's diffident wooing. He was cultured and well spoken. He had been abroad, talked of exotic sports: ice hockey, downhill skiing. He took her to fancy restaurants she'd only heard of, that her other, young, unestablished boyfriends would never have been able to afford, and would probably only have embarrassed her if they had taken her. Samuel had polish. But he was humble, too, like the way he grew his own vegetables, or the self-deprecating tone in which he spoke of himself. He was always punctual, always courteous to her and her mother. Beatrice could count on him for little things, like picking her up after class, or driving her mother to the hairdresser's. With the other men, she always had to be on guard: pouting until they took her somewhere else for dinner, not another free meal in her mother's restaurant, wheedling them into using the condoms. She always had to hold something of herself shut away. With Samuel, Beatrice relaxed into trust.

"Beatrice, come! Come quick, nuh!"

Beatrice ran in from the backyard at the sound of her mother's voice. Had something happened to Mummy?

Her mother was sitting at the kitchen table, knife still poised to crack an egg into the bowl for the pound cake she was making to take to the shop. She was staring in open-mouthed delight at Samuel, who was fretfully twisting the long stems on a bouquet of blood-red roses. "Lord, Beatrice; Samuel say he want to marry you!"

Beatrice looked to Sammy for verification. "Samuel," she asked unbelievingly, "what you saying? Is true?"

He nodded yes. "True, Beatrice."

Something gave way in Beatrice's chest, gently as a long-held breath. Her heart had been trapped in glass, and he'd freed it.

They'd been married two months later. Mummy was retired now; Samuel had bought her a little house in the suburbs, and he paid for the maid to come in three times a week. In the excitement of planning for the wedding, Beatrice had let her studying slip. To her dismay she finished her final year of university with barely a C average.

"Never mind, sweetness," Samuel told her. "I didn't like the idea of you studying, anyway. Is for children. You're a big woman now." Mummy had agreed with him too, said she didn't need all that now. She tried to argue with them, but Samuel was very clear about his wishes, and she'd stopped, not wanting anything to cause friction between them just yet. Despite his genteel manner, Samuel had just a bit of a temper. No point in crossing him, it took so little to make him happy, and he was her love, the one man she'd found in whom she could have faith.

Too besides, she was learning how to be the lady of the house, trying to use the right mix of authority and jocularity with Gloria, the maid, and Cleitis, the yardboy who came twice a month to do the mowing and the weeding. Odd to be giving orders to people when she was used to being the one taking orders, in Mummy's shop. It made her feel uncomfortable to tell people to do her work for her. Mummy said she should get used to it, it was her right now.

The sky rumbled with thunder. Still no rain. The warmth of the day was nice, but you could have too much of a good thing. Beatrice opened her mouth, gasping a little, trying to pull more air into her lungs. She was a little short of breath nowadays as the baby pressed on her diaphragm. She knew she could go inside for relief from the heat, but Samuel kept the air-conditioning on high, so cold that they could keep the butter in its dish on the kitchen counter. It never went rancid. Even insects refused to come inside. Sometimes Beatrice felt as though the house were really somewhere else, not the tropics. She had been used to waging constant war against ants and cockroaches, but not in Samuel's house. The cold in it made Beatrice shiver, dried her eyes out until they felt like boiled eggs sitting in their sockets. She went outside as often as possible, even though Samuel didn't like her to spend too much time in the sun. He said he feared that cancer would mar her soft skin, that he didn't want to lose another wife. But Beatrice knew he just didn't want her to get too brown. When the sun touched her, it brought out the sepia and cinnamon in her blood, overpowered the milk and honey, and he could no longer pretend she was white. He loved her skin pale. "Look how you gleam in the moonlight," he'd say to her when he made gentle, almost supplicating love to her at night in the four-poster bed. His hand would slide over her flesh, cup her breasts with an air of reverence. The look in his eyes was so close to worship that it sometimes frightened her. To be loved so much! He would whisper to her, "Beauty. Pale Beauty, to my Beast," then blow a cool breath over the delicate membranes of her ear, making her shiver in delight. For her part, she loved to look at him, his molasses-dark skin, his broad chest, the way the planes of flat muscle slid across it. She imagined tectonic plates shifting in the earth. She loved the bluish-black cast the moonlight lent him. Once, gazing up at him as he loomed above her, body working against and in hers, she had seen the moonlight playing glints of deepest blue in his trim beard.

"Black Beauty," she had joked softly, reaching to pull his face closer for a kiss. At the words, he had lurched up off her to sit on the edge of the bed, pulling a sheet over him to hide his nakedness. Beatrice watched him, confused, feeling their blended sweat cooling along her body.

"Never call me that, please, Beatrice," he said softly. "You don't have to draw attention to my colour. I'm not a handsome man, and I know it. Black and ugly as my mother made me."

"But, Samuel . . . !"

"No."

Shadows lay between them on the bed. He wouldn't touch her again that night.

Beatrice sometimes wondered why Samuel hadn't married a white woman. She thought she knew the reason, though. She had seen the way that Samuel behaved around white people. He smiled too broadly, he simpered, he made silly jokes. It pained her to see it, and she could tell from the desperate look in his eyes that it hurt him too. For all his love of creamy white skin, Samuel probably couldn't have brought himself to approach a white woman the way he'd courted her.

The broken glass was in a neat pile under the guava tree. Time to make Samuel's dinner now. She went up the verandah stairs to the front door, stopping to wipe her sandals on the coir mat just outside the door. Samuel hated dust. As she opened the door, she felt another gust of warm wind at her back, blowing past her into the cool house. Quickly, she stepped inside and closed the door, so that the interior would stay as cool as Sammy liked it. The insulated door shut behind her with a hollow sound. It was air-tight. None of the windows in the house could be opened. She had asked Samuel, "Why you want to live in a box like this, sweetheart? The fresh air good for you."

"I don't like the heat, Beatrice. I don't like baking like meat in the sun. The sealed windows keep the conditioned air in." She hadn't argued.

She walked through the elegant, formal living room to the kitchen. She found the heavy imported furnishings cold and stuffy, but Samuel liked them.

In the kitchen she set water to boil and hunted a bit—where did Gloria keep it?—until she found the Dutch pot. She put it on the burner to toast the fragrant coriander seeds that would flavour the curry. She put on water to boil, stood staring at the steam rising from the pots. Dinner was going to be special tonight. Curried eggs, Samuel's favourite. The eggs in their cardboard case put Beatrice in mind of a trick she'd learned in physics class, for getting an egg unbroken into a narrow-mouthed bottle. You had to boil the egg hard and peel it, then stand a lit candle in the bottle. If you put the narrow end of the egg into the mouth of the bottle, it made a seal, and when the candle had burnt up all the air in the bottle, the vacuum it created would suck the egg in, whole. Beatrice had been the only one in her class patient enough to make the trick work. Patience was all her husband needed. Poor, mysterious Samuel had lost two wives in this isolated country home. He'd been rattling about in the airless house like the egg in the bottle. He kept to himself. The closest neighbours were miles away, and he didn't even know their names.

She was going to change all that, though. Invite her mother to stay for a while, maybe have a dinner party for the distant neighbours. Before her pregnancy made her too lethargic to do much.

A baby would complete their family. Samuel *would* be pleased, he would. She remembered him joking that no woman should have to give birth to his ugly black babies, but she would show him how beautiful their children would be, little brown bodies new as the earth after the rain. She would show him how to love himself in them.

It was hot in the kitchen. Perhaps the heat from the stove? Beatrice went out into the living room, wandered through the guest bedroom, the master bedroom, both bathrooms. The whole house was warmer than she'd ever felt it. Then she realised she could hear sounds coming from the outside, the cicadas singing loudly for rain. There was no whisper of cool air through the vents in the house. The air conditioner wasn't running.

Beatrice began to feel worried. Samuel liked it cold. She had planned tonight to be a special night for the two of them, but he wouldn't react well if everything wasn't to his liking. He'd raised his voice at her a few times. Once or twice he had stopped in the middle of an argument, one hand pulled back as if to strike, to take deep breaths, battling for self-control. His dark face would flush almost blue-black as he fought his rage down. Those times she'd stayed out of his way until he was calm again.

What could be wrong with the air conditioner? Maybe it had just come unplugged? Beatrice wasn't even sure where the controls were. Gloria and Samuel took care of everything around the house. She made another circuit through her home, looking for the main controls. Nothing. Puzzled, she went back into the living room. It was becoming thick and close as a womb inside their closed-up home.

There was only one room left to search. The locked third bedroom. Samuel had told her that both his wives had died in there, first one, then the other. He had given her the keys to every room in the house, but requested that she never open that particular door.

"I feel like it's bad luck, love. I know I'm just being superstitious, but I hope I can trust you to honour my wishes in this." She had, not wanting to cause him any anguish. But where else could the control panel be? It was getting so hot!

As she reached into her pocket for the keys she always carried with her, she realised she was still holding a raw egg in her hand. She'd forgotten to put it into the pot when the heat in the house had made her curious. She managed a little smile. The hormones flushing her body were making her so absent-minded! Samuel would tease her, until she told him why. Everything would be all right.

Beatrice put the egg into her other hand, got the keys out of her pocket, opened the door.

A wall of icy, dead air hit her body. It was freezing cold in the room. Her exhaled breath floated away from her in a long, misty curl. Frowning, she took a step inside and her eyes saw before her brain could understand, and when it did, the egg fell from her hands to smash open on the floor at her feet. Two women's bodies lay side by side on the double bed. Frozen mouths gaped open; frozen, gutted bellies, too. A fine sheen of ice crystals glazed their skin, which like hers was barely brown, but laved in gelid, rime-covered blood that had solidified ruby red. Beatrice whimpered.

"But Miss," Beatrice asked her teacher, "how the egg going to come back out the bottle again?"

"How do you think, Beatrice? There's only one way; you have to break the bottle."

This was how Samuel punished the ones who had tried to bring his babies into the world, his beautiful black babies. For each woman had had the muscled sac of her womb removed and placed on her belly, hacked open to reveal the purplish mass of her placenta. Beatrice knew that if she were to dissect the thawing tissue, she'd find a tiny foetus in each one. The dead women had been pregnant too.

A movement at her feet caught her eyes. She tore her gaze away from the bodies long enough to glance down. Writhing in the fast congealing yolk was a pin-feathered embryo. A rooster must have been at Mister Herbert's hens. She put her hands on her belly to still the sympathetic twitching of her womb. Her eyes were drawn back to the horror on the beds. Another whimper escaped her lips.

A sound like a sigh whispered in through the door she'd left open. A current of hot air seared past her cheek, making a plume of fog as it entered the room. The fog split into two, settled over the heads of each woman, began to take on definition. Each misty column had a face, contorted in rage. The faces were those of the bodies on the bed. One of the duppy women leaned over her own corpse. She lapped like a cat at the blood thawing on its breast. She became a little more solid for having drunk of her own life blood. The other duppy stooped to do the same. The two duppy women each had a belly slightly swollen with the pregnancies for which Samuel had killed them. Beatrice had broken the bottles that had confined the duppy wives, their bodies held in stasis because their spirits were trapped. She'd freed them. She'd let them into the house. Now there was nothing to cool their fury. The heat of it was warming the room up quickly.

The duppy wives held their bellies and glared at her, anger flaring hot behind their eyes. Beatrice backed away from the beds. "I didn't know," she said to the wives. "Don't vex with me. I didn't know what it is Samuel do to you."

Was that understanding on their faces, or were they beyond compassion?

"I making baby for him too. Have mercy on the baby, at least?"

Beatrice heard the *snik* of the front door opening. Samuel was home. He would have seen the broken bottles, would feel the warmth of the house. Beatrice felt that initial calm of the prey that realises it has no choice but to turn and face the beast that is pursuing it. She wondered if Samuel would be able to read the truth hidden in her body, like the egg in the bottle.

"Is not me you should be vex with," she pleaded with the duppy wives. She took a deep breath and spoke the words that broke her heart. "Is . . . is Samuel who do this."

She could hear Samuel moving around in the house, the angry rumbling of his voice like the thunder before the storm. The words were muffled, but she could hear the anger in his tone. She called out, "What you saying, Samuel?"

She stepped out of the meat locker and quietly pulled the door in, but left it open slightly so the duppy wives could come out when they were ready. Then with a welcoming smile, she went to greet her husband. She would stall him as long as she could from entering the third bedroom. Most of the blood in the wives' bodies would be clotted, but maybe it was only important that it be *warm*. She hoped that enough of it would thaw soon for the duppies to drink until they were fully real.

When they had fed, would they come and save her, or would they take revenge on her, their usurper, as well as on Samuel?

Eggie-Law, what a pretty basket.

The radio arm of the Canadian Broadcasting Corporation was once looking for emerging writers from whom to commission new fiction. Writer Olive Senior recommended me to them. CBC Radio asked me for a story, but cautioned me that I'd have to "watch the sex and the violence," since it was public radio (in fact, they said that they were actually more worried about the sex, since they got way more angry phone calls about sexual content in their programmes than about violence). But after that warning, it seemed that all I could see was the sex and the violence. "Slow Cold Chick" is the result of my effort to restrain those twin energies.

SLOW COLD CHICK

They'd cut off the phone. Blaise slammed the receiver back into its cradle. "Oonuh couldn't wait just a little more?" she asked resentfully of the silent instrument. "I get paid Friday, you know." Now she couldn't ask her mother to put milk or water in the cornbread. Chuh. Blaise flounced into the kitchen and scowled at the mixing bowl on the counter.

Mummy used milk, she was almost sure of it. Blaise poured milk and oil, remembering her mother's home-made cornbread, yellow-warm smelling, hot from the oven, with butter melting more yellow into it. Yes, Mummy used milk.

And eggs. And Blaise didn't have any. "Damn." It was almost a week until payday. She made a sucking sound of irritation. Frustration burned deep in her chest.

A movement through her kitchen window caught her eye. From her main-floor apartment, Blaise could easily see the Venus-built lady in the next-door garden. The Venus-built lady's cottage always gave the appearance of having just popped into existence, unexpected and anachronistic as Doctor Who's call box.

Chocolate-dark limbs peeking out of her plush white dressing gown, the Venus-built lady waded indolently through rioting ivy, swollen red roses, nasturtiums that pursed into succulent lips. Blaise had often thought to ask the beautiful woman what her name was. But to meet the eyes of someone so self-possessed, much less speak to her . . .

Branches laden, an otaheite tree bobbed tumescent maroon fruit, so low that the lady could have plucked them with her mouth. Blaise's mother sometimes sent her otaheite apples from Jamaica, but how did the tropical tree flourish in this northern climate?

As ever, the Venus-built lady's gingered brown hair flung itself in crinkled dreadknots down her back, tangled as lovers' fingers. Blaise had chemically straightened all the kinks out of her own hair.

The Venus-built lady was laying a circle of conch shells around a bed of bleeding hearts. She reached out to caress the plants' pink flowers. At her touch, they shivered delicately. Blaise looked down at her own dull brown hands. The Venus-built lady's skin had the glow of full-fat chocolate.

The woman bent and straightened, bent and straightened, leaving a pouting conch shell behind her each time, until pink echoed pink in a circle around the bleeding hearts. Blaise thought of the shells singing as the wind blew past their lips.

The lady turned away from the flower bed and swayed amply up her garden path. As her foot touched the first step of the cottage, a fat, velvet-petaled rose leaned beseechingly towards her. She tugged the rose from its stem and ate it. Then she opened her ginger-bread door and sashayed inside.

Weird. Blaise imagined a spineless green grub squirming voluptuously in the heart of the overblown rose. And an avid mouth descending towards it. She shuddered. *I don't want to eat the worm.*

It had gotten hot in the apartment. The fridge burped. Distractedly, Blaise went to it and opened it.

There was an egg huddling in one of the little cups inside the fridge door. Where had that come from? Exactly what she needed. She was reaching eagerly for it when a stench from deep inside the fridge slid into her nostrils, a poisonous, vinegary tang. The Scotch Bonnet pepper sauce she'd made, last year sometime? was rotting in its glass jar. The pepper crusting the jar's lid had begun to corrode the metal. A vile greenness bloomed on the surface of the red liquid. Blaise kissed her teeth in disgust and dumped the mouldering sauce into the sink.

Cornbread now.

The egg was a little too big for its cradle, a little rounder than eggs usually were. Blaise picked it up. Its cold, mercurial weight shifted in her palm, sucking warmth from her hand. She cracked it into the bowl. With a hollow *clomp!* a mass disappeared below the surface of the liquid. A sulphur-rot stench filled the kitchen.

"Backside!" Blaise swallowed a wave of anger. A

bubble of foetid air popped from the depths of the bowl. Blaise grimaced and began to pour the swampy goop down the drain. The tainted milk and oil mingled with the pepper sauce.

Something rubbery thumped into the mouth of the drain and lay there. It was small and grey and jointed. A naked, fully formed chicken foetus. Blaise's gorge rose. When the thing moved, wallowing in the pepper sauce remaining in the sink, she nearly spewed the coffee she'd drunk that morning.

"*Urrrr . . .* " rattled the cold-grown chick. Slowly, slowly, it extended a peeled head on a wobbly neck. Its tiny beak was thin as nail parings. Its eyes creaked open, stretching a red film of pepper sauce from lid to lid. It shrieked tinnily as the pepper made contact with its eyes. Frantically it shook its head. Its pimply grey body contorted in agony. It shrieked again. Fighting revulsion, Blaise grabbed a cooking spoon and scooped it up.

"Shh, shh." She wadded a tea towel in her free hand and deposited the bird into it. It wailed and stropped its own head against the tea towel. Through the fabric Blaise could feel the bird's cartilaginous body writhing against her palm. Her skin crawled.

"*Arr . . .* " the chick complained. Blaise filled the cooking spoon with water and trickled it over the grey, bald head. The bird fought and spluttered. Reddened eyes glared accusingly at Blaise.

"Make up your mind," she flared. "You want fire in your eyes, or cool water?" The chick tried to peck. Blaise hissed angrily, "Well here, then, take that!"

She scooped some drops of pepper sauce from the sink with her fingers and flicked it at the bird's head. It yowped in indignation. Then, worm-blind, a tiny grey tongue snaked out of its mouth and licked some of the pepper sauce off its beak. "*Urrrr . . .* " This time it didn't seem to mind the taste of the pepper. It licked it off, then blinked its burned eyes clear.

Its body a blur, it shook the water off. It sat up straight in her palm, staring alertly at her. It seemed a little bigger. It did have a few feathers after all. Blaise must have just not noticed them before.

Her anger cooled. She'd let loose the heat of her temper on such a little thing.

The chick opened its mouth wide; Blaise nearly dropped it in alarm. Its hungry red maw looked bigger than its head.

Well, it had seemed to like the pepper, after all. Blaise scraped a stringy mass of it out of the sink and dangled it in front of the cold chick's beak. The chick gaped even wider, begging to be fed. Blaise let slimy tendrils fall. Red threads wriggled down the bird's throat. Ugh.

The chick swallowed, withdrew its pinny head into its ugly neck, and closed its eyes.

"That do you for now?" Blaise asked it.

The chick purred, a low, rattling sound. It radiated heat into her hand. It wasn't so ugly, really. She tucked its warmth close to her breast.

Someone knocked at the door. Blaise gasped, jolted out of her peaceful moment. She dumped the chick into a soup bowl. It squawked and toppled, legs kicking at the air. "Stay there," she hissed, and went to answer the knock.

It was the guy next door, lanky and pimply in a frowsty leather jacket. "Hi there, Blaise," he leered. "Whatcha up to?"

The red tongues of his construction boots hung loose and floppy. He was gnawing on the gooey tag end of a cheap chocolate bar, curled wrapper ends wilting from his fist.

"Nothing much," Blaise replied.

Tethered by a leash through its studded leather collar, the guy's ferret humped around and around in sad circles at his feet. Something about its furtive slinkiness brought to mind a furry penis with teeth.

The guy took a hopeful step closer. "Want some company?"

Not this again. "Um, maybe another time." She remained blocking the doorway, hoping he'd get the point. The ferret sneezed and rubbed fretfully at its snout. Oh, goody: The guy next door's ferret had a head cold. Gooseflesh rose on Blaise's arms.

"What, like this evening, maybe?" asked the guy. His eyes roamed eagerly over her face and body. The familiar steam of stifled anger bubbled through Blaise. Why couldn't he ever take a hint? She wished he'd just dry up and fly away.

There was a thump from the kitchen. The ferret arched sinuously up onto its hind legs, its fur bristling. Blaise turned; her blood froze cold. A creature something between a chicken and an eagle was stalking menacingly out of her kitchen. It was the cold chick, grown to the size of a spaniel. Its down-feathered neck wove its raptor's head in a serpentine dance. Its feet had become cruel, ringed claws. It stared at her with a fierce intelligence.

The guy goggled. "What the . . . ?"

At the sound, the chick's fiery-red comb went erect. Nictitating membranes slid clear of its eyes, which glowed red. Blaise felt a peppery warmth flood her body briefly. Frightened, she stepped aside. The chick turned its gaze full on the guy. It hissed, a sound like steam escaping. The guy next door looked down at it, and seemed immediately held by its stare. He whimpered softly. Heat danced between the chick and the guy next door, then he just, well, vaporized. In a second, all that was left of him was a grey smear of ash on the hallway carpet, and a faint whiff of cheap chocolate.

"Oh my God," Blaise said, feeling frantically for the open doorway.

The ferret growled. The chick pounced. Blaise leapt out of the way. Jesus, now they were between her and the way out.

The ferret wound itself around the creature. The chick's beak slashed. The ferret yipped, sneezed. Drops of ferret blood and mucus flew. The cold chick flexed a meaty thigh to slice a talon through the ferret's middle. The ferret arched and writhed in extremis. Knots of bloody intestine trailed from its belly. The cold chick twisted the ferret's head between the cruel tines of its beak. Blaise heard the ferret's neck snap. Holding it down with its claws, the cold chick began to devour the ferret with a wet crunching sound. Blaise could hear her own panicked sobbing.

The chick sucked up looped coils of gut with little chirps of pleasure. Then it blurred. When Blaise could see it clearly again, it was the size of a rottweiler. Its feathers had sprouted into rich burgundy and green plumes. It snapped up the rest of the ferret, then crouched in the doorway. It looked at her, and Blaise knew it would burn her to death. A keening sound came from her mouth. Heat washed over her, but then the membranes slid down over the chick's open eyes. Blaise could still see its piercing stare, slightly opaqued.

"Mmrraow?" it enquired fondly. It had a satisfied look on its beaky face.

It wasn't going to eat her. It had done this to please her, and now the guy next door was really dried up and gone. "That isn't what I meant," Blaise wailed. The chick cocked its head adoringly at the sound of her voice.

Blaise sat down heavily in her tattered armchair, trying to figure out what to do next. The chick groomed, rattling its beak through its jewel-coloured feathers. Its meal was still altering its body. It blurred again, it morphed. Four clawed, furred front legs sprouted to replace its chicken feet. The chick—cocka-trice—looked down at its own body, stomped around experimentally on its new limbs. It made a chuckling noise. Would it have stayed a slow, cold chick if it hadn't eaten the ferret? Or the burning pepper sauce?

It belched, spat up a slimy black thread; the ferret's leash. It pounced on the leash and started worrying at it. Sunlight danced motes of colour through its plumage. It was very beautiful. And it would probably need to feed again soon.

I not going to be second course, Blaise thought. She moved to the door. Happily torturing the leash, the cockatrice ignored her. She grabbed her jacket from its peg and locked her door behind her. She left the apartment.

The clean fall air cleared her mind a little. The animal shelter, yeah, they'd come and take the beast away.

She had to pass the Venus-built lady's garden on the way. There was a man in the yard with his back to her: a slim, bald man with a wiry strength to his build. Shirt-less, he was digging beside the otaheite tree. His tanned shoulders made a V with the narrowness of his waist. With each thrust of the shovel, corded muscles flexed like cables in his arms and back. Blaise slowed to admire him. He pumped the shovel smoothly into the earth with one bare, sturdy foot, but something stopped it from sinking any farther. He went down on one knee and began tenderly pulling up clods of dirt, crumbling them between his fingers. Blaise crept closer to the gate and craned her neck to see better. The man sniffed at the dark soil in his hands and poured a handful of it down his throat. His Adam's apple jumped when he swallowed.

Was everybody eating something strange today? All Blaise had wanted was cornbread.

The man looked round, saw her, and grinned. It was a friendly expression; there were well-worn smile lines pared into his cheeks. She grinned back. His lean face had the rough texture of chipped rock. Not handsome, but striking.

He reached into the womb of soil again and tugged out the rock that had stopped his shovel. His fingers flexed. He crushed the rock between them like a sugar cube and reverently licked up the powdery bits.

The cottage door opened, letting the Venus-built lady out. She had changed into a sweater and close-fitting jeans that made her hips heart-shaped. She had a basket slung over one shoulder.

A smile broke onto the man's face the way the stone had cracked between his fingers. He offered a stone-powdered palm. "It's sweet," he said in a voice like gravel being ground underfoot. "The fruit will be sweet too."

The Venus-built lady smiled back. Then she looked at Blaise. "So come and help us then, nuh?" she asked in a warm alto that sang of the tropics. "Instead of standing there staring?"

Blaise felt heat warming her face.

But what about the cockatrice?

The problem was too big for her to deal with for the moment. With an "Um, okay," she chose denial. She let herself into the garden, trying shyly to avoid eye contact with either of them. "What you doing?"

"Getting the otaheite tree ready for winter," the man replied. "It won't last out in the open like this."

"I bury it in the soil every winter," the Venus-built lady told her. "Then I dig it up in summer, and it blooms for me by the fall."

"And that works?"

"It works, yes," the Venus-built lady replied. "It bears, and it feeds my soul. Is a flavour of home. You going to help me pick, or you want to help Johnny dig?"

Standing this close to her neighbour, Blaise could taste the warm rose spice of her breath. Even her skin had the scent of the roses she ate. Blaise looked at Johnny. He was resting comfortably on the shovel, watching both of them. He grinned, jade eyes bright.

Who to help? Who to work close beside? "I will help you pick for now," she told the Venus-built lady. "But when Johnny get tired, I could help him dig."

Johnny nodded. "The more, the merrier." He returned to his task.

The otaheite apples seemed to leap joyfully from their stems into the Venus-built lady's hands. She and Blaise picked all the fruit, ate their fill of maroon-skinned sweetness and melting white flesh, fed some to sweaty Johnny as he dug. The woman owned a flower shop over in Cabbagetown. "Is called Rose of Sharon," she laughed. "Sharon is my name." Blaise inhaled her flower-breathed words.

Johnny was a metalworker. He pointed proudly at Sharon's wrought-iron railings. "Made those."

The ruddiness of this white man came from facing down fire every day. Blaise imagined him shirtless at the forge, forming the molten iron into beautiful shapes.

"I need help at the shop," Sharon told her. "You don't like the job you have now, and you have a gentle hand with that fruit you're picking. You want to come by Monday and talk to me about it?"

Blaise thought she might like to work amongst flowers, coaxing blooms to fullness. "Okay. Monday evening," she replied.

She and Johnny dug out most of the soil from around the tree's roots while Sharon steadied its trunk. Then all three of them laid the tree in its winter bed, clipped its branches, and covered it with soil.

"Good night, my darling," whispered Sharon. "See you soon." The bleeding hearts quivered daintily. The roses dipped their weighty heads.

The sun was lowering by the time they were done. The shelter would be closed, but probably the cockatrice was asleep by now. Blaise stood with Sharon and Johnny beside the giant's grave that held the otaheite tree. She ached from all the picking and digging; a good hurt. Johnny put a hand lightly on her shoulder. She felt the heat of it through the fabric. He smelt of sweat and fire and earth. On Johnny's other side, Sharon took his free hand. She and Johnny kissed, slowly. They looked into each other's eyes and smiled. Sharon slid an arm around Blaise's waist. Blaise relaxed into the touch, then caught herself. Ears burning, she eased away, stood apart from the warmth of the two.

"I should go now," she said.

Sharon replied, "Johnny likes to take earth into himself. Soil and rock and iron."

"What?"

"It's what I crave," Johnny told her helpfully. "And plants nourish Sharon. What do you eat?"

"How you mean? I don't understand."

Sharon said, "You must know the things that nourish you. Sometimes you have to reach out for them."

No, that couldn't be right. The bird birthed of the heat of Blaise's anger had eaten as it pleased, and it had turned into a monster.

"Um, I really have to go now. Things to take care of."

"Something we can do?" Johnny asked. Both his face and Sharon's held concern.

Blaise looked at this man who ingested the ore he forged, and the woman to whom flowers gave themselves to be supped. She took a deep breath and told them the story of the cockatrice.

Blaise's hallway still had the oily smell of cheap chocolate, burnt. She stepped guiltily around the ash smear on the carpet. "This is my place."

"Careful as you go in," Sharon warned.

The apartment was close and hot. It reeked of sulphur. Blaise flicked on the light.

The TV had been gutted. It lay crumpled on its side, a stove-in, smoking box.

"Holy," Johnny growled. The couch was in shreds, the plants steamed and wilting. The casing of the telephone was melted, adding its own acrid smell to the reek.

Blaise could feel the tears filling her eyes. Sharon put an arm around her shoulders. Blaise leaned into the comfort of Sharon's petal-soft body and sobbed, a part of her still aware of Sharon's rosiness and duskiness.

A bereft screech; a flurry of feathers and fur and heat; a stinking hiss of pepper and rotten eggs. The cockatrice rammed full weight into Blaise and Sharon, bearing them to the floor. Sharon rolled out, but the cockatrice sat on Blaise's chest. Its wordless howl carried all the anguish of *Mummy gone and leave me*, and the rage of *Oh, so she come back now? Well, I going show her.*

Blaise cringed. The cockatrice spat a thick red gobbet at her face. It burned her cheek. The drool smelled like rotting pepper sauce. Blaise went cold with horror.

Suddenly the creature's weight was lifted off her. Johnny was holding the cockatrice aloft by its thick, writhing neck. Blaise scrabbled along the floor, putting Johnny between herself and the monster. Johnny's biceps bulged; the rock-crushing fingers flexed; the cockatrice's furred hindquarters kicked and clawed. It spat. Johnny didn't budge. Fire had met stone.

"Kill it for me, Johnny, do!" Blaise shoved herself to her feet.

"Oh God, Johnny; you all right?" Sharon asked.

"Yes," he muttered, all his concentration on the struggle. But his voice rang flat, a hammer on flawed steel.

The cockatrice thrashed. Blaise's belly squirmed in response. The animal made a choking sound. It was dying. Blaise felt warmth begin to drain from her body. Her heat, her fire was dying.

"You have to go," Blaise whispered at it. "You can't do as you want, lash out at anything you don't like."

Sharon gripped Blaise's shoulder. Where was the softness? Sharon's hand was knotted and tough as iron-wood. "You want to kill your every desire dead?" she asked.

The cockatrice sobbed. It turned a hooded look of sorrow and rage on Blaise. Then it glowered at Johnny. Blaise saw the membranes slide back from its eyes. She lunged at it.

Too late. The heat of its glare was full on. The air sizzled, and Johnny was caught. Sharon screamed. Johnny glowed, red as the iron in his forge fires.

But he didn't melt or burn. Yet. Blaise could see him straining to break the pull of the cockatrice's glare, see him weakening. Her beast would kill this man.

"Bloodfire!" Furious, she charged the cockatrice, dragged it out of Johnny's grasp. She heard Johnny crash to the floor.

The cockatrice broke away, fluttered to the carpet. It glared at her. Hot, hot. She was burning up with heat, with the bellyfires of anger, of wanting, of hunger.

"Talk to it," Sharon told her. "Tell it what you want."

Blaise took a step towards the cockatrice. Birdlike, it cocked its head. It mewed a question.

"I want," she said, her voice quaking out the unfamiliar word, "to be able to talk what I feel." God, feverhot. "I want to be able to say, *You hurt me*." The cockatrice hissed. "Or, *I'm not interested*." The cockatrice chortled wickedly. "Or," Blaise hesitated, took in a burning breath, *"I like you."*

The cockatrice sighed. It leapt into her arms, its dog-heavy weight nearly buckling her knees. Its claws scratched her and its breath was rank, but somehow she hung on, feeling its strength flex against her. She held the heat of its needing body tight.

Suddenly, it shoved its beak between her lips. Blaise choked, tried to drop the beast, but its flexed claws grasped her tightly. Impossibly, it crammed its whole head into her mouth. Blaise gagged. She could feel its beak sliding down her throat. It would sear her, like a hot poker. She fought, looking imploringly at Sharon and Johnny, but they just sat on the floor, watching.

Blaise tried to vomit the beast out, but it kept pushing more of itself inside her. How, how? It was unbelievable. Her mouth was stretched open so wide, she thought it would tear. Heat filled her, her ribs would crack apart. The beast's head and neck snaked down towards her belly. Its wings beat against her teeth, her tongue. Her throat, it was in her throat, stopping her air! Terrified, she pulled at the cockatrice's legs. It clawed her hands away. With a great heave, its whole bulk slid into her stomach. She could feel its muscly writhing, its fire that now came from her core. She could breathe, and she was angry enough to spit fire.

"What oonuh were thinking!" she raged at them. "Why you didn't help me!"

Johnny only said, "I bet you feel good now."

Oh. She did. Strong, sure of herself. Oh.

Sharon leaned over Johnny and blew cool, aloe-scented breath on his blisters. Blaise admired the way that the position emphasized the fullness of her body. Johnny's burns healed as Blaise watched. "I enjoyed your company this afternoon," she said to them both. Simple, risky words to say with this new-found warmth in her voice.

Sharon smiled. "You must come and visit again soon, then."

Blaise giggled. She reached a hand to either of them, feeling the blood heat of her palms flexing against theirs.

The mutant fish that K.C. mentions is the only thing remotely fantastical about this next story. It felt like a tale that needed to be grounded in the potential for reality.

FISHERMAN

You work as what, a fisherman?"

I nearly jump clean out my skin at the sound of she voice, tough like sugarcane when you done chew the fibres dry. "Fisherm . . . ?" I stutter.

She sweet like cane, too? Shame make me fling the thought 'way from me. Lord Jesus, is what make me come here any atall? I turn away from the window, from the pure wonder of watching through one big piece of clear glass at the hibiscus bush outside. Only Boysie house in the village have a glass window, and it have a crack running crossways through it. The rest of we have wooden jalousie shutters. I look back at she proud, round face with the plucked brows and the lipstick red on she plump lips. The words fall out from my mouth: "I . . . I stink of fish, don't it?"

A smile spread on she beautiful brown face, like when you draw your finger through molasses on a plate. "Sit down nuh, doux-doux, you in your nice clean pressed white shirt? I glad you dress up to come and see me."

"All right." I siddown right to the edge of the chair with my hands in my lap, not holding the chair arms. I frighten for leave even a sniff of fish on the expensive tapestry. Everything in this cathouse worth more than me. I frighten for touch anything, least of all the glory of the woman standing in front of me now, bubbies and hips pushing out of she dress, forcing the cloth to shape like the roundness of she. The women where I living all look like what them does do: market woman, shave ice seller, baby mother. But she look like a picture in a magazine. Is silk that she wearing? How I to know, I who only make for wear crocus bag shirt and Daddy old dungarees?

She move little closer, till she nearly touching my knees. From outside in the parlour I hearing two-three of the boys and them laughing over shots of red rum and talking with some of the whores that ain't working for the moment. I hear Lennie voice, and Two-Tone, though I can't really make out what them saying. Them done already? I draw back little more on the fancy chair.

The woman frown at me as if to say, *Who you is any atall?* The look on she face put me in mind of how you does look when you pull up your line out of the water sometimes to find a ugly fish gasping on the end of it, and instead of a fin, it have a small hand with three boneless fingers where no hand supposed to grow. She say, "You have a fainty smell of the sea hanging round you, is all, like this seashell here."

She lean over and pick up a big conch shell from she windowsill. It clean and pink on the inside with pointy brown parts jooking out on the outside.

She wearing a perfume I can't even describe, my

head too full up with confusion. Something like how Granny did smell that time when I was small and Daddy take me to visit she in town. Granny did smell all baby powder and coconut grater-cake. Something like the Ladies-of-the-Night flowers too, that does bloom in my garden.

I slide back little more again in the chair, but she only move closer. "Here," she say, putting the shell to my nose. "Smell."

I sniff. Is the smell I smell every living day Papa God bring, when I baking my behind out on the boat in the sun hot and callousing up my hands pulling in the net next to the rest of the fishermen and them. I ain't know what to say to she, so I make a noise like, "Mm . . . ?"

"Don't that nice?" She laugh a little bit, siddown in my lap, all warm, covering both my legs, the solid, sure weight and the perfume of she.

My heart start to fire *budupbudup* in my chest.

She say, "Don't that just get all up inside your nose and make you think of the blue waves dancing, and the little red crabs running sideways and waving they big gundy claw at you, and that green green frilly seaweed that look like it would taste fresh like lettuce in your mouth? Don't that smell make your mind run on the sea?"

"It make my mind run on work," I tell she.

She smile little bit. She put the shell back. "Work done for tonight," she tell me. "Now is time to play." She smoky laugh come in cracked and full up of holes. She voice put me in mind of the big rusty bell down by the beach what we does ring when we pull in the catch to let the women and them know them could come and buy fish. Through them holes in the bell you could hear the sea waves crashing on the beach. Sometimes I does feel to ring the bell just for so, just to hear the tongue of the clapper shout "fish, fish!" in it bright, break-up voice, but I have more sense than to make the village women mad at me.

She chest brush my arm as she lean over. She start to undo my shirt buttons. *No, not the shirt.* I take she hands and hold them in my own, hold her soft hands in my two hard own that smell like dead fish and fish scale and fish entrails.

The madam smile and run a warm, soft finger over my lips. I woulda push she off me right then and run go home. In fact I make to do it, but she pick up she two feet from off the floor and is then I get to feel the full weight and solidness of she.

"You go throw me off onto the hard ground, then?" she say with a flirty smile in she voice.

One time, five fifty-pound sack of chicken feed tumble from Boysie truck and land on me; two hundred fifty pounds drop me *baps* to the ground. Boysie had was to come and pull me out. Is heavy same way so she feel in my lap, grounding me. This woman wasn't going nowhere she ain't want to go.

"I . . . " I start to reply, and she lean she face in close to mine, frowning at me the whole while like if I is a grouper with a freak hand. She put she two lips on my own. I frighten I frighten I frighten so till my breath catch like fish bone in my throat. Warm and soft she mouth feel against mine, so soft. My mouth was little bit open. I ain't know if to close it, if to back back, if to laugh. I ain't know this thing that people does do, I never do it before. The sea bear Daddy away before he could tell me about it.

She breath come in between my lips. Papa God, why nobody ever tell me you could taste the spice and

warmth of somebody breath and never want to draw
your face away again? Something warm and wet touch
inside my lips and pull away, like a wave on a beach.
She tongue! Nasty! I jerk my head, but she have it
holding between she two hands, soft hands with the
strength of fishing net. I feel the slip slip slip of she
tongue again. She must be know what she doing. I let
myself taste, and I realise it ain't so nasty in truth, just
hot and wet with the life of she. My own tongue reach
out, trembling, and tip to twiny conch tip touch she
own. She mouth water and mine mingle. It have a tear
in the corner of one of my eyes, I feel it twinkling there.
I hear a small sound start from the back of my throat.
When she move she face away from me, I nearly beg she
not to stop.

She grin at me. My breath only coming in little sips,
I feeling feverish, and what happening down between
my legs I ain't even want to think about. I strong. I
could move my head away, even though she still
holding it. But I don't want to be rude. I cast my eyes
down instead and find myself staring at the two fat bubbies spilling out of she dress, round and full like the
hops bread you does eat with shark, but brown, skin-
dark brown.

I pull my eyes up into she face again.

"Listen to me now," she say. "I do that because I feel
to. If you want to kiss the other women so you must ask
permission first. Else them might box you two lick and
scream for Jackobennie. You understand me?"

Jackobennie is the man who let me in the door of
this cathouse, smirking at me like he know all my
secrets. Jackobennie have a chest a bull would give he
life to own and a right arm to make a leg of ham jealous.
I don't want to cross Jackobennie atall atall.

"You understand me?" she ask again.

Daddy always used to say my mouth would get me in trouble. I open it to answer she yes, and what the rascal mouth say but, "No, I ain't understand. Why I could lick inside your mouth like that but not them own? I could pay."

She laugh that belly laugh till I think my thighs go break from the shaking. "Oh sweetness, I believe a treasure come in my door this day, a jewel beyond price."

"Don't laugh at me." If is one thing I can't brook, is nobody laughing at me. The fishermen did never want me to be one of them. I had was to show up at the boat every blessèd morning and listen to the nasty things them was saying about me. Had to work beside people who would spit just to look on me. Till them come to realise I could do the work too. I hear enough mockery, get enough mako make 'pon me to last all my days.

She look right in my eyes, right on through to my soul. She nod. "I would never laugh after you, my brave one, to waltz in here in your fisherman clothes."

Is only the fisherman she could see? "No, is not my work clothes I wearing. Is my good pair of pants and my nice brown shoes."

"And you even shine the shoes and all. And press a crease into the pants. I see that. I does notice when people dress up for me. And Jackobennie tell me you bring more than enough money. That nice, sweetness. I realise is your first time here. Is only the rules of my house I telling you; whatever you want to do, you must ask the girls and they first. And them have the right to refuse."

After I don't even know what to ask! Pastor would call it the sin of pride, to waltz in the place thinking my money could stand in place of good manners. "I sorry, Missis; I ain't know."

Surprise flare on she face. She draw back little bit to look at me good. "And like you really sorry, too. Yes, you is a treasure, all right. No need to be sorry, darling. You ain't do nothing wrong."

The Ladies-of-the-Night scent of she going all up inside my nostrils. The other men and they does laugh after me that I have a flower bush growing beside the pigeon peas and the tomatoes, so womanish, but I like to cut the flowers and put inside the house to brighten up the place with their softness and sweet smell. I have a blue glass bottle that I find wash up on the shore one day. The sand had scour it so it wasn't shining like glass no more. But all the waves smash it, it ain't break yet. From the licking of the sea and the scraping of the sand, it had a texture under my fingertips like stone. I like that. I does put the flowers in it and put them on my table, the one what Daddy help me make.

"So, why you never come with the other fishermen? When you pull up to the dock all by yourself in that little dinghy, I get suspicious one time. I never see you before."

All the while she talking, and me mesmerized by she serious brown eyes, and too much to feel and think about at once, I never realise she did sliding she hand down inside my blouse, down until she fingers and thumb slide round one of my bubbies and feel the weight of it. Jesus Lord, she go call Jackobennie now! I make to jump up again, terror making me stronger, but this time she look at me with kindness. It make me weak. "Big strong woman," she whisper.

She know! All this time, she know? I couldn't move from that chair, even if Papa God heself was to come down to earth and command me. I just sitting there, weak and trembling, while she undo the shirt slow, one button at a time, drag it out of my pants, and lay my bubbies bare to the open air. The nipples crinkle up one time and I shame I shame. Nothing to do but sit there, exposed and trembling like conch when you drag it out of the shell to die.

I squinch my eyes closed tight, but I feel a hot tear escape from under my eyelid and track down my face. So long nobody ain't see me cry. I feel to dead. I wait to hear the scorn from she dry-ashes voice.

"Sweetheart?" Gentle hands closing back my shirt, but not drawing away; resting warm on the fat shameful weight of my bubbies. "Mister Fisherman?"

Yes. Is that I is. A fisherman. I draw in the breath I been keeping out, a long, shuddery one. She hands rise and fall with my chest. I open my eyes, but I can't stand to look in she face. I away gaze out the window, past the clean pink shell to the blue wall of the sea far away. What make me leave my home this day any atall, eh?

"Look at me, nuh? What you name?"

I dash way the tear with the back of my hand, sniff back the snot. "K.C."

"Casey?"

"Letter K, letter C. For 'Kelly Carol': K.C. I sorry I take up your time, Missis. You want me to go?" I chance a quick glance at her. She get that weighing and measuring look again. The warmth of she hands through my shirt feeling nice. Can't think 'bout that.

"Why you come here in the first place, K.C.?"

I tilt my head away from her, look down at my shoes, my nice shine shoes. Oh God, how to explain? "Is just I . . . look, I not make for this, I not a . . . I did only want some company, the way the other men and they does talk about all the time. All blessèd week we pulling on the nets together, all of we. And some of the men does even treat me like one of them, you know? A fisherman, doing my job. Then Saturday nights after we go to market them does leave me and come here, even Lennie, and I hear next day how sweet allyou is, all of allyou in this cathouse. Every week it happen so and every Saturday night I stay home in my wattle and daub hut and watch at the kerosene lamp burning till is time to go to bed. Nobody but me. But I catch plenty fish and sell in the market today, I had enough money, and after them all come here I follow them in one of Lennie small boats. I just figure is time, my turn now . . . But I will go away. I don't belong here." My heart feeling heavy in my chest. I sit and wait for she to banish me.

She laugh like a dolphin leaping. "K.C., you don't have to go nowhere. Look at me, nuh?"

The short distance I had was to drag my eyes from the window to she face was like I going to dead, like somebody dragging a sharp knife along the belly of a fish that twisting in your hands. My two eyes and she own make four, and I feel my belly bottom drop out same way so that fish guts would tumble like rope from it body.

She start to count off on she fingers: "You come in clean clothes; you bathe too, I could smell the carbolic soap on your skin; you not too drunk to have sense; you come prepared to pay; you have manners. Now tell me: Why I would turn away such a ideal customer?"

"I . . . because I . . . "

"You ever fuck before?"

"No!" My face burning up for shame. I hear the word plenty time. I see dogs doing it in the road. I not sure what it have to do with me. But I want to find out.

She give me one mischievous grin. "Well, doux-doux, is your lucky night tonight; you going to learn from the mistress of this house!"

Oh God.

Softly she say, "You go let me touch you, K.C.? Mister fisherman?"

My heart flapping in my chest like a mullet on a jetty. She must be can feel it jumping under she hands. I whisper, "Yes, please."

And next thing I know, my shirt get drag open all the way. She say, "Take it off, nuh? I want to see the muscles in your arms."

My arms? I busy feeling shamed, 'fraid for she to watch at my bubbies—nobody see them all these years—but is my arms she want to see? For the first time this night, I crack one little smile. I pull off the shirt, stand there holding it careful by the collar so it wouldn't get rampfle. She step in closer and squeeze my one arm, and when she look at me, the look make something in my crotch jump again. Is a look of some-body who want something. My smile freeze. I ain't know what to do with my face. My eyes start to drop to the floor again. But she put she hand under my chin. "Watch at me in my eyes, K.C.; like man does look at woman."

My blasted tongue run away with me again. "And what it have to look at? You seeing more of me than I seeing of you."

A grin that could swallow a house. "True. Help me fix that then, nuh?" And she present me with she back, one hand cock-up on she hip. "Undo my dress for me, please?"

She had comb she hair up onto her head with a sweep and a frill like wedding cake icing, only black.

The purple silk of the gown come down low on she back so I could see all that brown skin, smelling like sweet flowers. The fancy dress-back fasten with one set of hook and eye and button and bow. I tall, nearly tall like Two-Tone, but this woman little bit taller than me, even. I reach up to the top of she dress-back. I manage to undo three button and a hook before a button just pop off in my hand. "Fuck, man, I can't manage these fancy things; I ain't make for them. Missis, I done bust up your dress, I sorry."

She feel behind she, run one long brown finger over the place where the button tear from. Quicker than my eyes could follow, she undo the dress the rest of the way. I see she big round bamsie naked and smooth under there, but she step away and turn to face me before I could see enough. "Give me the button."

I hand it to she. She laugh little bit and drop it down between she bubbies. "Oh. Look what I gone and do. Come and find it for me, nuh?"

Is like somebody nail my two foot-them to the floor. I couldn't move. I feel like my head going to bust apart. I just watch at she. She step so close to me I could smell she breath warm on my lips. I want to taste that breath again. She whisper, "Find my button for me, K.C."

I don't know when my hands reach on she shoulders. Is like I watching a picture film of me sliding my hands down that soft skin to the opening of the dress, moving my hands in and taking she two tot-tots in each hand. They big and heavy, would be about three pound each on the scale. If I was to price this lady pound for pound, I could never afford she. I move my hand in to the warm, damp place in between she bubbies. The flower smell rising warm off she. My fingers only trembling, trembling, but I pick out the button. I give it back. She stand there, watching in my eyes. Is when I see she smile that I realise I put the fingers that reach the button in my mouth. She taste salt and smell sweet. She push the dress off one shoulder, then the next one. It land on she hips and catch there. Can't go no farther past the swelling of she belly and bamsie without help. And me, I only watching at the full and swing and round of she bubbies and is like my tongue swell up and my whole body it hot it hot it hot like fire.

"You like me?" she say.

"I . . . I think so."

"Help me take off my dress the rest of the way?" She telling me I could touch she. My mother was the last somebody what make me touch their body, when I was helping Daddy look after she before she dead. Mummy was wasting away them times there. She skin was dry and crackly like the brown paper we does wrap the fish in. But this skin on this lady belly and hips put me in mind of that time Daddy take me to visit my granny in the town, how Granny put me on she knee and give me cocoa-tea to drink that she make by grating the cocoa and nutmeg into the hot milk, how Granny did wearing a brown velvet dress and I never touch velvet, before neither since, and I just sit there so on Granny knee, running my thumb across a little piece of she sleeve over and over again, drinking hot cocoa-tea with plenty condensed milk. This woman skin under my hands put me in mind of that somehow, of velvet and hot cocoa with thick, sweet condensed milk and the delicious fat floating on top. As I pass my hands over she hips to draw down the dress the rest of the way, I feel to just stop there and do that all evening, to just touch she flesh over and over again like a piece of brown velvet.

Then she make a kind of little wiggle and the dress

drop right down on the ground and is like I get transfix. My two eye-them get full up of beauty and if God did strike me dead right there I woulda die happy.

She only smiling, smiling. "Like you like what you see, eh, Fisherman?"

"Yes, Ma'am."

She step out the dress and go over to the bed. She lie back on it and I mark how she bubbies roll to either side when she do so. Today I bring back two fat, round pumpkin from the market, rolling around in my basket. The soup from those pumpkins going to be nice. I taste the salt on my lips still from when I touch she bubbies and lick my fingers after.

She say, "Come over here, K.C."

I go and sit on the edge of the bed, not too close. And now I shame again, for it have a white crochet spread on the bed, and white pillowcases on the pillows and them, with some yellow and pink embroidery edging the pillowcases. I can't get my fisherman stink all over this lady nice bed!

"Take off your shoes and your pants, K.C."

So I do that, giving thanks that I could turn my back on she and not see she watching when I get naked.

"The underwears too."

I drag off my underpants, the one good ones with no stain. I fold them up small small and put them at the foot of the bed. I leave my hand on them. They still warm from my body. I feel to never leave that warmth.

"Come into bed with me."

So then I had was to turn around to climb on the bed. I feel so big and boobaloops and clumsy. I roll back the bedspread, careful, and sit down on the sheet. I pull my knees up to my chest. I watch at she feet. Pretty feet. No callus though.

She rise up in the bed, sit facing me. She ease the crochet bedspread out from under she body and roll it all the way down to the end of the bed. What she go do now? I nearly perishing for fright. "Lie back, K.C."

So I do that, stiff like one piece of plank. She lean over me, she chest hanging nearly in my face. If she come down any lower, how I go breathe? She start passing she hands over my two shoulders, side to side. Big, warm hands. Big like mine. All these years, is this my skin been hungry for. I feel my whole body getting warm, melting into the soft bed. I close my eyes.

"Nice?" she ask.

"Mm-hmm."

She hands pass side to side, side to side, so hot and nice on my skin. And then the hands go under my bubbies, weighing. I jump and my eyes start open, but the look on she face ain't telling me nothing. I turn a piece of board again, just lying there. She run she thumbs over my nipples and I swear I feel it right down to my crotch. Is so I does do myself nights when the skin hunger get too bad, but Jesus God, how it powerful when somebody else do it for you! My breath coming hard, making little sounds. Can't make she see, can't make she hear. I go to push she hands away.

"Is all right, K.C. Nothing for shame. Relax, nuh?"

"I doing it right?"

"When it feeling good, you doing it right."

I must be doing it plenty right, then. I put my head on the pillow again. She start to squeeze my bubbies, to pull and tug at them. I ain't know how much time past, I just get lost in what she hands doing. The little noises I making coming louder now. I wonder if Lennie could hear me, and Two-Tone, but I decide I ain't care.

The woman hands on my belly now, massaging the

big swell of it. Between my legs my blood only beating, beating. I want . . . no, I ain't want that. How anybody could want that? But when she push my legs apart, when that big, warm hand cover my whole pum-pum and squeeze, I swear it try to leap into she hands. She push apart my legs little more, spread my pum-pum lips open. Oy-oy-oy, I shame, but I couldn't stand to stop she. She press on that place, the place between my legs I find to rub so long ago. I forget how to breathe. "Look your little parson's nose there," she giggle. She take she hand away and I nearly beg she to put it back. She lick she fingers. She must be did watching my face, how it get disgust, for she say, "You never taste yourself?"

"Yes." My voice come out small.

"Well, then." She put the fingers back. Oh God, the wetness she bring on she fingers just sliding and sliding on the button. And she rub and she rub and little more I thrashing round on the bed till she had was to lie over me with all she weight to make me keep still, make me stay open under she fingers and something coming from deep inside me it buzzing buzzing buzzing from way inside my body like I don't know what but it coming and I can't stop it, don't want to stop it, and I barely hear myself and the noises I making and then it hit me like lightning and it ride me like a storm and I shout something, I ain't know what, and inside my pum-pum squeezing so hard and nice. I only sweating and trembling when the something drop me back on the bed. "Fuck."

"Exactly." She laugh, move off me. "You have a mouth like a fisherman, too."

Sweat drenching me, salt drying on my skin. My belly feeling all fluttery inside. I couldn't look at she. One time long long ago, one nighttime in my bed, I touch myself long time like she just touch me and I get a feeling little bit like she just give me, but it frighten me. I thought I was deading. I thought is because is nastiness I was doing. I pull my hand away, and the feeling stop. And though I figure out afterwards that I wasn't go dead, though I do that thing between my legs plenty times since and it feel nice, I never manage after that to make the feeling come back so strong again. "What we go do now?" I ask she.

"How you know we ain't finish, K.C.?"

I peek over my bubbies and belly at she. She sitting in between my legs like if it ain't have nothing wrong with that. She two massive legs pinning my own big ones down, brown on brown. I see she cocoa pod pum-pum, spread open pink and glistening, going to brown at the edges. Lord, what a thing. "I ain't feel finish yet, I feel like it have more."

She give me that rapscallion smile. "Oh yes, it could have plenty more."

She start to stroke my button again, gentle. I glad for that, for it feeling tender. Nice, though. I ain't really get surprised when she push a finger inside my pum-pum. Then another one. I do that myself, plenty times. I thought is only me do that. Me and my nastiness. I start to relax back on she fine white bedspread again, but all of a sudden I sitting up and pulling she hands away. "No. Stop."

She stop one time. "You don't like it?"

"I . . . I don't know." Then I bust out with, "I just feel . . . I not a glove you does wear for you to go inside me like that."

She just stroke my thighs, with a look on she face like she thinking. "All right, then. Let we try something else."

Just like that? "Is all right?"

"Yes, K.C. Everybody different. You must tell me what you like and don't like. Move over so I could lie down."

I make room for she. She lie down on she back with one knee bend. "Touch me like I touch you."

Lord, but this thing hard to do. The way the boys and them talk, I did think it would be easy; just pay the woman and she fix you up.

I do she like she do me. I massage she shoulders, I play with she bubbies. So strange. Like touching my own, almost.

"Pull them."

I ain't know what she mean. She put she nipples between my fingers.

"Pull."

I tug little bit.

"Harder."

So I 'buse up she breasts for she. It look like she good and like it, though. She breathing coming in heavy. It make me feel good. Powerful. I knead she belly, and she spread open she legs for me. The pum-pum smell rise from she, like I used to smelling it on myself. I know that smell like my life. I start to relax. I rub she little button, but that ain't seem to sweet she so much. She only screwing up she face and twitching little bit when I touch she. I stop. "I not doing it right."

"It ain't have no right nor wrong, my fisherman. Just stroke it from the top to the bottom, very gentle."

Oho. Treat she tot-tots hard on top, she pum-pum soft down below. I could do that. I make the touch light, so light. In two-twos she start to say, "Mm," and "Ah," quiet-quiet like the first soft breeze of morning. I look at she face. She head only rolling from side to side, she eyes shut tight. She nipples crinkle-up and jooking out. I feel if to kiss them. I wonder if I could do that? She belly shuddering. I think she liking it.

Something wetting my hand, down there where I stroking she. I look down. She pum-pum getting wet and warm and sticky. The salt and sweat smell rising up from she stronger. Now what to do? I ain't know what to do.

Do me like I do you, that is what she tell me. Maybe she don't mind being a glove. So I slip one finger inside the pum-pum. She kinda give a little squeak. It hot in there, and slippery. It only squeezing and squeezing my finger, tight. "Like this, Missis?"

"Oh God like that. Go in and out for me, nuh? No, no; only partway out. Yes, yes, K.C., like that."

I get a rhythm going; in, out, in.

"More fingers, K.C."

I could do that.

"More."

Four fingers inside she, fulling she up. She squeezing tight like a handshake now, and only getting wetter. And every push I push, my hand going in farther. I get lost in the warm wet and sucking and the little moans she making. She spreading she knees wider, tilting up she hips to get my fingers deeper in.

"Oh God more."

More? Is only my thumb leave behind. I tuck it in close with the others and push that inside she too. She start to groan. I say, "I hurting you?" I start to pull my hand out.

"If you only take it out," she pant, "I swear I box you here tonight." She spread she two feet to either side of the bed, move she pum-pum up to meet me hand. "Push it, K.C. Push."

And is like a space opening up deep inside the poonani. Like it pulling. Like it hungry. I push a few little
minutes more, with she groaning and rolling she head
around. And next thing I know, is no lie, my whole
hand pass through the tightest place inside she and
slide into she poonani right up to the wrist! She groan,
"Fuck me, K.C.!"

She hips bucking like anything. A strong woman this.
I had was to brace myself, wrap one arm around she
thigh, and hold on tight. So close in there, I close my
hand up into a fist. I pull back my hand partway, and
push it in again. Pull back, push in. Pull back, push in.
She start to bawl 'bout don't stop, fuck she, don't stop. I
could do that. I hold on to she bucking body and I fuck
she. Me, K.C. She only throwing sheself around steady
on the bed. The way she head tossing, all she hair come
loose from that pretty hairstyle. It twisting and knotting
all over the two pillows. She belly shaking, she bubbies
bouncing up and down, she thighs clamp onto me. And
she bawling, bawling. This woman bawling like any baby
here in this bed. I ride with she. I feel my own pum-pum
getting warm, my button swelling and throbbing
between my legs. I fuck she, I fuck she. She moan, she
twist herself up. My shoulders burning from all the work
I doing, but I just imagine I pulling in the net with the
boys and them. Push your hand out, pull it back. Push it
out, pull it back. Push, pull. I smelling pum-pum all
round me and my sweat and she own.

All of a sudden, something deep inside she start to
squeeze my hand fast-fast-fast like a pounding heart, so
strong I frighten my hand going to sprain. She arch she
back up right off the bed and she scream, "Oh GOD I
love a mannish woman!" And more too besides, but
them wasn't exactly words.

Hmm. Mannish woman. I like better to be she fisherman. Now is not the time to tell she that, though.

The pounding inside she stop. She give a little sigh and reach down and grab my wrist to hold it quiet. She flop back down on the bed with that mischevious grin on she face again.

Somebody knock on the door. I jump and freeze. If I come out too fast, I might hurt she.

"Mary Anne? Everything all right?" Is a man voice.

She start to laugh. I could feel it right down in she belly. "Jackobennie, you too fast. I with a customer. Leave we some privacy."

A deep chuckle roll into the room. "Sorry, girl. I ain't mean to disturb allyou; I gone."

I could hear the heavy weight of he footsteps as he walk away. Jackobennie is a giant of a man. My whole body start to feel cold one time. "You is Jackobennie woman?"

She lie back and close she eyes, squeeze my hand that jam up inside she. She smile. "Jackobennie is my right-hand man. He and me know one other since God was a little boy in short pants. Jackobennie does make sure me and the rest of the girls stay safe. Sometimes customers does act stupid. Don't fret your head about Jackobennie, K.C. You is a well-behaved customer."

I smile.

"Move the heel of your hand up and down for me, nuh? Ai! Gentle!"

I could do that. A sucking sound come from inside she poonani as she flesh move away little bit from my hand.

"Good. Now come out, slow."

My shoulder muscles burn as I pull out. My hand

come back to me wet and wrinkly. I raise the hand to my mouth. It smell like she, like me. I taste it. I know that taste.

"Here." Mary Anne hand me a towel from out the bedside table. I wipe my hands.

My bubbies tingling.

Mary Anne sit up, she belly resting on she thighs like a calabash. When she grin at me again, I feel all warm inside.

"So, Fisherman," she say, "what you think of your first time?"

"Nice. Strange. But nice."

"Like you. You going to come back and see me sometimes?"

"You want me to come back?"

"It have plenty more I could show you, sweetness."

My pum-pum feeling like a big, warm smile. I just done fuck somebody. The grin that break out on my face must be did brighter than the sun.

For that grin, she say, she kiss me again.

After she and me done clean weselves up she count the money and tuck it into she bosom. She take my hand. Nobody ain't do that since I was a small child. We step outside the room and walk down the hall to the parlour.

Bright lights. All the chatting stop one time. Everybody looking at we. Lennie skinning up he face like he smelling something rotten. Two-Tone, with the cards still in he hand, busting a grin from one side of he jaw to the next and shaking he head. "Lord, K.C.," he laugh. "Is what you was doing inside there with that woman?"

Mary Anne walk with me over to the bar. "Is what you think he was doing, Two-Tone? Bartender, give the man a beer there. House paying."

I hear the chair scrape and I turn round one time to face the storm. I did know it was coming. Everything I get in this life, I had was to fight for. Lennie throw down his cards and slam his hand on the table. The shot glasses jump. "'Man'? Don't make joke, woman! Is nastiness allyou was doing! Is against nature!"

I step between Lennie and Mary Anne, but she come out from behind me. She push out one broad hip and cotch up she hand on it. "Lennie," she say, loud so everyone in the bar was looking now. "Against nature? And the way you too love to push your totie up inside my behind—ain't that is against nature too?"

And one set of belly laugh cut loose in the place. Jackobennie, man mountain, thundering, slapping his hand on the bar. The little, light-skin bartender with he long fingers only giggling and snapping he white towel in the air. The rest of my crew holding their sides and shaking with laugh. Ramesh. Errol. Matchstick. Two of the whores jump up from their tables and start to wind each other down, back to belly. "Like this, Lennie? Eh?" the one in back shout, jooking she crotch in she miniskirt, up against the behind of the one in front of she. Lennie face just shut down.

I barely have time to notice how the miniskirt woman voice hard, how she shoulders broader than my own, when Lennie rush Mary Anne, reach for she neck. Jackobennie jump and hold he, but is my hand grab Lennie wrist. Lennie spit at me: "Bullah woman!"

He try to break my hold. I hang on. I could do that.

"Lennie man, calm down!" Jackobennie say, wrestling Lennie by he shoulders. But Lennie not paying him no mind. He only trying to box me, he eyes boring hate into me like them could jook inside my brain and strike me dead. Mary Anne not saying anything. I can't see she. She all right? I holding Lennie back with the arm I had inside she. It getting weary. But I hang on. Lennie know he could pull net twice as hard as me. But like he forget I could go longer.

"Lennie," Jackobennie rumble right beside Lennie ear. He put he hand on Lennie shoulder. Lennie try to shrug it away.

"Let me go, I say! Fucking bullah woman and she fucking whore! I going knock she head right off she shoulders!"

I just keep holding on. My hand trembling, but I don't let go. Mary Anne step in between me and Lennie, and I see Jackobennie fingers tighten on Lennie shoulder. "Lennie," Mary Anne say, hard and fast, "if you make anymore comess in my house tonight, you never going set foot in here again."

Lennie look from me to she, he eyes bull-red in he angry face.

"No more of this sweet behind for you, Lennie. Who else you going find to let you do that thing with them?"

Lennie shake my hand off he wrist. It look like he cool down little bit, so I let he. He try to stare down Mary Anne. Jackobennie never move away from he the whole time, that big, heavy hand resting like a threat on Lennie shoulder. From behind the two of them I hear Two-Tone say, "The woman right you know, Lennie. You have to have some manners inside she establishment. And all these years K.C. been doing everything else we men does do, you think she ain't go do this, too?"

"It not right!" Lennie spit, glaring at Mary Anne.

I barely hear what Jackobennie whisper to Lennie, grinning the whole while: "And what you pay me and Mary Anne to do to you that time? That wrong too?"

Lennie glance over he shoulder like is the devil heself latch on there. He go still. It get quiet in the place again. I see he shoulders sag. "All right," he mutter. "Let me go. I ain't go hurt nobody."

Jackobennie release him. Lennie dust heself off and sit back down to table. He growl to Two-Tone, "Let we finish we game and go home, yes."

I glance at the whore with the deep voice and the broad shoulders and the tiny, tiny skirt. She? smile and roll she eyes at me.

Mary Anne throw she arms round my waist. I smile at she. "Thanks."

"Only the best for the best customers."

I hug she back, this armful of woman. I think the perfume smell and woman smell of she going stay with me whole week.

But I know Lennie and me story ain't done yet. I have to stand up to he now, in the light, else I go be looking over my shoulder every time it get dark from now on. "Just now," I excuse myself to Mary Anne.

"All right, darling."

Lennie and Two-Tone look up when I reach to their table. I pull a chair, I turn it backwards. I throw my leg over it (poonani still feeling warm and nice under my clothes) and I sit down. "Lennie," I say. He ain't say nothing.

Mary Anne and Jackobennie come to the table with three beers. "On the house," Jackobennie tell we. "To thank everybody for being gentlemen." He look hard at Lennie as he and Mary Anne put down the beers. Two-Tone thank them, but Lennie just pick up his and start guzzling it down. Mary Anne wink at me as they walk away.

I take a sip from my beer. Cold and nice, just so I like it. I swallow two more times, think about what I going to say. "Lennie, you is a man, right?"

"Blasted right!" He slam the empty bottle down onto the table.

"Big, hard-back, long-pants-wearing man?"

"Yes." He look at me with suspicion.

"Work and sweat for your living? Try to treat everybody fair?"

"I never cheat you, K.C.!"

"Is true. You wish if I never try to work with allyou neither, but once you see I could pull my weight, you treat me like all the rest."

"So long as you know your place!" He scowl and shake the beer bottle at me. "But coming in here brazen like this!"

"You is a man, yes."

He look at me, confused. I see Two-Tone frowning too. I nod my head, sip some more beer. "Work hard in the hot sun, don't do nobody wrong. Have a right to fuck any way you want."

"But not you! You is a woman!"

To rass. Time to done with this. "Lennie, you is a man. And I? I is a fisherman."

And I swear all the glasses in the place ring like the fishing bell, the way Two-Tone start to make noise in the place. "Oh God, K.C., in all my born days, I never meet no one like you!" He put down he cards and he hold he belly and he laugh.

"What, you taking the bullah woman side now?" Lennie sulk.

"Man, Lennie, hold some strain," Two-Tone say. "K.C. not judging you for what you like to do. I not judging you, and you know Mary Anne not judging you, for you bringing you good good dollars and give she. K.C. work hard beside you every day, she never ask no man to look after she. She have a right to play hard too."

Is not only me does work hard, neither. Mary Anne. All the whores. I realise is not only man have a right to fuck how he want. When a truth come to you simple like that, it does full you up and make you feel warm, make you want to tell everybody. I must ask Mary Anne sometime if she think I right. But for now I just smile and look down at my nice clean shine shoes. I drink some more beer and look Lennie right in he eye, friendly. He scowl at me, but I ain't look away. Is he glance down finally.

He pick up he cards. "You playing or what?" he say to Two-Tone.

"Deal me in next hand," I say. God, he go do it?

Lennie glance sideways at me over he cards. Look down at the cards. Then quiet, "You have money after you done spending everything on Mary Anne?"

"Yes, man." I done being careful. "I have enough to whip both of allyou behind."

"Oh, yes?" Lennie say. "Well, don't get too attached to it. I bet you I leave this place tonight with you money and my own."

He throw down he cards. Two-Tone inspect them, make a face, drop he cards on the table, and pull out two bills and lay them down. Lennie pocket the bills. He pick up the whole deck of cards and hand them to me. "Deal. Fisherman."

I feel the grin lighting up my face as I take the cards from he. "I could do that."

*T*he Caribbean folktale about what happens to the greedy spider man Anansi when he encounters Dry Bone is one of the eeriest, most sinister I've ever read. In my novel Midnight Robber, *the* heroine Tan-Tan discovers that her deeds are becoming so legendary that they're passing into folklore. Tan-Tan hears a tale about herself that refers to incidents in her life, but which casts them as fable. People are beginning to confuse her in their minds with Anansi.

TAN-TAN AND DRY BONE

If you only see Dry Bone: one meager man, with arms and legs thin so like matches stick, and what a way the man face just a-hang down till it favour jackass when him sick!

Duppy Dead Town is where people go when life boof them, when hope left them and happiness cut she eye 'pon them and strut away. Duppy Dead people drag them foot when them walk. The food them cook taste like burial ground ashes. Duppy Dead people have one foot in the world and the next one already crossing the threshold to where the real duppy-them living. In Duppy Dead Town them will tell you how it ain't have no way to get away from Dry Bone the skin-and-bone man, for even if you lock you door on him, him body so fine him could slide through the crack and all to pass inside your house.

Dry Bone sit down there on one little wooden crate in the open market in Duppy Dead Town. Him a-think about food. Him hungry so till him belly a-burn him, till it just a-prowl round inside him rib cage like angry bush cat, till it clamp on to him backbone, and a-sit there so and a-growl.

And all the time Dry Bone sitting down there in the market, him just a-watch the open sky above him, for Dry Bone nah like that endless blue. Him 'fraid him will just fall up into it and keep falling.

Dry Bone feel say him could eat two-three of that market woman skinny little fowl-them, feathers and all, then wash them down with a dry-up breadfruit from the farmer cart across the way, raw and hard just so, and five-six of them wrinkle-up string mango from the fruit stand over there. Dry Bone coulda never get enough food, and right now, all like how him ain't eat for days, even Duppy Dead people food looking good. But him nah have no money. The market people wouldn't even prekkay 'pon him, only a-watch him like stray dog so him wouldn't fast himself and thief away any of them goods. In Duppy Dead Town them had a way to say if you only start to feed Dry Bone, you can't stop, and you pickney-them go starve, for him will eat up all your provisions. And then them would shrug and purse-up them mouth, for them know say hunger is only one of the crosses Duppy Dead pickney go have to bear.

Duppy Dead Town ain't know it waiting; waiting for the one name Tan-Tan.

So—it had Dry Bone sitting there, listening to he belly bawl. And is so Tan-Tan find he, cotch-up on the wooden crate like one big black anansi-spider.

Dry Bone watch the young woman dragging she sad self into the market like monkey riding she back. She nah have no right to look downpressed so; she body tall and straight like young cane, and she legs strong. But the look on she pretty face favour puppy what lose it mother, and she carrying she hand on she machäte handle the way you does put your hand on your friend shoulder. Dry Bone sit up straight. He lick he lips. A stranger in Duppy Dead Town, one who ain't know to avoid he. One who can't see she joy for she sorrow; the favourite meat of the one name Dry Bone. He know she good. Dry Bone know all the souls that feed he. He recognize she so well, he discern she name in the curve of she spine. So Dry Bone laugh, a sound like the dust blowin' down in the dry gully. "Girl pickney Tan-Tan," he whisper, "I go make you take me on this day. And when you pick me up, you pick up trouble."

He call out to Tan-Tan, "My beautiful one; you enjoying the day?"

Tan-Tan look at the little fine-foot man, so meager you could nearly see through he. "What you want, Grandpa?" she ask.

Dry Bone smile when she say "Grandpa." True, Duppy Dead townspeople have a way to say that Dry Bone older than Death it own self. "Well doux-doux darlin', me wasn't going to say nothing; but since you ask, beg you a copper to buy something to eat, nuh? I ain't eat from mornin'."

Now, Tan-Tan heart soft. Too besides, she figure maybe if she help out this old man who look to be on he last legs, she go ease up the curse on she a little. For you must know the story 'bout she, how she kill she only family on New Half Way Tree. Guilt nearly breaking she heart in two, but to make it worse, the douen people nah put a curse on she when she do the deed? Yes, man: She couldn't rest until she save two people life to make up for the one she did kill. Everywhere she go, she could hear the douen chant following she:

> *It ain't have no magic in do-feh-do.*
> *If you take one, you mus' give back two.*

Tan-Tan reach into she pocket to fling the old man couple-three coppers. But she find it strange that he own people wasn't feeding he. So she raise she voice to everyone in the market place: "How oonuh could let this old man sit here hungry so? Oonuh not shame?"

"Lawd, Missus," say the woman selling the fowl, "you ain't want to mix up with he. That is Dry Bone, and when you pick he up, you pick up trouble!"

"What stupidness you talking, woman? Hot sun make you bassourdie, or what? How much trouble so one little old man could give you?"

A man frying some hard johnny cake on a rusty piece of galvanized iron look up from he wares. "You should listen when people talk to you, girl pickney. Make I tell you: You even self touch Dry Bone, is like you touch Death. Don't say nobody ain't tell you!"

Tan-Tan look down at the little old man, just holding he belly and waiting for somebody to take pity on he. Tan-Tan kiss she teeth *steuups*. "Oonuh too craven, you hear? Come, Daddy. I go buy you a meal, and I go take you where I staying and cook it up nice for you. All right?"

Dry Bone get excited one time; he almost have she

now! "Thank you, my darlin'. Granny Nanny bless you, doux-doux. I ain't go be plenty trouble. Beg you though, sweetheart: Pick me up. Me old bones so weak with hunger, I ain't think I could make the walk back to your place. I is only a little man, halfway a duppy meself. You could lift me easy."

"You mean to say these people make you stay here and get hungry so till you can't walk?" Tan-Tan know say she could pick he up; after he the smallest man she ever see.

The market go quiet all of a sudden. Everybody only waiting to see what she go do. Tan-Tan bend down to take the old man in she arms. Dry Bone reach out and hold on to she. As he touch she, she feel a coldness wrap round she heart. She pick up the old man, and is like she pick up all the cares of the world. She make a joke of it, though: "Eh-eh, Pappy, you heavier than you look, you know!"

That is when she hear Dry Bone voice good, whispering inside she head, *sht-sht-sht*, like dead leaf on a dead tree. And she realise that all this time she been talking to he, she never see he lips move. "I name Dry Bone," the old man say, "I old like Death, and when you pick me up, you pick up trouble. You ain't go shake me loose until I suck out all your substance. Feed me, Tan-Tan."

And Tan-Tan feel Dry Bone getting heavier and heavier, but she couldn't let he go. She feel the weight of all the burdens she carrying: alone, stranded on New Half Way Tree with a curse on she head, a spiteful woman so ungrateful she kill she own family.

"Feed me, Tan-Tan, or I go choke you." He wrap he arms tight round she neck and cut off she wind. She stumble over to the closest market stall. The lady selling the fowl back away, she eyes rolling with fright. Gasping for air, Tan-Tan stretch out she hand and feel two dead fowl. She pick them up off the woman stand. Dry Bone chuckle. He loosen up he arms just enough to let she get some air. He grab one fowl and stuff it into he mouth, feathers and all. He chew, then he swallow. "More, Tan-Tan. Feed me." He choke she again.

She body crying for breath, Tan-Tan stagger from one market stall to the next. All the higglers fill up a market basket for she. Them had warn she, but she never listen. None of them would take she money. Dry Bone let she breathe again. "Now take me home, Tan-Tan."

Tan-Tan grab the little man round he waist and try to dash he off, but she hand stick to he like he was tar baby. He laugh in she mind, the way ground puppy does giggle when it see carrion. "You pick me up by your own free will. You can't put me down. Take me home, Tan-Tan."

Tan-Tan turn she feet towards she little hut in the bush, and with every step she take along the narrow gravel path into the bush, Dry Bone only getting heavier. Tan-Tan mother did never want she; Ione make Antonio kidnap she away to New Half Way Tree. Even she daddy who did say he love she used to beat she, and worse things too besides. Tan-Tan never see the singing tree she always pass by on she way home, with the wind playing like harp in the leaves, or the bright blue furry butterflies that always used to sweet she, flitting through the bush carrying the flowers they gather in their little hands. With Dry Bone on her back and the full market basket in her arms, Tan-Tan had was to use she shoulders to shove aside the branches to make she way to she hut. Branches reach out bony fingers to pull at she dreads, but she ain't feel that pain. She only feel the pain of knowing what she is, a worthless, wicked woman that only good to feed a duppy like Dry Bone. How anybody could love she? She don't deserve no better.

"Make haste, woman," Dry Bone snarl. "And keep under the trees, you hear? I want to get out from under the open sky."

By the time them reach the thatch hut standing all by itself in the bush, Tan-Tan back did bend with the weight of all she was carrying. It feel like Dry Bone get bigger, oui? Tan-Tan stand up outside she home, panting under the weight of she burdens.

"Take me inside, Tan-Tan. I prefer to be out of the air."

"Yes, Dry Bone." Wheezing, she climb up the verandah steps and carry he inside the dark, mean one-room hut, exactly the kind of place where a worthless woman should live. One break-seat chair for sit in; a old ticking mattress for when sleep catch she; two rusty hurricane lamp with rancid oil inside them, one for light the inside of the hut, and one for light outside when night come, to keep away the ground puppy and mako jumbie-them; a dirty coal-pot, and a bucket full of stale water with dead spider and thing floating on top. Just good for she. With all the nice things she steal from people, she ain't keep none for she self, but only giving them away all the time.

Dry Bone voice fill up the inside of she head again: "Put me on the mattress. It look softer than the chair. Is there I go stay from now on."

"Yes, Dry Bone." She find she could put he down, but the weight ain't lift from off she. Is like she still carrying he, a heaviness next to she heart, and getting heavier.

"I hungry, Tan-Tan. Cook up that food for me. All of it, you hear?"

"Yes, Dry Bone." And Tan-Tan pluck the fowl, and chop off the head, and gut out the insides. She make a fire outside the hut. She roast the fowl and she boil water for topi-tambo root, and she bake a breadfruit.

"I want johnnycake, too."

So Tan-Tan find she one bowl and she fry pan, and she little store of flour and oil, and she carry water and make dumpling and put it to fry on the fire. And all she working, she could hear Dry Bone whispering in she head like knowledge: "Me know say what you is, Tan-Tan. Me know how you worthless and your heart hard. Me know you could kill just for so, and you don't look out for nobody but yourself. You make a mistake when you pick me up. You pick up trouble."

When she done cook the meal, she ain't self have enough plate to serve it all one time. She had was to bring a plate of food in to Dry Bone, make he eat it, and take it outside and fill it up again. Dry Bone swallow every last johhnycake whole. He chew up the topi-tambo, skin and all, and nyam it down. He ain't even wait for she to peel the roast breadfruit, he pop it into he maw just so. He tear the meat from the chicken bone, then he crunch up the bone-them and all. And all he eat, he belly getting round and hard, but he arms and legs only getting thinner and thinner. Still, Tan-Tan could feel the weight of he resting on she chest till she could scarcely breathe.

"That not enough," Dry Bone say. "Is where the fowl guts-them there?"

"I wrap them up in leaf and bury them in the back," Tan-Tan mumble.

"Dig them up and bring them for me."

"You want me to cook them in the fire?"

"No, stupid one, hard-ears one," Dry Bone say in he sandpaper voice. "I ain't tell you to cook them. I go eat them raw just so."

She own-way, yes, and stupid too. Is must be so. Tan-Tan hang she head. She dig up the fowl entrails and bring them back. Dry Bone suck down the rank meat, toothless gums smacking in the dark hut. He pop the bitter gallbladder in he mouth like a sea grape and swallow that too. "Well," he say, "that go do me for now, but a next hour or two, and you going to feed me again. It ain't look like you have plenty here to eat, eh, Tan-Tan? You best go and find more before evening come."

That is all she good for. Tan-Tan know she best be grateful Dry Bone even let she live. She turn she weary feet back on the path to Duppy Dead Town. She feel the weight on she dragging she down to the ground. Branch scratch up she face, and mosquito bite she, and when she reach where she always did used to find Duppy Dead Town, it ain't have nothing there. The people pick up lock, stock, and barrel and left she in she shame with Dry Bone. Tears start to track down Tan-Tan face. She weary, she weary can't done, but she had was to feed the little duppy man. Lazy, the voice in she head say. What a way this woman could run from a little hard work! Tan-Tan drag down some net vine from out a tree and weave she-self a basket. She search the bush. She find two-three mushroom under some rockstone, and a halwa tree with a half-ripe fruit on it. She throw she knife and stick a fat guinea lizard. Dry Bone go eat the bones and all. Maybe that would full he belly.

And is so the days go for she. So Dry Bone eat, so he hungry again one time. Tan-Tan had was to catch and kill and gut and cook, and she only get time to sneak a little bite for sheself was when Dry Bone sleeping, but it seem like he barely sleep at all. He stretch out the whole day and night on Tan-Tan one bed, giving orders. Tan-Tan had to try and doze the long nights through in the break-seat chair or on the cold floor, and come 'fore day morning, she had was to find sheself awake one time, to stoke up the fire and start cooking all over again. And what a way Dry Bone belly get big! Big like a watermelon. But the rest of he like he wasting away, just a skin-and-bone man. Sometimes, Tan-Tan couldn't even self see he in the dark hut; only a belly sticking up on the bed.

One time, after he did guzzle down three lizard, two breadfruit, a gully hen, and four gully hen eggs, Dry Bone sigh and settle back down on the bed. He close he eyes.

Tan-Tan walk over to the bed. Dry Bone ain't move. She wave she hand in front of he face. He ain't open he eyes. Maybe he did fall to sleep? Maybe she could run away now? Tan-Tan turn to creep out the door, and four bony fingers grab she round she arm and start to squeeze. "You can't run away, Tan-Tan. I go follow you. You have to deal with me."

Is must be true. Dry Bone was she sins come to haunt she, to ride she into she grave. Tan-Tan ain't try to get away no more, but late at night, she weep bitter, bitter tears.

One day, she had was to go down to the river to dip

some fresh water to make soup for Dry Bone. As she lean out over the river with she dipping bowl, she see a reflection in the water: Master Johncrow the corbeau-bird, the turkey buzzard, perch on a tree branch, looking for carrion for he supper. He bald head gleaming in the sun like a hard boil egg. He must be feeling hot in he black frock coat, for he eyes look sad, and he beak drooping like candle wax. Tan-Tan remember she manners. "Good day to you, Sir Buzzard," she say. "How do?"

"Not so good, eh?" Master Johncrow reply. "I think I going hungry today. All I look, I can't spy nothing dead or even ready to dead. You feeling all right, Tan-Tan?" he ask hopefully.

"Yes, Master Buzzard, thanks Nanny."

"But you don't look too good, you know. Your eyes sink back in your head, and your skin all grey, and you walking with a stoop. I could smell death around here yes, and it making me hungry."

"Is only tired I tired, sir. Dry Bone latch onto me, and I can't get any rest, only feeding he day and night."

"Dry Bone?" The turkey buzzard sit up straight on he perch. Tan-Tan could see a black tongue snaking in and out of he mouth with excitement.

"Seen, Master Buzzard. I is a evil woman, and I must pay for my corruption by looking after Dry Bone. It go drive me to me grave, I know, then you go have your meal."

"I ain't know about you and any corruption, doux-doux." Johncrow leap off the tree branch and flap down to the ground beside Tan-Tan. "You smell fresh like the living to me." Him nearly big as she, he frock-coat feathers rank and raggedy, and she could smell the carrion on he. Tan-Tan step back a little.

"You don't know the wicked things I do," she say.

"If a man attack you, child, don't you must defend yourself? I know this, though: I ain't smell no rottenness on you, and that is my favourite smell. If you dead soon, I go thank you for your thoughtfulness with each taste of your entrails, but I go thank you even more if you stay alive long enough to deliver Dry Bone to me."

"How you mean, Master Crow?"

"Dry Bone did dead and rotten long before Nanny was a girl, but him living still. Him is the sweetest meat for a man like me. I could feed off Dry Bone for the rest of my natural days, and him still wouldn't done. Is years now I trying to catch he for me larder. Why you think he so 'fraid the open sky? Open sky is home to me. Do me this one favour, nuh?"

Tan-Tan feel hope start to bud in she heart.

"What you want me to do, Master Crow?"

"Just get he to come outside in your yard, and I go do the rest."

So the two of them make a plan. And before he fly off Master Johncrow say to she, "Like Dry Bone not the only monkey that a-ride your back, child. You carrying around a bigger burden than he. And me nah want that one there. It ain't smell dead, but like it did never live. Best you go find Papa Bois."

"And who is Papa Bois, sir?"

"The old man of the bush, the one who does look after all the beast-them. He could look into your eyes, and see your soul, and tell you how to cleanse it."

Tan-Tan ain't like the sound of someone examining she soul, so she only say politely, "Thank you, Master Johncrow. Maybe I go do that."

"All right then, child. Till later." And Master Buzzard fly off to wait until he part of the plan commence.

Tan-Tan scoop up the water for the soup to carry back to she hut, feeling almost happy for the first time in weeks. On the way home, she fill up she carry sack with a big, nice halwa fruit, three handful of mushroom, some coco yam that she dig up, big so like she head, and all the ripe hog plum she could find on the ground. She go make Dry Bone eat till he foolish, oui?

When she reach back at the hut, she set about she cooking with a will. She boil up the soup thick and nice with mushroom and coco yam and cornmeal dumpling. She roast the halwa fruit in the coal pot, and she sprinkle nutmeg and brown sugar on top of it too besides, till the whole hut smell sweet with it scent. She wash the hog plum clean and put them in she best bowl. And all the time she work, she humming to sheself:

> *Corbeau say so, it must be so,*
> *Corbeau say so, it must be so.*

Dry Bone sprawl off on she bed and just a-watch she with him tiny jumby-bead eye, red with a black centre. "How you happy so?"

Tan-Tan catch sheself. She mustn't make Dry Bone hear Master Johncrow name. She make she mouth droop and she eyes sad, and she say, "Me not really happy, Dry Bone. Me only find when me sing, the work go little faster."

Dry Bone still suspicious, though. "Then is what that you singing? Sing it louder so I could hear."

"Is a song about making soup." Tan-Tan sing for he:

Coco boil so, is so it go,
Coco boil so, is so it go.

"Cho! Stupid woman. Just cook the food fast, you hear?"

"Yes, Dry Bone." She leave off singing. Fear form a lump of ice in she chest. Suppose Dry Bone find she out?

Tan-Tan finish preparing the meal as fast as she could. She take it to Dry Bone right there on the bed.

By now, Dry Bone skin did draw thin like paper on he face. He eyes did disappear so far back into he head that Tan-Tan could scarce see them. She ain't know what holding he arms and legs-them together, for it look as though all the flesh on them waste away. Only he belly still bulging big with all the food she been cooking for he. If Tan-Tan had buck up a thing like Dry Bone in the bush, she would have take it for a corpse, dead and rotting in the sun. Dry Bone, the skin-and-bone man. To pick he up was to pick up trouble, for true.

Dry Bone bare he teeth at Tan-Tan in a skull grin. "Like you cook plenty this time, almost enough for a snack. Give me the soup first." He take the whole pot in he two hand, put it to he head, and drink it down hot hot just so. He never even self stop to chew the coco yam and dumpling, he just swallow. When he put down the pot and belch, Tan-Tan see steam coming out of he mouth, the soup did so hot. He scoop out all the insides of the halwa fruit with he bare hand, and he chew up the hard seed-them like them was fig. Then he eat the thick rind. And so he belly getting bigger. He suck down the hog plum one by one, then he just let go Tan-

Tan best bowl. She had was to catch it before it hit the ground and shatter.

Dry Bone lie back and sigh. "That was good. It cut me hunger little bit. In two-three hour, I go want more again."

Time was, them words would have hit Tan-Tan like blow, but this time, she know what she have to do. "Dry Bone," she say in a sweet voice, "you ain't want to go out onto the verandah for a little sun while I cook your next meal?"

Dry Bone open he eyes up big big. Tan-Tan could see she death in them cold eyes. "Woman, you crazy? Go outside? Like you want breeze blow me away, or what? I comfortable right here." He close he eyes and settle back down in the bed.

She try a next thing. "I want to clean the house, Master. I need to make up the bed, put on clean sheets for you. Make me just cotch you on the verandah for two little minutes while I do that, nuh?"

"Don't get me vex." Tan-Tan feel he choking weight on she spirit squeeze harder. Only two-three sips of air making it past she throat.

The plan ain't go work. Tan-Tan start to despair. Then she remember how she used to love to play masque Robber Queen when she was a girl-pickney, how she could roll pretty words around in she mouth like marble, and make up any kind of story. She had a talent for the Robber Queen patter. Nursie used to say she could make yellow think it was red. "But Dry Bone," she wheeze, "look at how nice and strong I build my verandah, fit to sit a king. Look at how it shade off from the sun." She gasp for a breath, just a little breath of air. "No glare to beware, no open sky to trouble you, only sweet breeze to dance over your face, to soothe you as you lie and daydream. Ain't you would like me to carry you out there to lounge off in the wicker chair, and warm your bones little bit, just sit and contemplate your estate? It nice and warm outside today. You could hear the gully hens-them singing cocorico, and the guinea lizards-them just a-relax in the sun hot and drowse. It nice out there for true, like a day in heaven. Nothing to cause you danger. Nothing to cause you harm. I could carry you out there in my own two arm, and put you nice and comfortable in the wicker chair, with two pillow at your back for you to rest back on, a king on he own throne. Ain't you would like that?"

Dry Bone smile. The tightness in she chest ease up little bit. "All right, Tan-Tan. You getting to know how to treat me good. Take me outside. But you have to watch out after me. No make no open sky catch me. Remember, when you pick me up, you pick up trouble! If you ain't protect me, you go be sorry."

"Yes, Dry Bone." She pick he up. He heavy like a heart attack from all the food he done eat already. She carry he out onto the verandah and put he in the wicker chair with two pillow at he back.

Dry Bone lean he dead-looking self back in the chair with a peaceful smile on he face. "Yes, I like this. Maybe I go get you to bring me my food out here from now on."

Tan-Tan give he some cool sorrel drink in a cup to tide he over till she finish cook, then she go back inside the hut to start cooking again. And as she cooking, she singing soft-soft,

> *Corbeau say so, it must be so,*
> *Corbeau say so, it must be so.*

And she only watching at the sky through the one little window in the hut. Suppose Master Johncrow ain't come?

"Woman, the food ready yet?" Dry Bone call out.

"Nearly ready, Dry Bone." *Is a black shadow that she see in the sky? It moving? It flying their way?* No. Just a leaf blowing in the wind. "The chicken done stew!" she called out to the verandah. I making the dumpling now!" And she hum she tune, willing Master Johncrow to hear.

A-what that? Him come? No, only one baby raincloud scudding by. "Dumpling done! I frying the banana!"

"What a way you taking long today," grumbled Dry Bone.

Yes. Coasting in quiet-quiet on wings the span of a big man, Master Johncrow the corbeau-bird float through the sky. From her window Tan-Tan see him land on the bannister rail right beside Dry Bone, so soft that the duppy man ain't even self hear he. She heart start dancing in she chest, light and airy like a masque band flag. Tan-Tan tiptoe out to the front door to watch the drama.

Dry Bone still have he eyes closed. Master Johncrow stretch he long, picky-picky wattle neck and look right into Dry Bone face, tender as a lover. He black tongue snake out to lick one side of he pointy beak, to clean out the corner of one eye. "Ah, Dry Bone," he say, and he voice was the wind in dry season, "so long I been waiting for this day."

Dry Bone open up he eye. Him two eyes make four with Master Johncrow own. He scream and try to scramble out the chair, but he belly get too heavy for he skin-and-bone limbs. "Don't touch me!" he shout.

"When you pick me up, you pick up trouble! Tan-Tan, come and chase this buzzard away!" But Tan-Tan ain't move.

Striking like a serpent, Master Johncrow trap one of Dry Bone arm in he beak. Tan-Tan hear the arm snap like twig, and Dry Bone scream again. "You can't pick me up! You picking up trouble!" But Master Johncrow haul Dry Bone out into the yard by he break arm, then he fasten onto the nape of Dry Bone neck with he claws. He leap into the air, dragging Dry Bone up with him. The skin-and-bone man fall into the sky in truth.

As he flap away over the trees with he prize, Tan-Tan hear he chuckle. "Ah, Dry Bone, you dead thing, you! Trouble sweet to me like the yolk that did sustain me. Is trouble you swallow to make that belly so fat? Ripe like a watermelon. I want you to try to give me plenty, plenty trouble. I want you to make it last a long time."

Tan-Tan sit down in the wicker chair on the verandah and watch them flying away till she couldn't hear Dry Bone screaming no more and Master Johncrow was only a black speck in the sky. She whisper to sheself:

> Corbeau say so, it must be so,
> Please, Johncrow, take Dry Bone and go,
> Tan-Tan say so,
> Tan-Tan beg so.

Tan-Tan went inside and look at she little home. It wouldn't be plenty trouble to make another window to let in more light. Nothing would be trouble after living with the trouble of Dry Bone. She go make the window tomorrow, and the day after that, she go re-cane the break-seat chair.

Tan-Tan pick up she kerosene lamp and went outside to look in the bush for some scraper grass to polish the rust off it. That would give she something to do while she think about what Master Johncrow had tell she. Maybe she would even go find this Papa Bois, oui?

Wire bend,
Story end.

"Craven choke puppy" means that puppies frequently choke on their food because they're too greedy to eat slowly.

GREEDY CHOKE PUPPY

I see a Lagahoo last night. In the back of the house, behind the pigeon peas."

"Yes, Granny." Sitting cross-legged on the floor, Jacky leaned back against her grandmother's knees and closed her eyes in bliss against the gentle tug of Granny's hands braiding her hair. Jacky still enjoyed this evening ritual, even though she was a big hard-back woman, thirty-two years next month.

The moon was shining in through the open jalousie windows, bringing the sweet smell of Ladies-of-the-Night flowers with it. The ceiling fan beat its soothing rhythm.

"How you mean, 'Yes, Granny'? You even know what a Lagahoo is?"

"Don't you been frightening me with jumby story from since I small? I putting a section on it in my thesis paper. Is a donkey with gold teeth, wearing a waistcoat with a pocket watch and two pair of tennis shoes on the hooves."

"Washekong, you mean. I never teach you to say 'tennis shoes.'"

Jacky smiled. "Yes, Granny. So, what the Lagahoo was doing in the pigeon peas patch?"

"Just standing, looking at my window. Then he pull out he watch chain from out he waistcoat pocket, and he look at the time, and he put the watch back, and he bite off some pigeon peas from off one bush, and he walk away."

Jacky laughed, shaking so hard that her head pulled free of Granny's hands. "You mean to tell me that a Lagahoo come all the way to we little house in Diego Martin, just to sample we so-so pigeon peas?" Still chuckling, she settled back against Granny's knees. Granny tugged at a hank of Jacky's hair, just a little harder than necessary.

Jacky could hear the smile in the old woman's voice. "Don't get fresh with me, young lady. You turn big woman now, Ph.D. student and thing, but is still your old nen-nen who does plait up your hair every evening, oui?"

"Yes, Granny. You know I does love to make mako 'pon you, to tease you a little."

"This ain't no joke, child. My mammy used to say that a Lagahoo is God horse, and when you see one, somebody go dead. The last time I see one is just before your mother dead." The two women fell silent. The memory hung in the air between them, of the badly burned body retrieved from the wreckage of the car that had gone off the road. Jacky knew that her grandmother would soon change the subject. She blamed herself for the argument that had sent Jacky's mother raging from the house in the first place. And whatever Granny didn't want to think about, she certainly wasn't going to talk about.

Granny sighed. "Well, don't fret, doux-doux. Just be careful when you go out so late at night. I couldn't stand to lose you, too."

"You self too, Granny. Always off to prayer meeting, sometimes 'fore day morning before you come home. I does worry about you, you know?"

Granny just grunted, "Mm-hmm."

Jacky closed her eyes, dreamy in the gentle tugs on her hair, the cool stripes of oil that Granny laid down with a finger in the parts between each plait. "Granny, you want to hear how my thesis going?"

"Mm?"

"I write about La Diablesse already, the devil lady, how she pretty for so, but with sharpened teeth and one goat hoof, you did right about that part, Granny."

"I know."

"And you ever notice is only men she does appear to? I talk about how she represent masculine fears of female sexua—"

"Hold this plait here, Jacky. Yes, keep it out of the way."

"Yes, Granny. That Lagahoo, now, that we was just talking about? Well, it have a Jamaican equivalent. They call it the Rolling Calf—"

"All right, girl: I done." Granny finished off the last braid and gently stroked Jacky's head. "Go and wrap up your head in a scarf, so the plaits will stay nice while you sleeping."

"Thank you, Granny. What I would do without you to help me make myself pretty for the gentlemen, eh?"

Granny smiled, but with a worried look on her face.

"Never you mind all that. You just mind your studies. It have plenty of time to catch man."

Jacky stood and gave the old woman a kiss on one warm, soft cheek and headed towards her bedroom in search of a scarf. Behind her, she could hear Granny settling back into the faded wicker armchair, muttering distractedly to herself, "But why this Lagahoo come to bother me again, eh?"

The first time, I ain't know what was happening to me. I was younger them times there, and sweet for so, you see? Sweet like julie mango, with two ripe tot-tot on the front of my body and two ripe maami-apple behind. I only had was to walk down the street, twitching that maami-apple behind, and all the boys-them on the street corner would watch at me like them was starving, and I was food.

But I get to find out know how it is when the boys stop making sweet eye at you so much, and start watching after a next younger thing. I get to find out that when you pass you prime, and you ain't catch no man eye, nothing ain't left for you but to get old and dry-up like cane leaf in the fire. Is just so I was feeling that night. Like something wither-up. Like something that once used to drink in the feel of the sun on it skin, but now it dead and dry, and the sun only drying it out more. And the feeling make a burning in me belly, and the burning spread out to my skin, till I couldn't take it no more. I jump up from my little bed just so in the middle of the night, and snatch off my nightie. And when I do so, my skin come with it, and drop off on the floor. Inside my skin I was just one big ball of fire, and Lord, the night air feel nice and cool on the flame! I know then I was a soucouyant, a hag-woman. I know what I had was to do. When your youth start to leave you, you have to steal more from somebody who still have plenty. I fly out the window and start to search, search for a newborn baby.

"Lagahoo? I know that word from somewhere, Jacky."

Jacky smiled at her friend Carmen, a librarian in the humanities section of the Library of the University of the West Indies. "You probably hear it from Granny. Is French creole for 'werewolf.' But as Trini people tell it, is a donkey, not a wolf. Only we could come up with something so jokey as a were-donkey, oui?"

Carmen giggled, leaning back in her chair behind the information desk, legs sprawled under the bulge of her advanced pregnancy. "And that and all going in your thesis paper, I suppose. You have a title for the paper yet?"

"'Magic in the Real: the Role of Folklore in Everyday Caribbean Life.'"

"'Magic in the Real': I like that." Carmen stretched, groaned. "Lord, girl, my back paining me for so, you see?"

"How much longer?" Jacky asked. A baby! To think Carmen would soon have a child.

"Two weeks. I could scarcely wait to get it out of me. I feel like I have a belly full of cement."

"Carmen!" Jacky was scandalised. "How you could talk so! I tell you, if it was me making baby, I would be happy, happy. I would be shining bright like the sun in the sky."

Carmen just chuckled. "From high school days you always been in such a hurry to turn big woman. Your turn to make baby will come, and then we will see how happy and shiny you talking by the time you due for labour."

Carmen was a little older than Jacky. They had known each other since they were girls together at Saint Alban's Primary School. Carmen was always very interested in Jacky's research.

"As far as I know, it doesn't change into a human being. Why does your granny think she saw a Lagahoo in the backyard?"

"You know Granny, Carmen. She sees all kinds of things, duppy and jumby and things like that. Remember the duppy stories she used to tell us when we were small, so we would be scared and mind what she said?"

Carmen laughed. "And the soucouyant, don't forget that. My mother used to tell me that one too." She smiled a strange smile. "It didn't really frighten me, though. I always wondered what it would be like to take your skin off, leave your worries behind, and fly so free."

"Well, you sit there so and wonder. I have to keep researching this paper. The back issues come in yet?"

"Right here." Sighing with the effort of bending over, Carmen reached under the desk and pulled out a stack of slim bound volumes of *Huracan,* a Caribbean literary journal that was now out of print. A smell of wormwood and age rose from them. In the 1940s, *Huracan* had published a series of issues on folktales. Jacky hoped that these would provide her with more research material.

"Thanks, Carmen." She picked up the volumes and looked around for somewhere to sit. There was an empty private carrel, but there was also a free space at one of the large study tables. Terry was sitting there, head bent over a fat textbook. The navy blue of his shirt suited his skin, made it glow like a newly unwrapped chocolate. Jacky smiled. She went over to the desk, tapped Terry on the shoulder. "I could sit beside you, Terry?"

Startled, he looked up to see who had interrupted him. His handsome face brightened with welcome. "Uh, sure, no problem. Let me get . . ." He leapt to pull out the chair for her, overturning his own in the process. At the crash, everyone in the library looked up. "Shit." He bent over to pick up the chair. His glasses fell from his face. Pens and pencils rained from his shirt pocket.

Jacky giggled. She put her books down, retrieved Terry's glasses just before he would have stepped on them. "Here." She put the spectacles onto his face, let the warmth of her fingertips linger briefly at his temples.

Terry stepped back, sat quickly in the chair, even though it was still at an odd angle from the table. He crossed one leg over the other. "Sorry," he muttered bashfully. He bent over, reaching awkwardly for the scattered pens and pencils.

"Don't fret, Terry. You just collect yourself and come and sit back down next to me." Jacky glowed with the feeling of triumph. Half an hour of studying beside him, and she knew she'd have a date for lunch. She sat, opened a copy of *Huracan*, and read:

SOUCOUYANT/OL' HIGUE
(Trinidad/Guyana)

Caribbean equivalent of the vampire myth. See also "Azeman." "Soucouyant," or "blood-sucker," derives from the French verb "sucer," to suck. "Ol'

Higue" is the Guyanese creole expression for an old hag, or witch woman. The soucouyant is usually an old, evil-tempered woman who removes her skin at night, hides it, and then changes into a ball of fire. She flies through the air, searching for homes in which there are babies. She then enters the house through an open window or a keyhole, goes into the child's room, and sucks the life from its body. She may visit one child's bedside a number of times, draining a little more life each time, as the frantic parents search for a cure, and the child gets progressively weaker and finally dies. Or she may kill all at once.

The smell of the soup Granny was cooking made Jacky's mouth water. She sat at Granny's wobbly old kitchen table, tracing her fingers along a familiar burn, the one shaped like a handprint. The wooden table had been Granny's as long as Jacky could remember. Grandpa had made the table for Granny long before Jacky was born. Diabetes had finally been the death of him. Granny had brought only the kitchen table and her clothing with her when she moved in with Jacky and her mother.

Granny looked up from the cornmeal and flour dough she was kneading. "Like you idle, doux-doux," she said. She slid the bowl of dough over to Jacky. "Make the dumplings then, nuh?"

Jacky took the bowl over to the stove, started pulling off pieces of dough and forming it into little cakes.

"Andrew make this table for me with he own two hand," Granny said.

"I know. You tell me already."

Granny ignored her. "Forty-two years we married, and every Sunday, I chop up the cabbage for the salt-fish on this same table. Forty-two years we eat Sunday morning breakfast right here so. Saltfish and cabbage with a little small-leaf thyme from the back garden, and fry dumpling and cocoa-tea. I miss he too bad. You grandaddy did full up me life, make me feel young."

Jacky kept forming the dumplings for the soup. Granny came over to the stove and stirred the large pot with her wooden spoon. She blew on the spoon, cautiously tasted some of the liquid in it, and carefully floated a whole, ripe Scotch Bonnet pepper on top of the bubbling mixture. "Jacky, when you put the dumpling-them in, don't break the pepper, all right? Otherwise this soup going to make we bawl tonight for pepper."

"Mm. Ain't Mummy used to help you make soup like this on a Saturday?"

"Yes, doux-doux. Just like this." Granny hobbled back to sit at the kitchen table. Tiny, graying braids were escaping the confinement of her stiff black wig. Her knobby legs looked frail in their too-beige stockings. Like so many of the old women that Jacky knew, Granny always wore stockings rolled down below the hems of her worn flower print shifts. "I thought you was going out tonight," Granny said. "With Terry."

"We break up," Jacky replied bitterly. "He say he not ready to settle down." She dipped the spoon into the soup, raised it to her mouth, spat it out when it burned her mouth. "Backside!"

Granny watched, frowning. "Greedy puppy does choke. You mother did always taste straight from the hot stove, too. I was forever telling she to take time. You come in just like she, always in a hurry. Your eyes bigger than your stomach."

Jacky sucked in an irritable breath. "Granny, Carmen have a baby boy last night. Eight pounds, four ounces. Carmen make she first baby already. I past thirty years old, and I ain't find nobody yet."

"You will find, Jacky. But you can't hurry people so. Is how long you and Terry did stepping out?"

Jacky didn't respond.

"Eh, Jacky? How long?"

"Almost a month."

"Is scarcely two weeks, Jacky, don't lie to me. The boy barely learn where to find your house, and you was pestering he to settle down already. Me and your grandfather court for two years before we went to Parson to marry we."

When Granny started like this, she could go on for hours. Sullenly, Jacky began to drop the raw dumplings one by one into the fragrant, boiling soup.

"Child, you pretty, you have flirty ways, boys always coming and looking for you. You could pick and choose until you find the right one. Love will come. But take time. Love your studies, look out for your friends-them. Love your old Granny," she ended softly.

Hot tears rolled down Jacky's cheeks. She watched the dumplings bobbing back to the surface as they cooked; little warm, yellow suns.

"A new baby," Granny mused. "I must go and visit Carmen, take she some crab and callaloo to strengthen she blood. Hospital food does make you weak, oui."

I need more time, more life. I need a baby breath. Must wait till people sleeping, though. Nobody awake to see a fire-ball flying up from the bedroom window.

The skin only confining me. I could feel it getting old, binding me up inside it. Sometimes I does just feel to take it off and never put it back on again, oui?

Three A.M. 'Fore day morning. Only me and the duppies going to be out this late. Up from out of the narrow bed, slip off the nightie, slip off the skin.

Oh, God, I does be so free like this! Hide the skin under the bed, and fly out the jalousie window. The night air cool, and I flying so high. I know how many people it have in each house, and who sleeping. I could feel them, skin-bag people, breathing out their life, one-one breath. I know where it have a new one, too: down on Vanderpool Lane. Yes, over here. Feel it, the new one, the baby. So much life in that little body.

Fly down low now, right against the ground. Every door have a crack, no matter how small.

Right here. Slip into the house. Turn back into a woman. Is a nasty feeling, walking around with no skin, wet flesh dripping onto the floor, but I get used to it after so many years.

Here. The baby bedroom. Hear the young breath heating up in he lungs, blowing out, wasting away. He ain't know how to use it; I go take it.

Nice baby boy, so fat. Drink, soucouyant. Suck in he warm, warm life. God, it sweet. It sweet can't done. It sweet.

No more? I drink all already? But what a way this baby dead fast!

Childbirth was once a risky thing for both mother and child. Even when they both survived the birth process, there were many unknown infectious diseases to which newborns were susceptible. Oliphant theorizes that the soucouyant lore was created in an attempt to explain infant deaths that would have seemed mysterious in more primitive times. Grieving parents could blame their loss on people who wished them ill. Women tend to have longer life spans than men, but in an even more superstitious age where life was hard and brief, old women in a community could seem sinister. It must have been easy to believe that the women were using sorcerous means to prolong their lives, and how better to do that than to steal the lifeblood of those who were very young?

Dozing, Jacky leaned against Granny's knees. Outside, the leaves of the julie mango tree rustled and sighed in the evening breeze. Granny tapped on Jacky's shoulder, passed her a folded section of newspaper with a column circled. *Births/Deaths*. Granny took a bitter pleasure in keeping track of whom she'd outlived each week. Sleepily, Jacky focused on the words on the page:

Deceased: Raymond George Lewis, 5 days old, of natural causes. Son of Michael and Carmen, Diego Martin, Port of Spain. Funeral service 5:00 p.m., November 14, Church of the Holy Redeemer.

"Jesus, Granny. Carmen's baby! But he was healthy, don't it?"

"I don't know, doux-doux. They say he just stop

breathing in the night. Just so. What a sad thing. We must go to the funeral, pay we respects."

Sunlight is fatal to the soucouyant. She must be back in her skin before daylight. In fact, the tales say that the best way to discover a soucouyant is to find her skin, rub the raw side with hot pepper, and replace it in its hiding place. When she tries to put it back on, the pain of the burning pepper will cause the demon to cry out and reveal herself.

Me fire belly full, oui. When a new breath fueling the fire, I does feel good, like I could never die. And then I does fly and fly, high like the moon. Time to go back home now, though.

Eh-eh! Why she leave the back door cotch open? Never mind; she does be preoccupied sometimes. Maybe she just forget to close the door. Just fly in the bedroom window. I go close the door after I put on my skin again.

Ai! What itching me so? Is what happen to me skin? Ai! Lord, Lord, it burning, it burning too bad. It scratching me all over, like it have fire ants inside there. I can't stand it!

Hissing with pain, the soucouyant threw off her burning skin and stood flayed, dripping.

Calmly, Granny entered Jacky's room. Before Jacky could react Granny picked up the Jacky-skin. She held it close to her body, threatening the skin with the sharp, wicked kitchen knife she held in her other hand. Her look was sorrowful.

"I know it was you, doux-doux. When I see the Lagahoo, I know what I have to do."

Jacky cursed and flared to fireball form. She rushed at Granny, but backed off as Granny made a feint at the skin with her knife.

"You stay right there and listen to me, Jacky. The soucouyant blood in all of we, all the women in we family."

You, too?

"Even me. We blood hot: hot for life, hot for youth. Loving does cool we down. Making life does cool we down."

Jacky raged. The ceiling blackened, began to smoke.

"I know how it go, doux-doux. When we lives empty, the hunger does turn to blood hunger. But it have plenty other kinds of loving, Jacky. Ain't I been telling you so? Love your work. Love people close to you. Love your life."

The fireball surged towards Granny. "No. Stay right there, you hear? Or I go chop this skin for you."

Granny backed out through the living room. The hissing ball of fire followed close, drawn by the precious skin in the old woman's hands.

"You never had no patience. Doux-doux, you is my life, but you can't kill so. That little child you drink, you don't hear it spirit when night come, bawling for Carmen and Michael? I does weep to hear it. I try to tell you, like I try to tell you mother: Don't be greedy."

Granny had reached the back door. The open back door. The soucouyant made a desperate feint at Granny's knife arm, searing her right side from elbow to scalp. The smell of burnt flesh and hair filled the little kitchen, but though the old lady cried out, she wouldn't drop the knife. The pain in her voice was more than physical.

"You devil!" She backed out the door into the cobalt

light of early morning. Gritting her teeth, she slashed the Jacky-skin into two ragged halves and flung it into the pigeon peas patch. Jacky shrieked and turned back into her flayed self. Numbly, she picked up her skin, tried with oozing fingers to put the torn edges back together.

"You and me is the last two," Granny said. "Your mami woulda make three, but I had to kill she too, send my own flesh and blood into the sun. Is time, doux-doux. The Lagahoo calling you."

My skin! Granny, how you could do me so? Oh God, morning coming already? Yes, I could feel it, the sun calling to the fire in me.

Jacky threw the skin down again, leapt as a fireball into the brightening air. *I going, I going, where I could burn clean, burn bright, and allyou could go to the Devil, oui!*

Fireball flying high to the sun, and oh God, it burning, it burning, it burning!

Granny hobbled to the pigeon peas patch, wincing as she cradled her burnt right side. Tears trickled down her wrinkled face. She sobbed, "Why allyou must break my heart so?"

Painfully, she got down to her knees beside the ruined pieces of skin and placed one hand on them. She made her hand glow red hot, igniting her grand-daughter's skin. It began to burn, crinkling and curling back on itself like bacon in a pan. Granny wrinkled her nose against the smell, but kept her hand on the smoking mass until there was nothing but ashes. Her hand faded back to its normal cocoa brown. Clambering to her feet again, she looked about her in the pigeon peas patch.

"I live to see the Lagahoo two time. Next time, God horse, you better be coming for me."

These are the latitudes of ex-colonised,
of degradation still unmollified,
imported managers, styles in art,
second-hand subsistence of the spirit,
the habit of waste,
mayhem committed on the personality,
and everywhere the wrecked or scuttled mind.
Scholars, more brilliant than I could hope to be,
advised that if I valued poetry,
I should eschew all sociology.

Slade Hopkinson, from
"The Madwoman of Papine: Two Cartoons with Captions"

A HABIT OF WASTE

I was nodding off on the streetcar home from work when I saw the woman getting on. She was wearing the body I used to have! The shock woke me right up: It was my original, the body I had replaced two years before, same full, tarty-looking lips; same fat thighs, rubbing together with every step; same outsize ass; same narrow torso that seemed grafted onto a lower body a good three sizes bigger, as though God had glued left-over parts together.

On my pay, I'd had to save for five years before I could afford the switch. When I ordered the catalogue from MediPerfiction, I pored over it for a month, drooling at the different options: Arrow-slim "Cindies" had long, long legs (*"supermodel quality"*). "Indiras" came with creamy brown skin, falls of straight, dark hair, and curvaceous bodies (*"exotic grace"*). I finally chose one of the "Dianas," with their lithe muscles and small, firm breasts (*"boyish beauty"*). They downloaded me into her as soon as I could get the time off work. I was back on the job in four days, although my fine muscle control was still a little shaky.

And now, here was someone wearing my old castoff. She must have been in a bad accident: too bad for the body to be salvaged. If she couldn't afford cloning, the doctors would have just downloaded her brain into any donated discard. Mine, for instance. Poor thing, I thought. I wonder how she's handling that chafing problem. It used to drive me mad in the summer.

I watched her put her ticket in the box. The driver gave her a melting smile. What did he see to grin at?

I studied my former body carefully as it made its way down the centre of the streetcar. I hated what she'd done to the hair—let it go natural, for Christ's sake, sectioned it off, and coiled black thread tightly around each section, with a puff of hair on the end of every stalk. Man, I hated that back-to-Africa nostalgia shit. She looked like a Doctor Seuss character. There's no excuse for that nappy-headed nonsense. She had a lot of nerve, too, wrapping that behind in a flower-print sarong miniskirt. Sort of like making your ass into a billboard. When it was my body, I always covered its butt in long skirts or loose pants. Her skirt was so short that I could see the edges of the bike shorts peeking out below it. Well, it's one way to deal with the chafing.

Strange, though; on her, the little peek of black shorts looked stylish and sexy all at once. Far from looking graceless, her high, round bottom twitched confidently with each step, giving her a proud sexiness that I had never had. Her upper body was sheathed in a white sleeveless T-shirt. White! Such a plain colour. To tell the truth, though, the clingy material emphasized her tiny waist, and the white looked really good against her dark skin. Had my old skin always had that glow to it? Such firm, strong arms . . .

All the seats on the streetcar were taken. Good. Let the bitch stand. I hoped my fallen arches were giving her hell.

Home at last, I stripped off and headed straight for the mirror. The boyish body was still slim, thighs still thin, tiny-perfect apple breasts still perky. I presented my behind to the mirror. A little flabby, perhaps? I wasn't sure. I turned around again, got up close to the mirror so that I could inspect my face. Did my skin have that glow that my old body's had? And weren't those the beginning of crow's-feet around my eyes? Shit. White people aged so quickly. I spent the evening sprawled on the sofa, watching reruns and eating pork and beans straight from the can.

That Friday afternoon at work, Old Man Morris came in for the usual. I stacked his order on the counter between us and keyed the contents into the computer. It bleeped at me: "This selection does not meet the customer's dietary requirements." As if I didn't know that. I tried to talk him into beefing up the carbs and beta-carotene. "All right, then," I said heartily, "what else will you have today? Some of that creamed corn? We just got a big batch of tins in. I bet you'd like some of that, eh?" I always sounded so artificial, but I couldn't help it. The food bank customers made me uncomfortable. Eleanor didn't react that way, though. She was so at ease in the job, cheerful, dispensing cans of tuna with an easy goodwill. She always chattered away to the clients, knew them all by name.

"No thanks, dear," Mr. Morris replied with his polite smile. "I never could stomach the tinned vegetables. When I can, I eat them fresh, you know?"

"Yeah, Cynthia," Eleanor teased, "you know that Mr. Morris hates canned veggies. Too much like baby food, eh, Mr. Morris?"

Always the same cute banter between those two. He'd flattened out his Caribbean accent for the benefit of us two white girls. I couldn't place which island he was from. I sighed and overrode the computer's objections. Eleanor and old man Morris grinned at each other while I packed up his weekend ration. Fresh, right. When could a poor old man ever afford the fresh stuff? I couldn't imagine what his diet was like. He always asked us for the same things: soup mix, powdered milk, and cans of beans. We tried to give him his nutritional quota, but he politely refused offers of creamed corn or canned tuna. I was sure he was always constipated. His problem, though.

I bet my parents could tell me where in the Caribbean he was from. Give them any inkling that someone's from "back home," and they'd be on him like a dirty shirt, badgering him with questions: *Which island you from? How long you been here in Canada? You have family here? When last you go back home?*

Old Man Morris signed for his order and left. One of the volunteers would deliver it later that evening. I watched him walk away. He looked to be in his sixties, but he was probably younger; hard life wears a person down. Tallish, with a brown, wrinkled face and tightly curled salt-and-pepper hair, he had a strong, upright walk for someone in his circumstances. Even in summer, I had never seen him without that old tweed jacket, its pockets stuffed to bursting with God knew what type of scavenge; half-smoked cigarette butts that people had dropped on the street, I supposed, and pop cans he would return for the deposit money. At least he seemed clean.

I went down to shipping to check on a big donation of food we'd received from a nearby supermarket. Someone was sure to have made a mistake sorting the cans. Someone always did.

My parents had been beside themselves when they found out I'd switched bodies. I guess it wasn't very diplomatic of me, showing up without warning on their suburban doorstep, this white woman with her flippy blond hair, claiming to be their daughter. I'd made sure my new body would have the same vocal range as the old one, so when Mom and Dad heard my voice coming out of a stranger's body, they flipped. Didn't even want to let me in the door, at first. Made me pass my new I.D. and the doctor's certificate through the letter slot.

"Mom, give me a break," I yelled. "I told you last year that I was thinking about doing this!"

"But Cyn-Cyn, that ain't even look like you!" My

mother's voice was close to a shriek. Her next words were for my dad:

"What the child want to go and do this kind of stupidness for? Nothing ain't wrong with the way she look!"

A giggled response from my father, "True, she behind had a way to remain in a room long after she leave, but she get that from you, sweetheart, and you know how much I love that behind!"

He'd aimed that dig for my ears, I just knew it. I'd had enough. "So, are the two of you going to let me in, or what?" I hated it when they carried on the way they were doing. All that drama. And I really wished they'd drop the Banana Boat accents. They'd come to Canada five years before I was even *born*, for Christ's sake, and I was now twenty-eight.

They did finally open the door, and after that they just had to get used to the new me.

I wondered if I should start saving for another switch. It's really a rich people's thing. I couldn't afford to keep doing it every few years, like some kind of vid queen. Shit.

"What's griping you?" Eleanor asked after I'd chewed out one of the volunteers for some little mistake. "You've been cranky for days now."

Damn. "Sorry. I know I've been bitchy. I've been really down, you know? No real reason. I just don't feel like myself."

"Yeah. Well." Eleanor was used to my moodiness. "I guess it *is* Thanksgiving weekend. People always get a little edgy around the holidays. Maybe you need a change. Tell you what; why don't you deliver Old Man Morris's ration, make sure he's okay for the weekend?"

"Morris? You want me to go to where he *lives?*" I couldn't imagine anything less appealing. "Where is that, anyway? In a park or something?"

Eleanor frowned at that. "So, even if he does, so what? You need to get over yourself, girl."

I didn't say anything, just thought my peevishness at her. She strode over to the terminal at her desk, punched in Mr. Morris's name, handed me the printout. "Just go over to this address, and take him his ration. Chat with him a little bit. This might be a lonely weekend for him. And keep the car till Tuesday. We won't be needing it."

Mr. Morris lived on the creepy side of Sherbourne. I had to slow the car down to dodge the first wave of drunken suits lurching out of the strip club, on their boozy way home after the usual Friday afternoon three-hour liquid lunch. I stared at the storey-high poster that covered one outside wall of the strip club. I hoped to God they'd used a fisheye lens to make that babe's boobs look like that. Those couldn't be natural.

Shit. Shouldn't have slowed down. One of the prostitutes on the corner began to twitch her way over to the car, bending low so she could see inside, giving me a flash of her tits into the bargain: "Hey, darlin', you wanna go out? I can swing lezzie." I floored it out of there.

Searching for the street helped to keep my mind off some of the more theatrical sights of Cabbagetown West on a Friday evening. I didn't know that the police *could* conduct a full strip search over the hood of a car, right out in the open.

The next street was Old Man Morris's. Tenement row houses slumped along one side of the short street, marked by sagging roofs and knocked-out steps. There were rotting piles of garbage in front of many of the houses. I thought I could hear the flies buzzing from where I was. The smell was like clotted carrion. A few people hung out on dilapidated porches, just staring. Two guys hunched into denim jackets stopped talking as I drove by. A dirty, greasy-haired kid was riding a bicycle up and down the sidewalk, dodging the garbage. The bike was too small for him and it had no seat. He stood on the pedals and pumped them furiously.

Mr. Morris lived in an ancient apartment building on the other side of the street. I had to double-park in front. I hauled the dolly out of the trunk and loaded Mr. Morris's boxes onto it. I activated the car's screamer alarm and headed into the building, praying that no weirdness would go down on the street before I could make it inside.

Thank God, he answered the buzzer right away. "Mr. Morris? It's Cynthia; from the food bank?"

The party going on in the lobby was only a few gropes away from becoming an orgy. The threesome writhing and sighing on the couch ignored me. Two men, one woman. I stepped over a pungent yellow liquid that was beetling its way down one leg of the bench, creeping through the cracks in the tile floor. I hoped it was just booze. I took the elevator up to the sixth floor.

The dingy, musty corridor walls were dark grey, peeling in places to reveal a bilious pink underneath. It was probably a blessing that there was so much dirt ground into the balding carpet. What I could glimpse of the original design made me queasy. Someone was frying Spam for dinner ("canned horse's cock," my dad called it). I found Mr. Morris's door and knocked. Inside, I could hear the sound of locks turning, and the curt "quack" of an alarm being deactivated. Mr. Morris opened the door to let me in.

"Come in quick, child," he said, wiping his hands on a kitchen towel. "I can't let the pot boil over. Don't Jake does deliver my goods?" He bustled back into a room I guessed was the kitchen. I wheeled the dolly inside. "Eleanor sent Jake home early today, Mr. Morris. Holiday treat."

He chuckled. "That young lady is so thoughtful, oui? It ain't have plenty people like she anymore."

"Hmm."

I took a quick glance around the little apartment. It was dark in there. The only light was from the kitchen, and from four candles stuck in pop bottles on the living room windowsill. The living room held one small, rump-sprung couch, two aluminum chairs, and a tiny card table. The gaudy flower-print cloth that barely covered the table was faded from years of being ironed. I was surprised; the place was spotless, if a little shabby. I perched on the edge of the love seat.

His head poked round the corner. "Yes," he said, "that's right. Siddown on the settee and rest yourself."

Settee. Oui. In his own home, he spoke in a more natural accent. "You from Trinidad, Mr. Morris?"

His face crinkled into an astonished grin. "Yes, doux-doux. How you know that?"

"That's where my parents are from. They talk just like you."

"You is from Trinidad?" he asked delightedly. "Is true Trini people come in all colours, but with that accent, I really take you for a Canadian, born and bred."

I hated explaining this, but I guess I'd asked for it, letting him know something about my life. "I was born here, but my parents are black. And so was I, but I've had a body switch."

A bemused expression came over his face. He stepped into the living room to take a closer look at me. "For true? I hear about people doin' this thing, but I don't think I ever meet anybody who make the switch. You mean to tell me, you change from a black woman body into this one? Lord, the things you young people does do for fashion, eh?"

I stood up and plastered a smile on my face. "Well, you've got your weekend ration, Mr. Morris; just wanted to be sure you wouldn't go hungry on Thanksgiving, okay?"

He looked pensively at the freeze-dried turkey dinner and the cans of creamed corn (I'd made sure to put them in his ration this time). "Thanks, doux-doux. True I ain't go be hungry, but . . ."

"But what, Mr. Morris?"

"Well, I don't like to eat alone. My wife pass away ten years now, but you know, I does still miss she sometimes. You goin' by you mummy and daddy for Thanksgiving?"

The question caught me off guard. "Yes, I'm going to see them on Sunday."

"But you not doing anything tonight?"

"Uh, well, a movie, maybe, something like that."

He gave me a sweet, wheedling smile. "You want to have a early Thanksgiving with a ol' man from back home?"

"I'm not from 'back home,'" I almost said. The hope on his face was more than I could stand. "Well, I . . ."

"I making a nice, nice dinner," he pleaded.

Eleanor would stay and keep the old man company for a few minutes, if it were her. I sat back down.

Mr. Morris's grin was incandescent. "You going to stay? All right, doux-doux. Dinner almost finish, you hear? Just pile up the ration out of the way for me." He bustled back into the kitchen. I could hear humming, pots and pans clattering, water running.

I packed the food up against one wall, a running argument playing in my head the whole time. Why was I doing this? I'd driven our pathetic excuse for a company car through the most dangerous part of town, just begging for a baseball bat through the window, and all to have dinner with an old bum. What would he serve anyway? Peanut butter and crackers? I knew the shit that man ate—I'd given it to him myself, every Friday at the food bank! And what if he pulled some kind of sleazy, toothless come-on? The police would say I asked for it!

A wonderful smell began to waft from the kitchen. Some kind of roasting meat, with spices. Whatever Mr. Morris was cooking, he couldn't have done it on food bank rations.

"You need a hand, Mr. Morris?"

"Not in here, darling. I nearly ready. Just sit yourself down at the table, and I go bring dinner out. I was going to freeze all the extra, but now I have a guest to share it with."

When he brought out the main course, arms straining under the weight of the platter, my mouth fell open. And it was just the beginning. He loaded the table with plate after plate of food: roasted chicken with a giblet stuffing, rich, creamy gravy, tossed salad with exotic greens; huge mounds of mashed potatoes, some kind of fruit preserve. He refused to answer my questions. "I go tell you all about it after, doux-doux. Now is time to eat."

It certainly was. I was so busy trying to figure out if he could have turned food bank rations into this feast, that I forgot all about calories and daily allowable grams of fat; I just ate. After the meal, though, my curiosity kicked in again.

"So, Mr. Morris, tell me the truth; you snowing the food bank? Making some money on the side?" I grinned at him. He wouldn't be the first one to run a scam like that, working for cash so that he could still claim welfare.

"No, doux-doux." He gave me a mischievous smile. "I see how it look that way to you, but this meal cost me next to nothing. You just have to know where to, um, *procure* your food, that is all. You see this fancy salad?" He pointed to a few frilly purple leaves that were all that remained of the salad. "You know what that is?"

"Yeah. Flowering kale. Rich people's cabbage."

Mr. Morris laughed. "Yes, but I bet you see it somewhere else, besides the grocery store."

I frowned, trying to think what he meant. He went on: "You know the Dominion Bank? The big one at Bathurst and Queen?" I nodded, still mystified. His smile got even broader. "You ever look at the plants they use to decorate the front?"

I almost spat the salad out. "Ornamental cabbage? We're eating ornamental cabbage that you *stole* from the front of a building?"

His rich laugh filled the tiny room. "Not 'ornamental cabbage,' darlin': 'flowering kale.' And I figure, I ain't really stealin' it; I recyclin' it! They does pull it all up and throw it away when the weather turn cold. All that food. It does taste nice on a Sunday morning, fry-up with a piece of saltfish and some small-leaf thyme. I does grow the herbs-them on the windowsill, in the sun."

Salted cod and cabbage. Flavoured with French thyme and hot pepper. My mother made that on Sunday mornings too, with big fried flour dumplings on the side and huge mugs of cocoa. Not the cocoa powder from the tin, either; she bought the raw chocolate in chestnut-sized lumps from the Jamaican store, and grated it into boiling water, with vanilla, cinnamon, and condensed milk. Sitting in Mr. Morris's living room, even with the remains of dinner on the table, I could almost smell that pure chocolate aroma. Full of fat, too. I didn't let my mom serve it to me anymore when I visited. I'd spent too much money on my tight little butt.

Still, I didn't believe what Old Man Morris was telling me. "So, you mean to say that you just . . . take stuff? From off the street?"

"Yes."

"What about the chicken?"

He laughed. "Chicken? Doux-doux, you ever see chicken with four drumstick? That is a wild rabbit I catch meself and bring home."

"Are you *crazy*? Do you know what's *in* wild food? What kind of diseases it might carry? Why didn't you tell me what we were eating?" But he was so pleased with himself, he didn't seem to notice how upset I was.

"Nah, nah, don't worry 'bout diseases, darlin'! I been eatin' like this for five-six years now, and I healthy like hog. De doctor say he never see a seventy-four-year-old man in such good shape."

He's seventy-four! He does look pretty damned good for such an old man. I'm still not convinced, though:

"Mr. Morris, this is nuts; you can't just go around helping yourself to leaves off the trees, and people's ornamental plants, and killing things and eating them! Besides, um, how do you catch a wild rabbit, anyway?"

"Well, that is the sweet part." He jumped up from his chair, started rummaging around in the pockets of his old tweed jacket that was hanging in the hallway. He came back to the table, clutching a fistful of small rocks and brandishing a thick, Y-shaped twig with a loose rubber strap attached. So that's what he kept in those pockets—whatever it was.

"This is a slingshot. When I was a small boy back home, I was aces with one of these!" He stretched the rubber strap tight with one hand, aimed the slingshot at one of his potted plants, and pretended to let off a shot. "*Plai!* Like so. Me and the boys-them used to practise shooting at all kind of ol' tin can and thing, but I was the best. One time, I catch a coral snake in me mother kitchen, and I send one boulderstone straight through it eye with me first shot!" He chuckled. "The stone break the window, too, but me mother was only too glad that I kill the poison snake. Well, doux-doux, I does take me slingshot down into the ravine, and sometimes I get lucky and catch something."

I was horrified. "You mean, you used that thing to kill a rabbit? And we just ate it?"

Mr. Morris's face finally got serious. He sat back down at the table. "You mus' understan', Cynthia; I is a poor man. Me and my Rita, we work hard when we come to this country, and we manage to buy this little apartment, but when the last depression hit we, I get lay off at the car plant. After that, I couldn't find no work again; I was already past fifty years old, nobody would hire me. We get by on Rita nurse work until she retire,

and then hard times catch we ass. My Rita was a wonderful woman, girl; she could take a half pound of
mince beef and two potatoes and make a meal that
have you feelin' like you never taste food before. She
used to tell me, 'Never mind, Johnny; so long as I have
a little meat to put in this cook pot, we not goin' to
starve.'

"Then them find out that Rita have cancer. She only
live a few months after that, getting weaker till she
waste away and gone. Lord, child, I thought my heart
woulda break. I did wish to dead too. That first year
after Rita pass away, I couldn't tell you how I get by; I
don't even remember all of it. I let the place get dirty,
dirty, and I was eatin' any ol' kaka from the corner store,
not even self goin' to the grocery. When I get the letter
from the government, telling me that them cuttin' off
Rita pension, I didn't know what to do. My one little
pension wasn't goin' to support me. I put on me coat,
and went outside, headin' for the train tracks to throw
myself down, oui? Is must be God did make me walk
through the park."

"What happened?"

"I see a ol' woman sittin' on a bench, wearing a tear-
up coat and two different one-side boots. She was
feedin' stale bread to the pigeons, and smiling at them.
That ol' lady with she rip-up clothes could still find
something to make she happy.

"I went back home, and things start to look up a
little bit from then. But pride nearly make me starve
before I find meself inside the food bank to beg some
bread."

"It's not begging, Mr. Morris," I interrupted.

"I know, doux-doux, but in my place, I sure you
woulda feel the same way. And too besides, even

though I was eatin' steady from the food bank, I wasn't eatin' good, you know? You can't live all you days on tuna fish and tin peas!"

I thought of all the tins of tuna I'd just brought him. I felt myself blushing. Two years in this body, and I still wasn't used to how easily blushes showed on its pale cheeks. "So, what gave you the idea to start foraging like this?"

"I was eatin' lunch one day, cheese spread and crackers and pop. One paipsy, tasteless lunch, you see? And I start thinkin' about how I never woulda go hungry back home as a small boy, how even if I wasn't home to eat me mother food, it always had some kinda fruit tree or something round the place. I start to remember Julie mango, how it sweet, and chataigne and peewah that me mother would boil up in a big pot a' salt water, and how my father always had he little kitchen garden, growin' dasheen leaf and pigeon peas and yam and thing. And I say to meself, 'But eh-eh, Johnny, ain't this country have plants and trees and fruit and thing too? The squirrels-them always looking fat and happy; they mus' be eatin' something. And the Indian people-them-self too; they must be did eat something else besides corn before the white people come and take over the place!'

"That same day, I find my ass in the library, and I tell them I want to find out about plants that you could eat. Them sit me down with all kinda book and computer, and I come to find out it have plenty to eat, right here in this city, growing wild by the roadside. Some of these books even had recipes in them, doux-doux!

"So I drag out all of Rita frying pan and cook spoon from the kitchen cupboard, and I teach meself to feed meself, yes!" He chuckled again. "Now I does eat fresh mulberries in the summer. I does dig up chicory root to take the bitterness from my coffee. I even make rowan-berry jam. All these things all around we for free, and people still starving, oui? You have to learn to make use of what you have.

"But I still think the slingshot was a master stroke, though. Nobody ain't expect a ol' black man to be hunting with a slingshot down in the ravine!"

I was still chuckling as I left Mr. Morris's building later that evening. He'd loaded me down with a container full of stuffed rabbit and a bottle of crabapple preserves. I deactivated the screamer alarm on the car, and I was just about to open the door when I felt a hand sliding down the back of my thigh.

"Yesss, stay just like that. Ain't that pretty? We'll get to that later. Where's your money, sweetheart? In this purse here?" The press of a smelly body pinned me over the hood. I tried to turn my head, to scream, but he clamped a filthy hand across my face. I couldn't breathe. The bottle of preserves crashed to the ground. Broken glass sprayed my calf.

"Shit! What'd you do that for? Stupid bitch!"

His hand tightened over my face. I couldn't *breathe!* In fury and terror, I bit down hard, felt my teeth meet in the flesh of his palm. He swore, yanked his hand away, slammed a hard fist against my ear. Things started to go black, and I almost fell. I hung on to the car door, dragged myself to my feet, scrambled out of his reach. I didn't dare turn away to run. I backed away, screaming, "Get away from me! Get away!" He kept coming, and he was big and muscular, and angry. Suddenly, he jerked, yelled, slapped one hand to his shoulder. "What the fuck . . . ?" I could see wetness seeping through the shoulder of his grimy sweatshirt. Blood? He yelled again, clapped a hand to his knee. This time, I had seen the missile whiz through the air to strike him. Yes! I crouched down to give Mr. Morris a clear shot. My teeth were bared in a fighter's grin. The mugger was still limping towards me, howling with rage. The next stone glanced by his head, leaving a deep gash on his temple. Behind him, I heard the sound of breaking glass as the stone crashed through the car window. He'd had enough. He ran, holding his injured leg.

Standing in the middle of the street, I looked up to Mr. Morris's sixth-floor window. He was on the balcony, waving frantically at me. In the dark, I could just see the Y of the slingshot in his hand. He shouted, "Go and stand in the entranceway, girl! I comin' down!" He disappeared inside, and I headed back towards the building. By the time I got there, I was weak-kneed and shaky; reaction was setting in, and my head was spinning from the blow I'd taken. I didn't think I'd ever get the taste of that man's flesh out of my mouth. I leaned against the inside door, waiting for Mr. Morris. It wasn't long before he came bustling out of the elevator, let me inside, and sat me down on the couch in the lobby, fussing the whole time.

"Jesus Christ, child! Is a good thing I decide to watch from the balcony to make sure you reach the car safe! Lawd, look at what happen to you, eh? Just because you had the kindness to spen' a little time with a ol' man like me! I sorry, girl; I sorry can't done!"

"It's okay, Mr. Morris; it's not your fault. I'm all right. I'm just glad that you were watching." I was getting a little hysterical. "I come to rescue you with my food bank freeze-dried turkey dinner, and you end up rescuing me instead! I have to ask you, though, Mr. Morris; how come every time you rescue a lady, you end up breaking her windows?"

That Sunday, I drove over to my parents' place for Thanksgiving dinner. I was wearing a beret, cocked at a chic angle over the cauliflower ear that the mugger had given me. No sense panicking my mom and dad. I had gone to the emergency hospital on Friday night, and they'd disinfected and bandaged me. I was all right; in fact, I was so happy that two days later, I still felt giddy. So nice to know that there wouldn't be photos of my dead body on the covers of the tabloids that week.

As I pulled up in the car, I could see my parents through the living room window, sitting and watching television. I went inside.

"Mom! Dad! Happy Thanksgiving!" I gave my mother a kiss, smiled at my dad.

"Cynthia, child," he said, "I glad you reach; I could start making the gravy now."

"Marvin, don't be so stupidee," my mother scolded. "You know she won't eat no gravy; she mindin' she figure!"

"It's okay, Mom; it's Thanksgiving, and I'm going to eat everything you put on my plate. If I get too fat, I'm just going to have to start walking to work. You've got to work with what you've got, after all." She looked surprised, but didn't say anything.

I poked around in the kitchen, like I always did. Dad stood at the stove, stirring the gravy. There was another saucepan on the stove, with the remains of that morning's cocoa in it. It smelt wonderful. I reached around my father to turn on the burner under the cocoa. He frowned at me.

"Is cocoa-tea, Cyn-Cyn. You don't drink that no more."

"I just want to finish what's left in the pot, Dad. I mean, you don't want it to go to waste, do you?"

*I*n 1971, the late Jamaican spiritual leader Imogene Elizabeth
Kennedy ("Miss Queenie") gave an interview. The words that
Sammie hears are taken from Miss Queenie's description of how she
came into her power. The sections in Miss Queenie's words are
reprinted with the kind permission of Savacou magazine.

AND THE LILLIES-THEM A-BLOW

Lilies. Nasty, dead people flowers.

Samantha held up the vase that she had found outside her apartment door that morning. Seven long-
stemmed white lilies wafted their funereal scent over
her. A single twig from a cotton plant, budding with
little white puffs, set off the arrangement. Who the rass
would send a cotton plant to a black woman? Like them
never hear of ancestral memory?

The vase was beautiful. Clear, round as a gourd, with
smooth ridges fluted up its sides, the solid weight of the
glass spread a pleasant warmth through her hands.
Someone had filled it with warm water to encourage
the scented blooms to open wide. Not to her liking, but
someone had taste.

There was a plain florist's shop card hanging from
one stem. It read, *One day, I remember one day I find
some lillies, and I plant the lillies-them in row, and one*

morning when I wake, all the lillies blow. Seven lillies, and the seven of them blow. Samantha felt the skin at the back of her neck prickle, like duppy walking on her grave. She stepped quickly back inside her apartment, locking the door and sliding the chain home. She took the vase into the small living room, shoved a bag of groceries aside to put the vase on the coffee table. She should unpack the bag soon—hadn't she bought strawberries or something last night?

The lilies nodded in the direction of her mother's intricately patched quilt, hanging kate-a-corner on the far wall. She really should straighten it, brush off the film of dust that clung to its top edge.

Not that that would help the rest of the apartment much. A bra was draped on the bookshelf, one strap hooked over a hand-rolled beeswax candle in a cast-iron holder. Like a dingy cotton ball, a dust bunny circled in an unseen draft in the corner of her living room by the door. Last night's dirty dinner plate sat on top the TV, a half-eaten carrot stick glued to its surface by a wet smear of congealing butter. Tucked under the plate, three glum sheets of scribbled notes gave Samantha a surge of guilt and panic. "A Chronological History of Provincial Government Support of Neighbourhood Centres in Ontario's North" was little more than a title at this point. And it was due today.

She went into the bathroom to commence the daily business of transforming herself into a semblance of a young career woman. She dressed and left for work, leaving the flowers pumping out their faint, sweet scent.

"Hey, Sam." Grant's cheerful face peered around the wobbly grey room divider that separated his desk from Samantha's. He must have nicked himself shaving again. A pinch of bloody cotton clung to his chin. "How was your weekend?"

"Could've been worse. Can't talk long, though. I've got a five P.M. deadline on this damned report. Why the hell does Barnes care if Asswipe County Community Centre got a $2,500 government grant in 1968 to repair their roof, huh?"

Grant chuckled. "Well, you know. What Barnes wants, she gets. Well, I better leave you to the joys of capital spending in our neighbourhood centres." He ducked out of sight, and Samantha returned to pounding at her computer keyboard, peering irritably at the screen. Nasty-smelling cologne Grant was wearing today, like rotting flowers.

Samantha slipped the finished report under Barnes's door at 4:48, but she still had to strike that administration budget and prepare the overheads for tomorrow's staff meeting on electronic access. Everybody else would leave at 5:00, but she'd be working late again. She went back to her cubicle, sat down, hit a button on her keyboard to wake her terminal up. On the screen she read, *seven lillies I plant and the seven of them blow. And I leave and go down in the gully bottom to go and pick some quoquonut. And when I go, I see a cottn tree and I just fell right down at the cottn tree root.*

This was too fucking bizarre. She was the only West Indian in the office. She'd only been away from her desk a second. Who could have typed those words and what the hell did they mean, anyway? She deleted the document, switched her computer off, stood up, and grabbed her purse out of her desk drawer. Screw this. She was going home early tonight.

The city air managed to smell almost fresh in the blustery spring evening. Samantha decided to walk home, a nice half-hour stroll. She couldn't avoid the tourist trap of the busy Yonge Street strip, though. It was a Monday evening, but Yonge Street never closed, was just as noisy as it would be on the weekend.

Three storeys tall and painted bright blue, a record store brayed out the latest dance hits. A video arcade squatted beside the store, a cacophony of flashing lights and bells. In its dark interior, wild-eyed young men and women pounded the levers on the video machines, feverishly jerking their bodies against the consoles with each hit, doing battle with monsters. The photos plastering the façades of the strip clubs displayed impossibly thin, impossibly busty women. A Thai restaurant faced a Columbian coffee shop, which was flanked by a franchise burger place, which overpowered a minuscule West Indian roti shop, which, despite the competition, was jammed full of customers.

People on the streets moved very slowly, walking three or four abreast, gawking, dawdling. At the corner of Yonge and Gerrard paced a young, gangly white man with stringy brown hair and wild blue eyes. The hem of his white robe had a rime of mud and salt. A smattering of people were watching him, waiting to see what he would do. He put a megaphone to his mouth and continued his harangue:

" . . . and when the Lord comes, brothers and sisters, and he asks what were your deeds on this Earth, what words will you speak? Will you be able to tell our Lord, *in the night, in the cottn tree come in like it hollow, and I inside there. And you have some grave arounn that cottn tree, right rounn it; some tombs. But those is some h'old-time h'African, you understand?* Have you accepted the

Lord as your Saviour in your hearts, brothers and sisters?"

Samantha felt her entrails curl tighter into her gut, her scalp prickle with gooseflesh. She couldn't have heard correctly. Looking back once over her shoulder at the Holy Roller, she hurried into the World's Biggest Bookstore, headed for the first quiet section. She paced up and down the rows, stopping here and there when a book caught her eye, paging through it half-heartedly before returning it to the shelf.

Maybe he had been Jamaican, that man?

The book drew her gaze by its sheer size. Too tall for the shelf, it had been put in at an angle. She eased the large, heavy volume down. It turned out to be a massive essay in photography of the various styles of adornment across the African continent.

Samantha eased the book open and ran her hand slowly down a full-page colour photograph of a young Berber woman in desert dress: a blue, billowing robe, lacy black designs painted on her bare feet and open palms, five or six stylized silver crosses around her neck, orange-sized balls of amber pinned into her hair. With her forefinger, Samantha traced the geometric outlines of the handbeaten crosses, each one different. She turned to the back cover. It cost more than she made in a day's work. She made to return the book to its shelf. Took it down again. Walked over to the cash register. "On my credit card, please."

She let herself into her apartment, kicked her boots off at the door, and went straight into the living room to throw herself onto the love seat. If anything, the flower arrangement on the coffee table looked more fresh than it had this morning. She could now see that the vase was not perfectly round, and that it was seamless, encysted here and there with tiny air bubbles. The vase was mouthblown glass. The flowers had that grave-side beauty, but the wonderfully imperfect vase was a treasure.

Who would have sent her such a lovely gift? Her friend David? She called him, but he only said, "Not me, girl. You getting bouquets from a secret admirer? What's the card say? Tell, tell!"

"Some weird shit about lilies blooming, and it's written like, well, kinda like my grandparents talk." Maybe her grandparents had sent it. But her grand-mother hated lilies too. Samantha called them, just in case. No, not them either. After a guilty promise to call more often, and a reassurance that she was dressing warmly as the days got colder, Samantha rang off, sat back on the couch, and opened her new purchase.

And was lost. Dinner forgotten, she spent hours curled up on the couch, reading the big book she'd bought. The master jewelers of Benin had been carving tiny, intricate brass and gold figures through the lost wax method for centuries. Ibo men wear their wealth in the form of intricate beaded corsets. Fulani women endure the weight of huge brass anklets because they like the seductive sway that it lends to their hips. Fulani men dye their lips and put kohl around their flirty eyes, wear all their sparkly finery on festival days to attract mates.

Samantha wandered into her bedroom, still gazing at the open book. The sweet fragrance of the lilies scented the air right through the apartment. No matter what room she was in, she was aware of their presence.

It was late. Samantha put the book down and went to bed.

The clock radio blared its wake-up call. Samantha

thumbed from alarm to a radio station and sat up in bed, eyes closed. In her half-awake state, it was a moment before her mind registered the tune coming from the radio. A capella, a little girl's voice sang threadily off-key:

Sammy plant piece a corn in the gully, mm-hmm.
An' 'ee grow till 'ee kill poor Sammy, mm-hmm.
Sammy dead, Sammy dead, Sammy dead-oi, mm-hmm.
Sammy dead, Sammy dead, Sammy dead-oi, mm-hmm.

Samantha threw the radio to the floor. It cracked apart, then went silent.

Once her shaking hands had managed to pick up the shards of plastic casing, Samantha headed for the garbage can in the kitchen.

She froze in the living room. The lilies were bare stalks, dried petals scattered all over the room as if they had been windblown. Like dead men's hair, withered wisps clung to the cotton-plant stick. The odour of water-rotted vegetation seeped into Samantha's nostrils.

"Your daddy sorry he didn't get to see you before he leave. He fly to Ottawa this morning, some conference or something. How things at work, sweetheart?" Samantha's mother fed layered squares of cloth and quilt batting under the sewing machine needle. Her sewing room took up half the basement, ceiling-high shelves of patterned cloth towering over a high-tech sewing machine encrusted with knobs, flashing lights, and diagrams. Samantha could remember any number of Sunday afternoons like this, herself and her mother cutting squares and triangles of fabric for quilts, chatting in the rhythms of her parents' birthplace that felt so easy in her mouth.

"Work okay. Not too nice sometimes. Come weekend, I don't feel to do nothing but sleep. But at least I have a job, right? Mummy, you know that song? The one that go, 'Sammy dead, Sammy dead'?"

"I used to sing it to you when you was small." Her mother snapped the pressure foot of the sewing machine down to hold the quilt in place, stood up, and arched her back to relieve the soreness. "You want some pimiento liqueur? Your grandfather just bring me some of his latest batch." Samantha nodded. Her mother walked over to the wet bar on the other side of the room and lifted out the cut-glass decanter. Ruby liquid sloshed inside it. When she removed the stopper, a warm, spicy scent floated up from the bottle.

Samantha's mother poured a measure of the liqueur into each of two brandy glasses. Sam accepted one, took a sip. The sweet, musky brew slid heavily down her throat, calming her. "What that song about, Mummy? Where it come from?"

"Is a old Jamaican song. I not too certain what about. It come from slavery days, and Papa tell me he think Sammy was a slave who had to work so hard it kill him. You should ask your grandfather—I teach maths, not history. Why you want to know?"

"No real reason. I just keep thinking about it a lot nowadays."

Mrs. Lewis smiled. "That song is so sad, but I loved it when I was a girl. Is Papa used to sing it to me. He tell me when I have children, I must sing it to them, so they wouldn't forget. It make me think of home. When I get pregnant with you, I tell your father that we was going to name you Sam or Samantha."

Great. Poor Sammy, worked to death.

Her mother's dinner had been wonderful, as usual. Samantha had lingered late, nibbling at the leftovers and hoping that if she just waited another half hour, she'd have room for that last slice of fried plantain. Replete, she dozed on the subway ride home, and didn't wake up until Dundas, one stop too far south. No matter. It wasn't a long walk. It was after 11 P.M. when she came up out of the subway station and started walking in the direction of her building.

Although never quite deserted, the downtown streets were still and quiet tonight. The windows of the roti shop were dark. As Samantha passed the fountain of the Polytechnic, she had the odd sensation that cotton wool had been stuffed in her ears, so softly did the spray of water fall back into the pond. The hookers strutting in front of the all-night burger place seemed morose, their usual banter with each other and their customers lacklustre. The long, empty stretch of pavement gleamed in the streetlight. It spooked her. Samantha decided to cut through the small park instead. It would be quicker, and it was brightly lit. She stepped onto the park grounds. There were the usual straggly knots of people gathered around the various benches under the trees; smoking up, cruising, or just hanging out. Sam started to feel a little better for having people around her. She kept going, left the section where the park benches were. In the dark, she could just make out the row of brass rectangles embedded along the perimeter of the park, plaques dedicated by people who had planted trees in memory of loved ones who had died. The trees danced and waved eerily at her. Samantha sped up. She rounded the big tree growing at the park's edge. She turned to check for traffic before crossing Carlton Street, and tripped on the uneven ground. She tumbled. Felt a sharp pain across the side of her skull as it cracked against a root of the tree. Then blackness.

. . . *well, those tombs arounn the cottn tree, and I inside the cottn tree lay down. And at night-time I see the cottn tree light up with candles and I resting now, put me hand this way and sleeping . . .*

"Hey, girl, you all right? That was some fall you took."

The chill of the icy earth made Samantha shiver. She opened her eyes to find two women bent over her. She was sitting with her back against the trunk of the tree that had tripped her. Stunned from the blow to her head, she stared bemusedly at the Day-Glo pink micromini one of the women was wearing. Hot pink was not her saviour's best colour. "I think I'm okay. Can you help me up?"

. . . *and I only hear a likkle voice come to me. And them talking to me, but those things is spirit talking to me, and them speaking to me now, and say now:*

"Sure." They helped her to her feet, their six-inch stilettos sinking into the thawing earth as they did so. The throbbing in Samantha's head was incredible, like someone pounding behind her eyes, trying to get out. Strangely, though, she could now hear very clearly, and the night had a pellucid clarity that let her see right to the other side of the park, even through the darkness.

The gently swaying oaks and maples now seemed venerable, not threatening. Samantha took a few deep breaths. The headache began to lessen. The woman in the Day-Glo mini smelt like apple blossoms. "I'm going to be all right. Thanks for helping me."

"Is a likkle nice likkle child, and who going get she right up now in the h'African world?

"Because you brains, you will take something, so therefore we going to teach you something."

"You sure? Maybe you should go to Emerge?"

Emerge. Oh, the emergency room. "'S'okay. If I start to feel sick I will, promise. But my home's right over there."

Samantha crossed the street safely this time. Five minutes later, she was in her apartment. The headache was completely gone, but she was still chilled and a little shaky.

Well, the first thing that them teach me is s'wikkidi; s'wikkidi lango, *which is sugar and water, see? And them teach me that.*

S'wikkidi lango. Yeah. At that moment, Sammie knew what to do for her chills. She went to the kitchen, put the kettle on to boil, fetched the ginger root from the crisper of the fridge and the Demerara sugar in its cookie tin from the cupboard, along with the nutmeg. As she waited for the water to boil, she heaped the sticky brown crystals into the bottom of her largest mug, then grated ginger and nutmeg into it. She filled the mug with boiling water and took it into her bedroom, where she changed into an oversized T-shirt while the infusion steeped. Sitting up in bed, Samantha clutched the mug to her and inhaled the spicy steam. She looked through the pages of the book while she did, at gold and silver, brass and copper: beauty made by hands, like her mother's quilt. Like the empty vase that now sat on her coffee table. She wondered what she could fill it with.

She sipped slowly at the tea until she had drunk it all, then put the mug on her bedside table and drifted into peaceful sleep.

Samantha strolled into work at 10 o'clock the next morning. It had taken longer at the university temp agency than she'd thought. She didn't worry about it. *Because you brains.*

Camille smiled and shook her head as Samantha walked by the reception desk. "Barnes has been asking for you. You were supposed to be in at eight-thirty."

"Yeah, I know."

As she passed Grant's cubicle, he stuck his head out. No cotton this morning. "Were you sick or something?" he asked.

"No, I'm fine." She went into her cubicle, dumped her coat, turned on her computer, started typing. The counsellor at the community college had said she stood a good chance of getting in, that it was never a very full course.

We going to teach you something. And them teach me my prayers, which is:

> *Dear Ms. Barnes: It is with regret that I tender my resignation . . .*

She printed the letter, slid it under Barnes's door. From inside, she could hear the creak of her boss's chair as she got up to investigate. Samantha went back to her

cubicle, fished the course calendar out of her purse, and
started to leaf through it. Two years to a certificate in
goldsmithing, and she could take an elective in forging
iron.

Toronto bags its trees in winter; New York ties theirs down. Tree bondage must be some kind of weird city thing.

WHOSE UPWARD FLIGHT I LOVE

That fall, a storm hailed down unseasonable screaming winds and fists of pounding rain. The temperature plummeted through a wet ululating night that blew in early winter. Morning saw all edges laced with frost.

In the city's grove, the only place where live things, captured, still grew from earth, the trees thrashed, roots heaving at the soil.

City parks department always got the leavings. Their vans were prison surplus, blocky, painted happy green. The growing things weren't fooled.

Parks crew arrived, started throwing tethers around the lower branches, hammering the other ends of twisted metal cables into the fast-freezing ground to secure the trees. Star-shaped leaves flick-

ered and flashed in butterfly-winged panic. Branches
tossed.

One tree escaped before they could reach it;
yanked its roots clear of the gelid soil, and flapping its
leafy limbs, leapt frantically for the sky. A woman of
the crew shouted and jumped for it. Caught a long,
trailing root as the tree rose above her. For a second
she hung on. Then the root tore away in her hand
and the tree flew free. Its beating branches soughed at
the air.

The woman landed heavily, knees bowing and
thighs flexing at the impact. She groaned, straightened, stared at the length of root she was clutching in
her garden glove. Liver-red, it wriggled like a worm.
Its clawed tip scratched feebly. A dark liquid welled
from its broken end. "We always lose a few when this
happens," she said. The man with her just stared at
the thing in her hand.

The tree was gaining altitude, purple leaves
catching the light as it winged its way to its warmer-
weathered homeland. She dropped the root. He tried
to kick dirt over it, his boot leaving dull indentations
in the earth. Then he gave a shout, not of surprise
exactly, rushed to another tree that had worked most
of its roots whipping out of the soil. She ran to help.
Cursing, they dodged flailing foliage, battened down
the would-be escapee.

He panted at her, "So, you and Derek still
fighting?"

Her heart tossed briefly. She hogtied the faint,
familiar dismay. "No, we worked it out again."

And Derek would stay, again. They would soldier

on. And quarrel again, neither sure whether they bat-
tled to leave each other or stay.

A burgundy gleam on the powder-dusted ground
caught her eye. The severed root was crawling jerkily,
trying to follow in the direction its tree had gone.

GANGER (BALL LIGHTNING)

ssy?"

"What."

"Suppose we switch suits?" Cleve asked.

Is what now? From where she knelt over him on their bed, Issy slid her tongue from Cleve's navel, blew on the wetness she'd made there. Cleve sucked in a breath, making the cheerful pudge of his tummy shudder. She stroked its fuzzy pelt.

"What," she said, looking up at him, "you want me wear your suit and you wear mine?" This had to be the weirdest yet.

He ran a finger over her lips, the heat of his touch making her mouth tingle. "Yeah," he replied. "Something so."

Issy got up to her knees, both her plump thighs on each side of his massive left one. She looked appraisingly at him. She was still mad from the fight they'd just had. But a good mad. She and Cleve, fighting always got them hot to make up. Had to be something good about that, didn't there? If they could keep finding their way back to each other like this? Her business if she'd wanted to make candy, even if the heat of the August night made the kitchen a hell. She wondered what the rass he was up to now.

They'd been fucking in the Senstim Co-operation's "wetsuits" for about a week. The toys had been fun for the first little while—they'd had more sex this week than in the last month—but even with the increased sensitivity, she was beginning to miss the feel of his skin directly against hers. "It not going work," Issy declared. But she was curious.

"You sure?" Cleve asked teasingly. He smiled, stroked her naked nipple softly with the ball of his thumb. She loved the contrast between his shovel-wide hands and the delicate movements he performed with them. Her nipple poked erect, sensitive as a tongue tip. She arched her back, pushed the heavy swing of her breast into fuller contact with the ringed ridges of thumb.

"Mmm."

"C'mon, Issy, it could be fun, you know."

"Cleve, they just going key themselves to our bodies. The innie become a outie, the outie become a innie . . . "

"Yeah, but . . . "

"But what?"

"They take a few minutes to conform to our body shapes, right? Maybe in that few minutes . . . "

He'd gone silent, embarrassment shutting his open countenance closed; too shy to describe the sensation he was seeking. Issy sighed in irritation. What was the big deal? Fuck, cunt, cock, come: simple words to say.

"In that few minutes, you'd find out what it feels like to have a poonani, right?'"

A snatch. He looked shy and aroused at the same time. "Yeah, and you'd, well, you know."

He liked it when she talked "dirty." But just try to get him to repay the favour. Try to get him to buzzingly whisper hot-syrup words against the sensitive pinna of her ear until she shivered with the sensation of his mouth on her skin, and the things he was saying, the nerve impulses he was firing, spilled from his warm lips at her earhole and oozed down her spine, cupped the bowl of her belly, filled her crotch with heat. That only ever happened in her imagination.

Cleve ran one finger down her body, tracing the faint line of hair from navel past the smiling crease below her tummy to pussy fur. Issy spread her knees a little, willing him to explore further. His fingertip tunneled through her pubic hair, tapped at her clit, making nerves sing. *Ah, ah.* She rocked against his thigh. What would it be like to have the feeling of entering someone's clasping flesh? "Okay," she said. "Let's try it."

She picked up Cleve's stim. So diaphanous you could barely see it, but supple as skin and thrice as responsive. Cocked up onto one elbow, Cleve watched her with a slight smile on his face. Issy loved the chubby chocolate-brown beauty of him, his fatcat grin.

Chortling, she wriggled into the suit, careful to ease it over the bandage on her heel. The company boasted that you couldn't tell the difference between the microthin layer of the wetsuits and bare skin. Bullshit. Like taking a shower with your clothes on. The suits made you feel more, but it was a one-way sensation. They dampened the sense of touch. It was like being trapped inside your own skin, able to sense your response to stimuli but not to feel when you had connected with the outside world.

Over the week of use, Cleve's suit had shaped itself to his body. The hips were tight on Issy, the flat chest part pressed her breasts against her rib cage. The shoulders were too broad, the middle too baggy. It sagged at knees, elbows, and toes. She giggled again.

"Never mind the peripherals," Cleve said, lumbering to his feet. "No time." He picked up her suit. "Just leave them hanging."

Just as well. Issy hated the way that the roll-on headpiece trapped her hair against her neck, covered her ears, slid sensory tendrils into her earholes. It amplified the sounds when her body touched Cleve's. It grossed her out. What would Cleve want to do next to jazz the skins up?

As the suit hyped the pleasure zones on her skin surface, Issy could feel herself getting wet, the mixture of arousal and vague distaste a wetsuit gave her. The marketing lie was that the suits were "consensual aids to full body aura alignment," not sex toys. Yeah, right. Psychobabble. She was being diddled by an oversized condom possessed of fuzzy logic. She pulled it up to her neck. The stim started to writhe, conforming itself to her shape. Galvanic peristalsis, they called its ability to move. Yuck.

"Quick," Cleve muttered. He was jamming his lubed cock at a tube in the suit, the innie part of it that would normally have slid itself into her vagina, the part that had been smooth the first time she'd taken it out of its case, but was now shaped the way she was shaped inside. Cleve pushed and pushed until the everted pocket slid over his cock. He lay back on the bed, his erection a jutting rudeness. "Oh. Wow. That's different. Is so it feels for you?"

Oh, sweet. Issy quickly followed Cleve's lead, spreading her knees to push the outie part of his wetsuit inside her. It was easy. She was slippery, every inch of her skin stimmed with desire. She palmed some lube from the bottle into the suit's pouched vagina. They had to hurry. She straddled him, slid onto his cock, making the tube of one wetsuit slither smoothly into the tunnel of the other. Cleve closed his eyes, blew a small breath through pursed lips.

So, so hot. "God, it's good," Issy muttered. Like being fucked, only she had an organ to push back with. Cleve just panted heavily, silently. As always. But what a rush! She swore she could feel Cleve's tight hot cunt closing around her dick. She grabbed his shoulders for traction. The massy, padded flesh of them filled her hands; steel encased in velvet.

The ganger looked down at its ghostly hands. Curled them into fists. Lightning sparked between the translucent fingers as they closed. It reached a crackling hand towards Cleve's shuddering body on the bathroom floor.

"Hey!" Issy yelled at it. She could hear the quaver in her own voice. The ganger turned its head towards the sound. The suits' sense-memory gave it some analog of hearing.

She tried to lift her head, banged it against the underside of the toilet. "Ow." The ganger's head elongated widthways, as though someone were pulling on its ears. Her muscles were too weakened from the aftershocks. Issy put her head back down. Now what? Think fast, Iss. "Y . . . you like um, um . . . chocolate fudge?" she asked the thing. Now, why was she still going on about the fucking candy?

The ganger straightened. Took a floating step away from Cleve, closer to Issy. Cleve was safe for the moment.

Coloured auras crackled in the ganger with each step. Issy laid her cheek against cool porcelain, stammered, "Well, I was making some last night, some fudge, yeah, only it didn't set, sometimes that happens, y'know? Too much humidity in the air, or something." The ganger seemed to wilt a little, floppy as the unhardened fudge. Was it fading? Issy's pulse leapt in hope. But then the thing plumped up again, drew closer to where she lay helpless on the floor. Rainbow lightning did a lava lamp dance in its incorporeal body. Issy whimpered.

Cleve writhed under her. His lips formed quiet words. His own nubbin nipples hardened. Pleasure transformed his face. Issy loved seeing him this way. She rode and rode his body, "Yes, ah, sweet, God, sweet," groaning her way to the stim-charged orgasm that would fire all her pleasure synapses, give her some sugar, make her speak in tongues.

Suddenly Cleve pushed her shoulder. "Stop! Jesus, get off! Off!"

Startled, Issy shoved herself off him. Achy suction at her crotch as they disconnected. "What's wrong?"

Cleve sat up, panting hard. He clutched at his dick. He was shaking. Shuddering, he stripped off the wetsuit, flung it to the foot of the bed. To her utter amazement, he was sobbing. She'd never seen Cleve cry.

"Jeez. Can't have been that bad. Come." She opened her thick, strong arms to him. He curled as much of his big body as he could into her embrace, hid his face from her. She rocked him, puzzled. "Cleve?"

After a while, he mumbled, "It was nice, you know, so different, then it started to feel like, I dunno, like my dick had been *peeled* and it was inside out, and you, Jesus, you were fucking my inside-out dick."

Issy said nothing, held him tighter. The hyped rasp of

Cleve's body against her stimmed skin was as much a turn-on as a comfort. She rocked him, rocked him. She couldn't think what to say, so she just hummed a children's song: *We're stirring cocoa beneath a tree / sikola o la vani / one, two, three, vanilla / chocolate and vanilla.*

Just before he fell asleep, Cleve said, "God, I don't want to ever feel anything like that again. I had breasts, Issy. They swung when I moved."

The wetsuit Issy was wearing soon molded itself into an innie, and the hermaphroditic feeling disappeared. She kind of missed it. And all the time she was swaying Cleve to sleep she couldn't help thinking: For a few seconds, she'd felt something of what he felt when they had sex. For a few seconds, she'd felt the things he'd never dared to tell her in words. Issy slid a hand between herself and Cleve, insinuating it into the warm space between her stomach and thigh till she could work her fingers between her legs. She could feel her own wetness sliding under the microthin fibre. She pressed her clit, gently, ah, gently, tilting her hips toward her hand. Cleve stirred, scratched his nose, flopped his hand to the bed, snoring.

And he'd felt what she was always trying to describe to him, the sensations that always defied speech. He'd felt what this was like. The thought made her cunt clench. She panted out, briefly, once. She was so slick. Willing her body still, she started the rubbing motion that she knew would bring her off.

Nowadays any words between her and Cleve seemed to fall into dead air between them, each not reaching the other. But this had reached him, gotten her inside him; this, this, this and the image of fucking Cleve pushed her over the edge and the pulseburst of her orgasm pumped again, again, again as her moans trickled through her lips and she fought not to thrash, not to wake the slumbering mountain that was Cleve.

Oh. "Yeah, man," Issy breathed. Cleve had missed the best part. She eased him off her, got his head onto a pillow. Sated, sex-heavy, and drowsy, she peeled off the wetsuit—smiled at the pouches it had moulded from her calabash breasts and behind—and kicked it onto the floor beside the bed. She lay down, rolled towards Cleve, hugged his body to her. "Mm," she murmured. Cleve muttered sleepily and snuggled into the curves of her body. Issy wriggled to the sweet spot where the lobes of his buttocks fit against her pubes. She wrapped her arm around the bole of his chest, kissed the back of his neck where his hair curled tightest. She felt herself beginning to sink into a feather-down sleep.

"I mean the boiled sugar kind of fudge," Issy told the ganger. It hovered over her, her own personal aurora. She had to keep talking, draw out the verbiage, distract the thing. "Not that gluey shit they sell at the Ex and stuff. We were supposed to have a date, but Cleve was late coming home and I was pissed at him and horny and I wanted a taste of sweetness in my mouth. And hot too, maybe. I saw a recipe once where you put a few flakes of red pepper into the syrup. Intensified the taste, they said. I wonder. Dunno what I was thinking, boiling fudge in this heat." Lightning-quick, the ganger tapped her mouth. The electric shock crashed her teeth together. She saw stars. "Huh, huh," she heard her body protesting as air puffed out of its contracting lungs.

Issy uncurled into one last, languorous stretch before sleep. Her foot connected in the dark with a warm, rubbery mass that writhed at her touch, then started to slither up her leg.

"Oh God! Shit! Cleve!" Issy kicked convulsively at

the thing clambering up her thigh. She clutched Cleve's shoulder.

He sprang awake, tapped the wall to activate the light. "What, Issy? What's wrong?"

It was the still-charged wetsuit that Cleve had thrown to the foot of the bed, now an outie. "Christ, Cleve!" Idiot.

The suit had only been reacting to the electricity generated by Issy's body. It was just trying to do its job. "S'all right," Cleve comforted her. "It can't hurt you."

Shuddering, Issy peeled the wetsuit from her leg and dropped it to the ground. Deprived of her warmth, it squirmed its way over to her suit. Innie and outie writhed rudely around each other; empty sacks of skin. Jesus, with the peripherals still attached, the damned things looked like they had floppy heads.

Cleve smiled sleepily. "Is like lizard tails, y'know, when they drop off and wiggle?"

Issy thought she'd gag. "Get them out of my sight, Cleve. Discharge them and put them away."

"Tomorrow," he murmured.

They were supposed to be stored in separate cases, outie and innie, but Cleve just scooped them up and tossed them together, wriggling, into the closet.

"Gah," Issy choked.

Cleve looked at her face and said, "Come on, Iss; have a heart; think of them lying side by side in their little boxes, separated from each other."

He was trying to joke about it.

"No," Issy said. "We get to do that instead. Wrap ourselves in fake flesh that's supposed to make us feel more. Ninety-six degrees in the shade, and we're wearing rubber body bags."

His face lost its teasing smile. Just the effect she'd

wanted, but it didn't feel so good now. And it wasn't true, really. The wetsuit material did some weird shit so that it didn't trap heat in. And they were sexy, once you got used to them. No sillier than strap-ons or cuffs padded with fake fur. Issy grimaced an apology at Cleve. He screwed up his face and looked away. God, if he would only speak up for himself sometimes! Issy turned her back to him and found her wadded-up panties in the bedclothes. She wrestled them on and lay back down, facing the wall. The light went off. Cleve climbed back into bed. Their bodies didn't touch.

The sun cranked Issy's eyes open. Its August heat washed over her like slops from a bucket. Her sheet was twisted around her, warm, damp and funky. Her mouth was sour and she could smell her own stink. "Oh God, I want it to be winter," she groaned.

She fought her way out of the clinging cloth to sit up in bed. The effort made her pant. She twisted the heavy mass of her braids up off the nape of her neck and sat for a while, feeling the sweat trickle down her scalp. She grimaced at the memory of last night.

Cleve wasn't there. Out for a jog, likely. "Yeah, that's how you sulk," she muttered. "In silence." Issy longed to know that he cared strongly about something, to hear him speak with any kind of force, the passion of his anger, the passion of his love. But Cleve kept it all so cool, so mild. Wrap it all in fake skin, hide it inside.

The morning sun had thrown a violent, hot bar of light across her bed. Heat. Tangible, almost. Crushed against every surface of her skin, like drowning in feathers. Issy shifted into a patch of shade. It made no difference. Fuck. A drop of sweat trickled down her neck, beaded a track down her left breast to drip off her nipple and splat onto her thigh. The trail of moisture it had left behind felt cool on her skin. Issy watched her aureole crinkle and the nipple stiffen in response. She shivered.

A twinkle of light caught her eye. The closet sliding door was open. The wetsuits, thin as shed snakeskin, were still humping each other beside their storage boxes. "Nasty!" Issy exclaimed. She jumped up from the bed, pushed the closet door shut with a bang. She left the room, ignoring the rhythmic thumping noise from inside the closet. Cleve was supposed to have discharged them; it could just wait until he deigned to come home again.

Overloading, crackling violently, the ganger stepped back. Issy nearly wept with release from its jolt. Her knees felt watery. Was Cleve still breathing? She thought she could see his chest moving in little gasps. She hoped. She had to keep the ganger distracted from him, he might not survive another shock. Teeth chattering, she said to the ganger, "You melt the sugar and butter—the salty butter's the best—in milk, then you add cocoa powder and boil it all to hard crack stage . . ." Issy wet her lips with her tongue. The day's heat was enveloping her again. "Whip in some more butter," she continued. "You always get it on your fingers, that melted, salty butter. It will slide down the side of your hand, and you lick it off—so you whip in some more butter, and real vanilla, the kind that smells like mother's breath and cookies, not the artificial shit, and you dump it onto a plate, and it sets, and you have it sweet like that; chocolate fudge."

The sensuality in her voice seemed to mesmerise the ganger. It held still, rapt. Its inner lightnings cooled to electric blue. Its mouth hole yawned, wide as two of her fists.

As she headed to the kitchen, Issy made a face at the salty dampness beneath her swaying breasts and the curve of her belly. Her thighs were sticky where they moved against each other. She stopped in the living room and stood, feet slightly apart, arms away from her sides, so no surface of her body would touch any other. No relief. The heat still clung. She shoved her panties down around her ankles. The movement briefly brought her nose to her crotch, a whiff of sweaty muskiness. She straightened up, stepped out of the sodden pretzel of cloth, kicked it away. The quick movement had made her dizzy. She swayed slightly, staggered into the kitchen.

Cleve had mopped up the broken glass and gluey candy from yesterday evening, left the pot to soak. The kitchen still smelt of chocolate. The rich scent tingled along the roof of Issy's mouth.

The fridge hummed in its own aura, heat outside making cold inside. She needed water. Cold, cold. She yanked the fridge door open, reached for the water jug, and drank straight from it. The shock of chilly liquid made her teeth ache. She sucked water in, tilting the jug high so that more spilled past her gulping mouth, ran down her jaw, her breasts, her belly. With her free hand, she spread the coolness over the pillow of her stomach, dipping down into crinkly pubic hair, then sliding up to heft each breast one at a time, sliding cool fingers underneath, thumb almost automatically grazing each nipple to feel them harden slightly at her touch. Better. Issy put the jug back, half full now.

At her back, hot air was a wall. Seconds after she closed the fridge door, she'd be overheated and miserable again. She stood balanced between ice and heat, considering.

She pulled open the door to the icebox. It creaked and protested, jammed with frost congealed on its hinges. The fridge was ancient. Cleve had joked with the landlady that he might sell it to a museum and use the money to pay the rent on the apartment for a year. He'd only gotten a scowl in return.

The fridge had needed defrosting for weeks now. Her job. Cleve did the laundry and bathroom and kept them spotlessly clean. The kitchen and the bedroom were hers. Last time she'd changed the sheets was about the last time she'd done the fridge. Cleve hadn't complained. She was waiting him out.

Issy peered into the freezer. Buried in the canned hoarfrost were three ice cube trays. She had to pull at them to work them free of hard-packed freezer snow. One was empty. The other two contained a few ice cubes between them.

The ganger took a step towards her. It paddled its hand in the black hole of its mouth. Issy shuddered, kept talking: "Break off chunks of fudge, and is sweet and dark and crunchy; a little bit hot if you put the pepper flakes in, I never tried that kind, and is softer in the middle, and the butter taste rise to the roof of your mouth, and the chocolate melt all over your tongue; man, you could almost come, just from a bite."

Issy flung the empty tray into the sink at the other end of the kitchen. Jangle-crash, displacing a fork, which leapt from the sink, clattered onto the floor. The thumping from inside the bedroom closet became more frenetic. "Stop that," Issy yelled in the direction of the bedroom. The sound became a rapid drubbing. Then silence.

Issy kicked the fridge door closed, took the two ice cube trays into the bathroom. Even with that short

walk, the heat was pressing in on her again. The bathroom was usually cool, but today the tiles were warm
against her bare feet. The humidity of the room felt like
wading through spit.

Issy plugged the bathtub drain, dumped the sorry
handful of ice in. Not enough. She grabbed up the mop
bucket, went back to the kitchen, fished a spatula out
of the sink, rinsed it. She used the spatula to dig out the
treasures buried in the freezer. Frozen cassava, some
unidentifiable meat, a cardboard cylinder of grape
punch. She put them on a shelf in the fridge. Those
excavated, she set about shoveling the snow out of the
freezer, dumping it into her bucket. In no time she had
a bucketful, and she'd found another ice cube tray, this
one full of fat, rounded lumps of ice. She was a little
cooler now.

Back in the bathroom, she dumped the bucket of
freezer snow on top of the puddle that had been the ice
cubes. Then she ran cold water, filled the bathtub calf-
deep, and stepped into it.

Sssss . . . The shock of cold feet zapped straight
through Issy's body to her brain. She bent—smell of
musk again—picked up a handful of the melting snow,
and packed it into her hair. Blessed, blessed cold. The
snow became water almost instantly and dribbled down
her face. Issy licked at a trickle of it. She picked up
another handful of snow, stuffed it into her mouth.
Crunchy-cold freon ice, melting on her tongue. She
remembered the canned taste from childhood, how her
dad would scold her for eating freezer snow. Her mother
would say nothing, just wipe Issy's mouth dry with a
silent, long-suffering smile.

Issy squatted in the bathtub. The cold water lapped

against her butt. Goose bumps pimpled the skin of her thighs. She sat down, hips pressing against either side of the tub. An ice cube lapped against the small of her back, making her first arch to escape the cold, then lean back against the tub with a happy shudder. Snow crunched between her back and the ceramic surface. Issy spread her knees. There was more snow floating in the diamond her legs made. In both hands, she picked up another handful, mashed it into the V of her crotch. She shivered at the sensation and relaxed into the cool water.

The fridge made a zapping, farting noise, then resumed its juddering hum. Damned bucket of bolts. Issy concentrated on the deliciously shivery feel of the ice melting in her pubic hair.

"Only this time," Issy murmured, *"the fudge ain't set. Just sat there on the cookie tin, gluey and brown. Not hard, not quite liquid, you get me? Glossy-shiny dark brown where it pooled, and rising from it, that chocolate-butter-vanilla smell. But wasted, 'cause it wasn't going to set."*

The television clicked on loudly with an inane laugh track. Issy sat up. "Cleve?" She hadn't heard him come in. With a popping noise, the TV snapped off again. "Cleve, is you?"

Issy listened. Nope, nothing but the humming of the fridge. She was alone. These humid August days made all their appliances schizo with static. She relaxed back against the tub.

"I got mad," Issy told the ganger. *"It was hot in the kitchen and there was cocoa powder everywhere and lumps of melting butter, and I do all that work 'cause I just wanted the taste of something sweet in my mouth and the fucker wouldn't set!*

"I backhanded the cookie tin. Fuck, it hurt like I crack a finger bone. The tin skidded across the kitchen counter, splanged off the side of the stove, and went flying."

Issy's skin bristled with goose bumps at the sight of the thing that walked in through the open bathroom door and stood, arms hanging. It was a human-shaped glow, translucent. Its edges were fuzzy. She could see the hallway closet through it. Eyes, nose, mouth were empty circles. A low crackling noise came from it, like a crushed Cheezies bag. Issy could feel her breath coming in short, terrified pants. She made to stand up, and the apparition moved closer to her. She whimpered and sat back down in the chilly water.

The ghost-thing stood still. A pattern of coloured lights flickered in it, limning where spine, heart, and brain would have been, if it had had those. It did have breasts, she saw now, and a dick.

She moved her hand. Water dripped from her fingertips into the tub. The thing turned its head towards the sound. It took a step. She froze. The apparition stopped moving too, just stood there, humming like the fridge. It plucked at its own nipples, pulled its breasts into cones of ectoplasm. It ran hands over its body, then over the sink, bent down to thrust its arms right through the closed cupboard doors. It dipped a hand into the toilet bowl. Sparks flew, and it jumped back. Issy's scalp prickled. Damn, the thing was electrical, and she was sitting in water! She tried to reach the plug with her toes to let the water out. Swallowing whimpers, she stretched a leg out: Slow, God, go slow, Issy. The movement sent a chunk of melting ice sliding along her thigh. She shivered. She couldn't quite reach the plug and if she moved closer to it, the movement would draw the apparition's attention. Issy breathed in short, shallow bursts. She could feel her eyes beginning to brim. Terror and the chilly water were sending tremors in waves through her.

What the fuck was it? The thing turned towards her. In its quest for sensation, it hefted its cock in its hand. Inserted a finger into what seemed to be a vagina underneath. Let its hands drop again. Faintly, Issy could make out a mark on its hip, a circular shape. It reminded her of something . . .

Logo, it was the logo of the Senstim people who'd invented the wetsuits!

But this wasn't a wetsuit, it was like some kind of, fuck, ball lightning. She and Cleve hadn't discharged their wetsuits. She remembered some of the nonsense words that were in the warning on the wetsuit storage boxes: "Energizing electrostatic charge," and "Kirlian phenomenon." Well, they hadn't paid attention, and now some kind of weird get of both suits was rubbing itself off in their bathroom. Damn, damn, damn Cleve and his toys. Sobbing, shivering, Issy tried to toe at the plug again. Her knee banged against the tub. The suit-ghost twitched towards the noise. It leaned over the water and dabbed at her clutching toes. Pop-crackle sound. The jolt sent her leg flailing like a dying fish. Pleasure crackled along her leg, painfully intense. Her knee throbbed and tingled, ached sweetly. Her thigh muscles shuddered as though they would tear free. The jolt slammed into her crotch and Issy's body bucked. She could hear her own grunts. She was straddling a live wire. She was coming to death. Her nipples jutted long as thumbs, stung like they'd been dipped in ice. Her head was banging against the wall with each deadly set of contractions. Issy shouted in pain, in glory, in fear. The suit-ghost leapt back. Issy's butt hit the floor of the tub, hard. Her muscles were twitching spasmodically. She'd bitten the inside of her mouth. She sucked in air like sobs, swallowed tinny blood.

The suit-ghost was swollen, bloated, jittering. Its inner lightning bolts were going mad. If it touched her again, it might overload completely. If it touched her again, her heart might stop.

Issy heard the sound of the key turning in the front door.

"Iss? You home?"

"No. Cleve." Issy hissed under her breath. He mustn't come in. But if she shouted to warn him, the suit-ghost would touch her again.

Cleve's footsteps approached the bathroom. "Iss? Listen, did you drain the wet—"

Like filings to a magnet, the suit-ghost inclined towards the sound of his voice.

"Don't come in, Cleve; go get help!"

Too late. He'd stuck his head in, grinning his open, friendly grin. The suit-ghost rushed him, plastered itself along his body. It got paler, its aura-lightnings mere flickers. Cleve made a choking noise and crashed to the floor, jerking. Issy levered herself out of the bath, but her jelly muscles wouldn't let her stand. She flopped to the tiles. Cleve's body was convulsing, horrible noises coming from his mouth. Riding him like a duppy, a malevolent spirit, the stim-ghost grew paler with each thrash of his flailing body. Its colour patterns started to run into each other, to bleach themselves pale. Cleve's energy was draining it, but it was killing him. Sucking on her whimpers, Issy reached a hand into the stim-ghost's field. Her heart went off like a machine gun. Her breathing wouldn't work. The orgasm was unspeakable. Wailing, Issy rolled away from Cleve, taking the ghost-thing with her. It swelled at her touch, its colours flared neon-bright, out of control. It flailed off her, floated back towards Cleve's more cooling energy.

Heart pounding, too weak to move, Issy muttered desperately to distract it the first thing that came to her mind: "Y . . . you like, um, chocolate fudge?"

The ghost turned towards her. Issy cried and kept talking, kept talking. The ghost wavered between Issy's hot description of bubbling chocolate and Cleve's cool silence, caught in the middle. Could it even understand words? Wetsuits located pleasurable sensation to augment it. Maybe it was just drawn to the sensuousness of her tone. Issy talked, urgently, carefully releasing the words from her mouth like caresses:

"So," she said to the suit-duppy, "I watching this cookie tin twist through the air like a Frisbee, and is like slow motion, 'cause I seeing gobs of chocolate goo spiraling from it as it flies, and they spreading out wider and wider. I swear I hear separate splats as chocolate hits the walls like slung shit and one line of it strafes the fridge door, and a gob somehow slimes the naked bulb hanging low from the kitchen ceiling. I hear it sizzle. The cookie tin lands on the floor, fudge side down, of course. I haven't cleaned the fucking floor in ages. There're spots everywhere on that floor that used to be gummy, but now they're layered in dust and maybe flour and desiccated bodies of cockroaches that got trapped, reaching for sweetness. I know how they feel. I take a step towards the cookie tin, then I start to smell burning chocolate. I look up. I see a curl of black smoke rising from the glob of chocolate on the light bulb."

Cleve raised his head. There were tears in his eyes and the front of his jogging pants was damp and milky. "Issy," he interrupted in a whisper.

"Shut up, Cleve!"

"That thing," he said in a low, urgent voice. "People call it a ganger; doppel—"

The ganger was suddenly at his side. It leaned a loving head on his chest, like Issy would do. "No!" she yelled. Cleve's body shook. The ganger frayed and tossed like a sheet in the wind. Cleve shrieked. He groaned like he was coming, but with an edge of terror and pain that Issy couldn't bear to hear. Pissed, terrified, Issy swiped an arm through its field, then rolled her bucking body on the bathroom tiles, praying that she could absorb the ganger's energy without it frying her synapses with sweet sensation.

Through spasms, she barely heard Cleve say to it, "Come to me, not her. Come. Listen, you know that song? '*I got a weakness for sweetness* . . . ' That's my Issy."

The ganger dragged itself away from Issy. Released, her muscles melted. She was a gooey, warm puddle spreading on the floor. The ganger reached an ectoplasmic hand towards Cleve, fingers stretching long as arms. Cleve gasped and froze.

Issy croaked, "You think is that it is, Cleve? Weakness?"

The ganger turned its head her way, ran a long, slow arm down its body to the floor, back up to its crotch. It stroked itself.

Cleve spoke to it in a voice that cracked whispery on the notes: "Yeah, sweetness. That's what my Issy wants most of all." The ganger moved towards him, rubbing its crotch. He continued, "If I'm not there, there's always sugar, or food, or booze. I'm just one of her chosen stimulants."

Outraged tears filled Issy's mouth, salty as butter, as flesh. She'd show him, she'd rescue him. She countered:

"The glob of burned sugar on the light? From the ruined fudge? Well, it goes black and starts to bubble."

The ganger extruded a tongue the length of an arm from its mouth. The tongue wriggled towards Issy. She rolled back, saying, "The light bulb explodes. I feel some shards land in my hair. I don't try to brush them away. Is completely dark now; I only had the kitchen light on. I take another step to where I know the cookie tin is on the floor. A third step, and pain crazes my heel. Must have stepped on a piece of light bulb glass. Can't do nothing about it now. I rise onto the toes of the hurting foot. I think I feel blood running down from heel to instep."

The ganger jittered towards her.

"You were always better than me at drama, Iss," Cleve said.

The sadness in his voice tore at her heart. But she said, "What that thing is?"

Cleve replied softly, "Is kinda beautiful, ain't?"

"It going to kill us."

"Beautiful. Just a lump of static charge, coated in the Kirlian energy thrown off from the suits."

"Why it show up now?"

"Is what happens when you leave the suits together too long."

The ganger drifted back and forth, pulled by one voice, then the other. A longish silence between them freed it to move. It floated closer to Cleve. Issy wouldn't let it, she wouldn't. She quavered:

"I take another step on the good foot, carefully. I bend down, sweep my hands around."

The ganger dropped to the floor, ran its long tongue over the tiles. A drop of water made it crackle and shrink in slightly on itself.

"There," Issy continued. "The cookie tin. I brush around me, getting a few more splinters in my hands. I get down to my knees, curl down as low to the ground as I can. I pry up the cookie tin, won't have any glass splinters underneath it. A dark sweet wet chocolate smell rising from under there."

"Issy, Jesus," Cleve whispered. He started to bellow the words of the song he'd taunted her with, drawing the ganger. It touched him with a fingertip. A crackling noise. He gasped, jumped, kept singing.

Issy ignored him. Hissing under his booming voice she snarled at the ganger, "I run a finger through the fudge. I lick it off. Most of it on the ground, not on the tin. I bend over and run my tongue through it, reaching for sweetness. Butter and vanilla and oh, oh, the chocolate. And crunchy, gritty things I don't think about. Cockroach parts, maybe. I swallow."

Cleve interrupted his song to wail, "That's gross, Iss. Why you had to go and do that?"

"So Cleve come in, he see me there sitting on the floor surrounded by broken glass and limp chocolate, and you know what he say?" The ganger was reaching for her.

"Issy, stop talking, you only drawing it to you."

"Nothing." The ganger jerked. "Zip." The ganger twitched. "Dick." The ganger spasmed, once. It touched her hair. Issy breathed. That was safe. "The bastard just started cleaning up; not a word for me." The ganger hugged her. Issy felt her eyes roll back in her head. She thrashed in the energy of its embrace until Cleve yelled:

"And what you said! Ee? Tell me!"

The ganger pulled away. Issy lay still, waiting for her breathing to return to normal. Cleve said, "Started carrying on with some shit about how light bulbs are such poor quality nowadays. Sat in the filth and broken glass, pouting and watching me clean up your mess. Talking about anything but what really on your mind. I barely get all the glass out of your heel before you start pulling my pants down."

Issy ignored him. She kept talking to the ganger. "Cool, cool Cleve. No 'What's up?'; no 'What the fuck is this crap on the floor?'; no heat, no passion."

"What was the point? I did the only thing that will sweet you every time."

"Encased us both in fake skin and let it do the fucking for us."

The ganger jittered in uncertain circles between the two of them.

"Issy, what you want from me?"

The ganger's head swelled obscenely towards Cleve.

"Some heat. Some feeling. Like I show you. Like I feel. Like I feel for you." The ganger's lower lip stretched, stretched, a filament of it reaching for Issy's own mouth. The black cavity of its maw was a tunnel, longing to swallow her up. She shuddered and rolled back farther. Her back came up against the bathtub.

Softly: "What do you feel for me, Issy?"

"Fuck you."

"I do. We do. It's good. But what do you feel for me, Issy?"

"Don't ridicule me. You know."

"I don't know shit, Issy! You talk, talk, talk! And it's all about what racist insult you heard yesterday, and who tried to cheat you at the store, and how high the phone bill is. You talk around stuff, not about it!"

"Shut up!"

The ganger flailed like a hook-caught fish between them.

Quietly, Cleve said, "The only time we seem to reach each other now is through our skins. So I bought something to make our skins feel more, and it's still not enough."

An involuntary sound came from Issy's mouth, a hooked, wordless query.

"Cleve, is that why . . . " She looked at him, at the intense brown eyes in the expressive brown face. When had he started to look so sad all the time? She reached a hand out to him. The ganger grabbed it. Issy saw fireworks behind her eyes. She screamed. She felt Cleve's hand on her waist, felt the hand clutch painfully as he tried to shove her away to safety with his other hand. Blindly she reached out, tried to bat the ganger away. Her hand met Cleve's in the middle of the fog that was the ganger. All the pleasure centres in her body exploded.

A popping sound. A strong, seminal smell of bleach. The ganger was gone. Issy and Cleve sagged to the floor.

"Rass," she sighed. Her calves were knots the size of potatoes. And she'd be sitting tenderly for a while.

"I feel like I've been dragged five miles behind a runaway horse," Cleve told her. "You all right?"

"Yeah, where'd that thing go, the ganger?"

"Shit, Issy, I'm so sorry. Should have drained the suits like you said."

"Chuh. Don't dig nothing. I could have done it too."

"I think we neutralized it. Touched each other, touched it: We canceled it out. I think."

"Touched each other. That simple." Issy gave a little rueful laugh. "Cleve, I . . . you're my honey, you know? You sweet me for days. I won't forget anymore to tell you," she said, "and keep telling you."

His smile brimmed over with joy. He replied, "You, you're my live wire. You keep us both juiced up, make my heart sing in my chest." He hesitated, spoke bashfully, "And my dick leap in my pants when I see you."

A warmth flooded Issy at his sweet, hot talk. She felt her eyelashes dampen. She smiled. "See, the dirty words not so hard to say. And the anger not so hard to show."

Tailor-sat on the floor, beautiful Buddha-body, he frowned at her. "I 'fraid to use harsh words, Issy, you know that. Look at the size of me, the blackness of me. You know what it is to see people cringe for fear when you shout?"

She was dropping down with fatigue. She leaned and softly touched his face. "I don't know what that is like. But I know you. I know you would never hurt me. You must say what on your mind, Cleve. To me, at least." She closed her eyes, dragged herself exhaustedly into his embrace.

He said, "You know, I dream of the way you full up my arms."

"You're sticky," she murmured. "Like candy." And fell asleep, touching him.

The ending of the folktale goes that when the old woman gives the peasant girl the gift of jewels that fall out of her mouth every time she speaks, the prince decides to marry the girl because she's so sweet and beautiful. Of course, the fact that she had just become a walking treasury can't have hurt her prospects either. I keep mixing that tale up with the one about the goose that laid the golden eggs and that ended up as dinner. That wasn't a happy ending either.

PRECIOUS

I stopped singing in the shower. I kept having to call the plumber to remove flakes of gold and rotted lilies from the clogged drain. On the phone I would say that I was calling for my poor darling cousin, the one struck dumb by a stroke at an early age. As I spoke, I would hold a cup to my chin to catch the pennies that rolled off my tongue. I would give my own address. If the plumber thought it odd that anyone could manage to spill her jewelry box into the bathtub, and more than once, he was too embarrassed to try to speak to the mute lady. I'm not sure what he thought about the lilies. When he was done, I would scribble my thanks onto a scrap of paper and tip him with a gold nugget.

I used to have the habit of talking to myself when I was alone, until the day I slipped on an opal that had tumbled from my lips, and fractured my elbow in the fall. At the impact, my cry of pain spat a diamond the size of an egg across the room, where it rolled under the couch. I pulled myself to my feet and called an ambulance. My sobs fell as bitter milkweed blossoms. I always hated to let the flowers die. Holding my injured arm close to my body, I clumsily filled a drinking glass with water from the kitchen and stuck the pink clusters into it.

The pain in my elbow made me whimper. Quartz crystals formed on my tongue with each sound, soft as pudding in the first instance, but gems always hardened before I could spit them out. The facets abraded my gums as they slipped past my teeth. By the time the ambulance arrived, I had collected hundreds of agonized whimpers into a bowl I had fetched from the kitchen.

During the jolting ride to the hospital, I bit nearly through my lip with the effort of making no sound. The few grunts that escaped me rolled onto the pillow as silver coins. "Ma'am," said a paramedic, "you've dropped your change. I'll just put it into your purse for you, okay?"

The anaesthetic in the emergency room was a greater mercy than the doctors could imagine. I went home as soon as they would allow.

My father had always told me that a soft answer would turn away wrath. As a young woman, I took his words to heart, tried to lull my stepmother with agreeableness, dull the edge of her taunts with a soft reply. I went cheerfully about my chores, and smiled till my teeth ached when she had me do her daughter Cass's work too. I pretended that it didn't burn at my gut to see mother and daughter smirking as I scrubbed. I always tried to be pleasant, and so of course I was pleasant when Cass and I met the old woman in the mall that day. She was thirsty, she said, so I fetched her the drink of water, though she seemed spry enough to run her own errands. Cass told her as much, scorn in her voice as she derided my instant obedience.

Sometimes I wonder whether that old woman wasn't having a cruel game with both of us, my sister and I. I got a blessing in return for a kind word, Cassie a curse as payment for a harsh one. That's how it seemed, but did the old lady know that I would come to fear attention almost as much as Cass feared slithering things? I believe I would rather taste the muscled length and cool scales of a snake shape themselves in my mouth, then slide headfirst from my lips, than look once more into the greedy gaze of my banker as I bring him another shoebox crammed with jeweled phrases, silver sentences, and the rare pearl of laughter.

Jude used to make a game of surprising different sounds from me, to see what wealth would leap from my mouth. He was playful then, and kind, the husband who rescued me from my stepmother's greed and wrath. My father's eyes were sad when we drove away, but he only waved.

Jude could make me smile, but he preferred it when I laughed out loud, raining him with wealth. A game of tickle would summon strings of pearly chuckles that gleamed as they fell at our feet. Once, a pinch on my bottom rewarded him with a turquoise nugget when I yelped. He had it strung on a leather thong, which he wore around his neck.

But it was the cries and groans of our lovemaking that he liked best. He would stroke and tongue me for hours, lick and kiss me where I enjoyed it most, thrust into me deeper with each wail of pleasure, until, covered in the fragrance of crushed lily petals, we had no strength for more. Afterwards, he would collect sapphires and jade, silver love knots and gold doubloons from the folds of the sheets. "I don't even need to bring you flowers," he would joke. "You speak better blossoms for yourself than I can ever buy."

It seemed as though only weeks had passed when my marriage began to sour. Jude's love-bites became painful nips that broke my skin and forced diamonds from my teeth. He often tried to scare me, hiding in the closet so I shrieked when he leapt out, grains of white gold spilling from my mouth. One night he put a dead rat in the kitchen sink. I found it in the morning, and platinum rods clattered to the ground as I screamed. I begged him to be kind, be pleasant, but he only growled that we needed more money, that our investments weren't doing well. I could hear him on the phone late at night, pleading for more time to pay his debts. He became sullen, and often came home with the smell of liquor on his breath. I grew nervous and quiet. Once he chided me for keeping too silent, not holding up my part of the marriage. I began to sob, withered tulips plummeting down. "Bitch!" he shouted. "Quit it with the damned flowers. More gold!" The backhand across my mouth drew blood, but along with two cracked teeth, I spat out sapphires. That pacified him for a short time.

From then on, the beatings happened often. It was eight months later—when Jude broke my arm—that I left, taking nothing with me. I moved to a different city. My phone number is unlisted. I pay all my bills through my bank, not through the mail. A high fence surrounds my house. The gate is always locked.

Since I have no need to work, my time is my own. I search the folklore databases of libraries all over the world, looking for a spell that will reach the old woman, beg her to take back her gift, her curse.

My stepmother will not say it, but Cassie is mad, driven to it by leathery bats and the wriggling legs of spiders uttering forth from her mouth. It's good that her mother loves her, cares for her out on that farm, because she sits and rocks now, her constant muttered curses birthing an endless stream of lizards and greasy toads. "It keeps the snakes fed," my stepmother says when she calls with sour thanks for her monthly cheque. "That way, they're not biting us." The mother and father that loved me are both long dead, but my stepmother still lives.

When the phone rang, I thought it was her, calling to complain about slugs in her lettuce.

"Hello?" I spat out a nasturtium.

"Precious. It *is* you." Jude's voice was honey dripped over steel. "Why have you been hiding, love?"

I clamped my lips together. I would not give him my words. I listened, though. I had always listened very carefully to Jude.

"You don't have to answer, Princess. I can see you quite clearly from here. You must have wanted me to find you, leaving the back curtains open like that. And the lock on that gate wouldn't keep an imbecile out."

"Jude, go away, or I'll call the police." Deadly nightshade fell from my lips. I paused to spit out the poisonous sap.

There was a crash in the living room as Jude came through the back sliding doors. He casually dropped the cell phone when he stepped through the ruined glass. He had a heavy mallet in the other hand. He let it fall too, to crunch on a shard of glass. Petrified, struck dumb as a stone, I made it to the front door before he slammed me against the wall, wrenching my arm behind my back. From years of habitual silence, my only sound was a hiss of pain. A copper coin rolled over my tongue, a metallic taste of fear.

"You won't call anyone, my treasure. You know it would ruin your life if people found out. Think of the tabloid media following you everywhere, the kidnapping attempts. You'd have every bleeding heart charity in the book breathing down your neck for donations. Let me protect you from all that, Jewel. I'm your husband, and I love you, except when you anger me. I only want my fair share."

Pressed against mine, Jude's body was tall as I remembered, and cruelly thin, driven by the strength of rage. He would have his due. Maybe I could talk my way out of this, be agreeable. "Let me go, Jude. I won't fight you anymore." I had to mouth the words around the petals of a dead rose. I carefully tongued the thorny stem past my teeth.

"You're sure?" He pushed my elbow higher up along my back, until I whimpered, grinding my teeth on more dry thorns. "I'm sure! Let go!" He did. I almost fainted as the wrenched muscles in my arm cramped. Jude grabbed my sore shoulder and pushed me ahead of him into the living room. He stopped and turned me to face him. Hatred glared back at me from his eyes.

"Okay, darling, you owe me. Left me in one hell of a mess back there, you know? They need to be paid, and soon. So, come on, make the magic. Spit it out."

"Jude, I'm sorry I ran away like that, but I was frightened." Two silver coins rolled to the ground.

"You can do better than that, Precious." Jude raised his fist level with my face. My jaw still ached where he dislocated it the first time he ever hit me. I forced a rush of words from my mouth, anything to make the wealth fall:

"I mean, I love you, darling, and I hope that we can work this out, because I know you were the one who rescued me from my stepmother, I'm grateful that you took care of me, so I didn't have to worry about anything . . . " A rain of silver was piling up around Jude's feet: bars, sheets, rods, wire. He grinned, reached down to touch the gleaming pile. I felt a little nudge of an emotion I didn't recognize, but no time to think about that; I had to placate him. I kept talking.

"It was so wonderful living with you, not like at my stepmother's, where I had to do all the cooking and cleaning, and my father never spoke up for me . . . " Semiprecious stones started piling up with the silver: rose quartz, jade, hematite. The mound reached Jude's knees, and the delight on his face made him look like the playful man I had married. He sat on the hillock of treasure, started shoveling it up over his lap. I had to keep the words flowing:

"If Daddy were a fair man, if he really loved me, he could have said something, and wouldn't it have been easier if the four of us had split the chores?" I couldn't stop, even if I dared. All those years of resentment gouted forth: emeralds green with jealousy; seething red garnets, cold blue chunks of lapis. The stones were larger now, the size of plums. I ejected them from my mouth with the force of thrown rocks. They struck Jude's chest, his chin. "Hey!" he cried. He tried to stand, but the bounty piled up over his shoulders, slamming him back down to the floor. My words were flying faster.

"So I fetched and I carried and I smiled and I simpered, while Daddy let it all wash over him and told me to be nicer, even nicer, and now he's dead and I can't tell him how mad I am at him, and the only thanks I got was that jealous, lazy hussy telling me it's *my* fault her daughter's spitting slugs, and then you come riding to my rescue so that I can spend the next year of my life trying to make you happy too, and you have the gall to lay hands on me, and to tell me that you have the right? Well, just listen to me, Jude: I am not your treasure trove, and I will not run anymore, and I shall be nice if and when it pleases me, and stop calling me Precious; my name is Isobel!"

As I shouted my name, a final stone formed on my tongue, soft at first, as a hen's egg forms in her body. It swelled, pushing my jaws apart until I gagged. I forced it out. It flew from my mouth, a ruby as big as a human heart, that struck Jude in the head, then fell onto the pile of treasure. He collapsed unconscious amidst the bounty, blood trickling from a dent in his temple. The red ruby gleamed as though a coal lit its core. I felt light-headed, exhilarated. I didn't bother to check whether Jude was still breathing. I stepped around him to the living room, saw the cell phone on the floor. I picked it up and dialled emergency. "Police? There's an intruder in my home."

It was when I was standing outside waiting for the police that I realised that nothing had fallen from my mouth when I made the telephone call. I chuckled first, then I laughed. Just sounds, only sounds.

About the Author

The daughter of a poet/playwright, NALO HOPKINSON was born in Jamaica and grew up in Guyana, Trinidad, Jamaica, and Canada, where she has lived since the age of sixteen. Her first novel, *Brown Girl in the Ring,* was the winner of the Locus Award for Best First Novel and a finalist for the Philip K. Dick Award. Her second novel, *Midnight Robber,* was also a finalist for the Philip K. Dick Award, as well as the Nebula and Hugo awards for Best Novel. She is the editor of the anthology *Whispers from the Cotton Tree Root: Caribbean Fabulist Fiction.* Her short fiction has appeared in a number of science-fiction and literary anthologies and magazines. She is writing her third novel, *Griffonne.*

"Precious" © 1999. First appeared in *Silver Birch, Blood Moon*, edited by Ellen Datlow and Terri Windling, Avon Eos, USA, 1999.